LISTENING
TO
BRAHMS

LISTENING
TO
BRAHMS

Rosemary Allen

Matador
9 Priory Business Park
Kibworth Beauchamp
Leicestershire LE8 0RX, UK
Tel: (+44) 116 279 2299
Fax: (+44) 116 279 2277
Email: books@troubador.co.uk
Web: www.troubador.co.uk/matador

ISBN 978 1780885 216

British Library Cataloguing in Publication Data.
A catalogue record for this book is available from the British Library.

Printed and bound in the UK by TJ International, Padstow, Cornwall
Typeset in 11pt Minion Pro by Troubador Publishing Ltd, Leicester, UK

Matador is an imprint of Troubador Publishing Ltd

PROLOGUE

Monday 1ˢᵗ January 1990

> *It's an hour into a new decade. The fireworks and church*
> *bells have stopped now. In the distance, I can still hear*
> *people singing and shouting and cheering.*

I pause and consider what I'm going to write next. I haven't
kept a journal for nearly thirty-six years. But if my life is to
change direction, it seems important to keep track of my
thoughts and feelings. I continue.

> *I can't believe that ten days ago, we hadn't even met…*

CHAPTER ONE

Part One

Thursday 21ˢᵗ December 1989

...because I haven't reached Blackheath yet. We won't meet until tomorrow. In fact, I'm still sitting on the train, which slows down again and grinds to a halt for no apparent reason. The young man opposite me shrugs resignedly. I tell him I'm going to stay with my sister and her husband in Blackheath for Christmas. He tells me he's only coming up for the day and at this rate it won't be worth it. After about five minutes we're off again and we don't say anything more for the rest of journey.

I open the paper I bought at the station. The headlines concentrate on the trouble in Panama. Last month the photos were of people streaming through the border between East and West Germany, and of Dubcek and Havel addressing the crowds in Wenceslas Square. Now it seems Havel will almost certainly be elected as the Czech president. Suddenly, anti-government protests are spreading to countries we know practically nothing about. At the bottom of the front page is an article about Romania – "Ceausescu Declares State of Emergency". Inside the paper there are photos of streets in Timisoara – a town I've never even heard of – where government troops fired on demonstrators, killing thousands. It's all happening so quickly. My thoughts inevitably go back to when I was in Germany, only nine years after the war had ended. The Hungarian Revolution and the Czech Revolt were still to come, the Berlin Wall hadn't yet been built, but the division between East and West seemed more enduring and invincible than any bricks and mortar.

When we eventually arrive in London, I trudge over the road to Waterloo East and find I have at least twenty minutes to wait for a train. I pull up my coat collar, stamp my feet and look forward to being enveloped in the colourful warmth of my sister's rather chaotic and welcoming house. Not for the first time, I wonder how I would cope with what seems to be a constant procession of people who arrive at the door without warning and stay for coffee, lunch, the night or even several weeks. Not well, I suspect.

Ruth is seven years older than me, and as far back as I can remember, I've envied her. Envied the fact that while I was growing up, she always seemed to be the centre of a group of rather eccentric friends, who would hardly give me a cursory glance before disappearing into her bedroom to have what I imagined to be unbelievably sophisticated and interesting discussions. Envied her for the seemingly endless string of young men arriving to take her to yet another party, while I was still at the jelly-and-pass-the-parcel stage. Envied her for the stir she had caused by insisting on marrying Geoffrey within two months of meeting him, when she was not yet twenty. Envied her for the fact that my parents' gloomy predictions – they were totally unsuited, she might be pregnant – were proved wrong. And still envy her. Never mind that I went on to get a good English degree and am now deputy head of an independent girls' school. Never mind that, seeing us together in family photographs, I realise that I was, and still am, rather better looking than Ruth, who has inherited my father's long, broad nose and my mother's tendency to put on weight.

The train, when it arrives at last, is very crowded and it's difficult to find somewhere to put my suitcase and the bag filled with presents. Whenever I come up by train I wish I'd driven, but when I'm stuck in a traffic jam I wish I'd taken the train. By the time I eventually climb the steps up to the vicarage, it's nearly two o'clock and I'm feeling distinctly peckish. The door is on the latch, so I walk straight in, leave my case in the hall and follow the sounds coming from the kitchen. Ruth is sitting at the table with her back to me, gesticulating wildly, just as she's been doing ever since I can remember. She is talking to a grey-haired woman I don't recognise, who is concentrating hard on cutting up a large, brown loaf. It's only when the dog's tail begins to thump on the side of her basket in greeting that they notice me.

'Oh good, you're here, Meg,' says Ruth, as if I'd just popped out to the shops for a minute. She gets up and gives me a brief but enthusiastic hug. 'You remember Shirley, don't you?' I don't, and I don't think Shirley remembers me, but I smile at her and she continues cutting up the bread. 'Geoffrey's hidden himself away in his study, as usual,' says Ruth. 'Can you go and tell him lunch is ready, Meg? I'll pour the soup.'

'I'll go, Ruth,' says Shirley. She jumps to her feet and hurries out into the hall. Geoffrey pretends he never notices the passions he arouses in middle-aged ladies. 'Another convert to the Angels of Mercy, darling,' Ruth will say. Now I look at her questioningly. She raises one eyebrow and nods slightly, and I suppress a grin.

Geoffrey comes into the kitchen with his familiar half smile on his face. For a moment I can't think why he looks different, until I realise he's shaved off his beard. I haven't seen him clean-shaven for years. He sits down at the table and grins at me through the steam rising from the soup bowls. He still likes to pretend he's the downtrodden male in a household of women. 'Even the cat and dog are female,' he always says.

As usual, Ruth's soup is delicious, but it's always the same soup. Chunks of whatever vegetables she happens to have, thrown into a saucepan and given the odd stir whenever she thinks about it. Rather like her life really. Everyone who walks through the front door is welcomed in with a minimum of fuss and is miraculously amalgamated into a homogeneous group. Now we all sit round the table, content for the moment just to concentrate on our lunch. I notice Shirley has been glancing at Geoffrey after every mouthful.

'Have some more soup, Shirley,' says Ruth.

'Oh dear, I don't know that I should.'

'Go on Shirley,' says Geoffrey, 'be a devil.' That line always goes down well with his ladies.

'Well, if you're having some… ' she simpers.

Afterwards, she insists on helping to clear away and I know Ruth will have to take everything out of the dishwasher and arrange it again when she's gone. And of course, she manages to slop the coffee on to the tray as she carries it into the sitting room. She's beginning to irritate me already, but Ruth and Geoffrey show no signs of being the least bit put out.

'What are you doing on Christmas Day, Shirley?' says Ruth. 'Are you going to your brother's again?'

Please don't ask her to come here, I find myself thinking.

'Well, he's not been well, actually. You know, his old trouble. But Betty has very kindly said I will be most welcome again.'

Thank goodness for that, I think uncharitably. Geoffrey sees it as part of the job to keep an open house at Christmas. It would be nice to have just family this year.

'I'll take my case upstairs,' I say.

When I come down again, Shirley has gone and I see Geoffrey disappearing once more into his study. I go in search of Ruth.

'Right,' she says, when I eventually find her outside in the back garden. 'You can help me carry the tree in before it gets too dark.'

They always wait until I arrive before decorating the tree. When Helen and Jane were tiny, they would both rush up and drag me into the sitting room before I could even take off my coat. The tree would be waiting, green and empty in the corner.

When we've managed to heave it indoors and put it in place, we decide to start putting the lights on it, but leave the rest of the decorations until Saturday, when Helen, Ian and the boys arrive.

'And I've got a surprise for you,' says Ruth, pointing to a cardboard box in the corner. I peer inside.

'Mother's decorations! I had no idea she still had them.'

'But that's not all. You wait.'

My mother moved into a flat near Ruth and Geoffrey when my father died about ten years ago, but refused to get rid of any of her "bits and pieces". We had no idea what was in the boxes, which were stacked up in her small spare bedroom. After she died in September, Ruth started sorting out her things – the piles of bills, the drawers stuffed with old underwear, the kitchen cupboards filled with out-of-date packets and jars. She would periodically ring me up to report her progress. But when she came to the spare bedroom, she refused to tell me anything. She said she wouldn't spoil it for me. Everything would be revealed at Christmas.

Geoffrey puts his head round the door.

'Just going over to the church for evening prayer.'

I still haven't quite got used to having a vicar for a brother-in-law and I can't help thinking his dog collar is some sort of fancy dress. When he and Ruth first met, he had just qualified as a solicitor and only decided to go into the church when he was forty, and already a partner in a local firm. Until then he'd always appeared to be the most secular of men, so it came as a bit of a surprise to us all, including Ruth, I think. The girls were just getting to the expensive stage and his sudden conversion had caused the only real disagreement over anything important he and Ruth had ever had, as far as I know.

'OK,' says Ruth. 'I'll start supper.'

'Good. I'll watch that James Bond video after *Eastenders*.'

Geoffrey has an almost passionate addiction to various soaps, as well as James Bond, Hammer Horror and American thrillers. Part of Christmas for me is lying in bed late at night, listening to the distant sounds of car chases, explosions and gunfire, while Geoffrey is still downstairs, slumped on the sofa in front of the television.

'I see you've shaved off your beard,' I say, as Geoffrey goes out. 'It suits you.'

'Well, I felt like a change. I'd almost forgotten what I looked like underneath all the hair.'

'We can look at mother's things in peace after supper,' says Ruth when he's gone.

We've finished hanging the lights on the tree and, miraculously, they come on first time. The room is beginning to look festive already. We go into the kitchen and I start on the salad, while Ruth finishes making a lasagne. For a while, we work in amicable silence.

'Jane's coming for Christmas Day,' says Ruth suddenly.

Jane is Ruth and Geoffrey's elder daughter. I've always thought of her as the more self-sufficient and imperturbable of the two girls – university, high-flying career, married to a merchant banker, no children. Helen, on the other hand, married Ian straight after university and now seems to be quite content to stay at home, looking after her three lively boys. Even as a little girl, she was the one who was happiest playing with her dolls, while Jane was outside falling out of trees.

'But not Philip,' she adds. 'He's left her.'

'Oh Ruth, no. I'm so sorry. When did you find out?'

'She came round last weekend – quite unexpectedly, actually. We hadn't seen her for about a month. She came out with it straight away. Philip's moved out and gone to live with this woman from his office. We all know he's had flings before, don't we, but this one is serious – not least because the wretched girl is pregnant. Philip is over the moon apparently. We all thought neither of them wanted a family, didn't we – careers and all that. Now it turns out they'd been trying for ages, so it makes it much worse of course.'

'I had no idea. How is she taking it?'

'She seems remarkably calm, really. But with Jane you never know what's going on under the surface, do you?'

'And what does Geoffrey say?'

'Well, he surprised me. Said she was probably better off without him.'

Good old Geoffrey. More astute than he appears. I decide not to say that Philip has always seemed a cold fish to me.

The phone rings. Knowing Ruth's talent for organisation and unflappability, I suppose I shouldn't be surprised at how well she acts the part of the vicar's wife. Although she goes to church every Sunday to support Geoffrey, she never takes Communion or joins in the Creed and only sings hymns because, as she says, they have some 'jolly good tunes'. She makes no secret of her agnosticism and Geoffrey has long ago given up trying to change her mind, even on occasion making her lack of belief part of a sermon.

I leave her trying to calm down whoever it is on the other end of the phone and go into the sitting room again. Ruth keeps a log fire alight all the time in the cold weather. When Geoffrey had a parish in the country for a while, one of the rituals of my visits was the foray into the copse above the church for the Christmas supply of logs. The wood I put on the fire now is much neater, properly dried and delivered in bags, instead of the untidy damp heap from the country, which tended to spit and splutter alarmingly. The room is lit just by the tree lights and the fire. I sit down on the sofa. The cat climbs on to my lap and purrs while I stroke her under her chin, in the way I know she likes. The dog has followed me in and settles down beside me, her head on my feet.

'What,' I ask them, 'has your mummy found in Granny's attic, I wonder?' Bella wags her tail enthusiastically and Sam twitches her ears and stares into the fire.

'Caught you,' says Ruth, coming in and switching on the light. 'They won't tell you, you know. We can look at everything after supper. Oh yes, remind me to ask Geoffrey to phone Mr Mason when he comes in.'

Ruth has brought in two mugs of tea and we sit for a while in silence.

'It's really strange without Mother, isn't it?' she says at last. 'Christmas is the one time of the year I always associate with her.' She pauses, gets up and puts another log on the fire. 'And actually this is our last year here. Geoffrey's decided to retire. The new man will be taking over in June. It's typical of him though, isn't it? He only told me quite casually last week. It's just like twenty-five years ago. He can discuss things like what bloody colour wine to buy until the cows come home, but any big decision – not a word. Good old Ruth is bound to go along with it.'

I'm rather taken aback. I've never heard her so bitter.

'You knew it would happen eventually, didn't you?'

'Yes, of course I did. It just came as a bit of a shock. It's ironic, isn't it? The church has been the most important thing in my life for nearly twenty-five years, and yet I still don't believe a word of it.'

'But I didn't think he had to retire until he's seventy?'

'He doesn't. That's what's so silly. He must have been thinking about it for ages without saying anything to me at all. I knew something was up when he shaved his beard off all of a sudden. He still refuses to discuss it, not even the practical things – like the little matter of where we're going to live. He's just assuming that we'll move into the cottage. But I think we ought to sell it and add our half of Mother's money to buy something near here. Or we could take whatever the church offers in the way of a rented house.'

'Well, I don't think the cottage would be a good idea at all. Wales is fine for the odd holiday, but I can't imagine you living anywhere else but here now. You'd miss your music for a start.'

'Yes, precisely. Anyway, I'm sure it will all work out. I suppose I'll just have to think of it as the next phase in my life.' She gets up abruptly and walks over to the window, as if to dismiss any more discussion on the subject. 'By the way, I haven't told the girls yet, so don't say anything. And I don't want to spoil Christmas for the boys, either. Helen says Max is getting beside himself at the thought of it all and Jack's feeling very important because he's been told not to let the cat out of the bag about Father Christmas. But I think Will is getting to the stage when it's not "cool", or whatever they say, to get excited about anything much except football. It hasn't stopped him from drawing up his usual all-inclusive present list, though.'

We both smile fondly. While we're waiting for Geoffrey to come back, we turn on the television and watch the six o'clock news. The demonstrations in Romania continue, despite the killing of protesters. And East German workers have begun dismantling the wall at the Brandenburg Gate in Berlin.

After supper, with Geoffrey safely settled down with James Bond, we can at last concentrate on Mother's "bits and pieces".

'Follow me,' says Ruth. We go into the dining room and I wait while she lifts six carefully labelled boxes on to the table. 'I hope you're impressed.'

'I am. But I seem to remember she had far more than this?'

'Well, I've done some careful whittling down. And there are some other things I'll show you later. Now, look at this one first.'

It's full of postcards and letters, some in their original envelopes.

'These are all the letters Mother and Dad ever sent to each other, I should think,' says Ruth. 'Not just the ones we knew about – you know, the ones Dad sent during the war – but from before they were married, too. I felt guilty reading them actually, because they're so personal and, well, loving.'

I draw one at random from its envelope. It's from my father and dated April 1927, nearly a year before their wedding. I read it out.

My own sweetheart, I hope you're not having any regrets. You know how much I love you and I couldn't bear to lose you, especially after yesterday.

Ruth and I look at each other.

'Well,' I say, 'I wonder what happened yesterday?'

'Some of the postcards are from when he went away to conferences and things, I think. And there are a few which are just notes really and a lovely one after they've obviously had a bit of a tiff and Mother sent him a "sorry" card. Anyway, you can read the rest later. These two boxes are all the old photos. Mother's written on the back of a lot of them and we've seen most of them before, of course, but there are some of people I don't recognise at all. We'll save those for a bit, shall we?'

She opens the fourth box. It's full to the brim with the

necklaces, bracelets, brooches and earrings my mother could never resist buying and could never throw away. She used to keep them in a drawer in her dressing table and when I was little, I used to spend hours sorting through them all, trying them on, posing in the mirror and prancing around. I look at the two remaining boxes.

'And what about those?'

Ruth almost ceremoniously hands me the one with "Meg" written on the top in her unmistakable scrawl.

'And the other one is mine,' she says.

I lift the lid off carefully. Silently, I begin to spread the contents over the dining room table. The box must contain a record of the whole of my childhood and adolescence. All my school reports are here, the certificates from my piano exams, a few of my childish drawings, some of my old school exercise books and the letters I'd sent to my parents while I was at college. And, right at the bottom, underneath some postcards and more letters, is the diary. It's more of a journal, really; I wrote it in a notebook with a dark-green cloth cover, now rather battered round the edges. I know without looking that it covers the first eight months of 1954 and stops abruptly on 20th of August. I realise that Ruth is waiting for my reaction.

'I had no idea she would have kept all this,' is all I can say. The memories I thought I had satisfactorily suppressed for all these years come flooding back. I realise I am actually shaking. I begin putting everything back in the box. I can't cope with seeing any more for a bit.

'Mine's much the same as yours, really,' says Ruth. 'And no, I didn't read your diary, or any of the letters, before you ask. There are quite a few things in my box I wouldn't want you to see either! I wonder if Mother had a good look, though. Knowing her, I can't imagine she wouldn't have.'

I don't think Ruth has noticed how shaken I am.

'You said there were some other things.'

'Oh yes! Quite a lot of books. Your old Enid Blytons, my Swallows and Amazons, that sort of thing. And would you believe she even kept some of our baby clothes? And all the things we had in the dressing-up box. Helen and Jane will remember all those too, of course.'

I suddenly feel incredibly weary.

'I don't think I can cope with any more today. Sorry, Ruth, I feel exhausted. I think I'll go up now.'

'All right, darling. See you in the morning. Sleep well.'

She gives me a brief kiss on the cheek. Ruth is still my big sister, after all. I put my head round the door to say goodnight to Geoffrey, but he is snoring gently, completely oblivious of the dreadful predicament James Bond has got himself into. Tomorrow he will insist he saw the whole film.

Clutching my box, I make my way upstairs to my room and sit down on the bed. All need for sleep suddenly evaporates. I take out the letters and postcards I sent home from Germany when I was not quite eighteen, beginning with…

PART TWO

Wednesday 11th August 1954

…the first duty postcard…

> *Volkmarshausen. Wednesday. 10 p.m.*
> *Dear Mummy and Daddy,*
> *We have all arrived safely. I am writing this in my room before going to sleep. The village is very picturesque.*

Gudrun's family live on the first floor, above the school and her parents are very nice. Tomorrow we have our official "Welcome to Germany" at what they call the Jugendhaus *– which means House of the Youth – in Hann. Münden. Will write more soon.*

Love Margaret.

...which says practically nothing about what I was actually thinking and feeling at the time.

It was the summer of 1954 and I was on an exchange trip to Münden in the province of Hannover in Germany, with the worthy aim on the part of our schools, I suppose, of cementing relationships between the youth of our countries. I was staying at the village school in the nearby village of Volkmarshausen. The German pupils had been to England earlier in the year, so I knew Gudrun already. The border with East Germany was less than thirty kilometres away. There were about twenty girls in the party, ranging in ages from fifteen to eighteen. We were accompanied by two teachers, Miss Harris and Miss Smithson. So much for the facts.

But then I look at the diary. My handwriting all those years ago was recognisably mine, but smaller, neater and written with a fountain pen, in blue ink. I quickly skip through the entries at the start of the year. They are all about relatively trivial things – friends, teachers, lessons, heavy colds, walks on the beach – and can wait. Until I get to August. And I gradually start reliving what seems to be someone else's life, as my seventeen-year-old self begins to emerge from the fog of memory.

By now, in Blackheath, it's nearly half past eleven. I decide to get into bed and just read a bit more before putting out the light. While I undress and clean my teeth, I try to put myself back in time and imagine what it was like to be me then.

I suppose you might say Ruth and I were from a privileged

background – no money worries or family traumas. My father was a doctor, so he had a car – a pre-war Austin 10 – which made me the envy of my friends. My mother had a cleaning lady and helped at my father's surgery. They voted Conservative and took the *Daily Telegraph*.

So, was I shy, reserved, introverted even? Yes, but only with strangers. Serious? Not really – one of my main memories of that time is of lots of giggling with my friends at school. Innocent? Definitely. I went to an all-girls school and had no male relations my own age. A few of my friends had brothers, but they were either little boys or unbelievably grown-up and unapproachable. Thinking, I suppose, that it was time to broaden my horizons, my mother had recently tried to persuade me to go to ballroom dancing classes. But although I remember having this vague idea of one day finding my perfect soul mate, even the mere thought of any kind of actual bodily contact with a boy filled me with horror.

I climb into bed, and decide to look for more clues. I turn back to the diary entry for 1st January 1954 and begin to read.

I saw the New Year in quite alone – in bed. I felt in a very reflective mood – rather wistfully looking back on last year. I think in 1953 I really grew up.

Hm, I don't think so. I read on.

In the winter I was quite enchanted by the snow. Before, I had only seen it as a means of playing snowballs, but last year I really saw the true beauty of it. And then in the spring I have memories of the joyful feeling of walking under waking trees, beneath a clear blue sky, with the birds singing as if their throats would burst – singing, because, like me, they felt the hope and expectation of the spring.

I smile somewhat ruefully to myself, because I realise this just about sums me up. I can remember seeing photographs of myself at that time looking, I hoped, wistful, but in reality just appearing vaguely unhappy about something. I was just beginning to think of myself as one of the great Romantics – definitely with a capital "R". And that was my downfall really. I continue to read.

> *Then I remember later in the year, I first wanted to discover the real meaning and aim of Life.* (Note the capital L) *But – oh dear – I've got so muddled up inside that I don't know what to think. Perhaps this year I shall sort myself out. Then about November, I formed a deep hatred of war – not so much a fear – but because of the injustice and folly of it.*

This must have been brought on by studying the First World War poets, in particular, I seem to remember, Siegfried Sassoon and Wilfred Owen.

> *At midnight all the ships' sirens in the harbour hooted and two cocks crowed. I wondered, perhaps with a little apprehension, what 1954 would bring, and regretfully saying goodbye to 1953. Gosh – I've rambled on. It is a little colder today. This morning I had a grand sort out of all my books. They give me a nice, comfortable feeling. We went down into town this afternoon to order our duffle coats.*

The other half of the "we", who would have teased me mercilessly had she read that entry, is, of course, Barbara. Barbara Hill. My best friend. Red hair. Freckles splattered over pale skin. Popular, confident, worldly, bossy. Frequently utterly infuriating. Whom I haven't seen since we left school.

I turn on to the entry for 11th August again. The journey from England to Germany lasted nearly thirty-six hours and led to the events that would change my life.

When we arrived at Münden, we were greeted by what seemed to be a large crowd gathered on the platform. The German girls had all come to meet us, bringing assorted parents, brothers, sisters, aunts and uncles, and they were all milling about, waving and shouting out names. Looking from the window as the train drew in, it was difficult to pick out individual faces.

In our befuddled state, we almost fell out on to the platform, heaving our luggage after us. And then Gudrun was standing in front of me, smiling and holding out her hand. She somehow looked different from how I remembered her in England. The tightly-plaited fair hair was the same and so were the rimless glasses. But she was more confident now, on her home territory, and looked me straight in the eye, rather than with the shy, rather formal look I remembered from her time in England. Behind her stood a rather plump young man, unsuitably dressed in view of the warm weather in a brown tweed jacket, thick socks, sturdy shoes and corduroy plus-fours, slightly worn at the knees.

'This is Fritz,' Gudrun said. 'You remember that I said to you about him?'

Of course, Fritz, the clergyman. Gudrun had not told us much about him except that he was living with her family, while he trained as a student teacher at her father's school. So, in my mind's eye I had seen a pale, tall, thin young man, dressed in black, with spectacles balanced on his long, thin nose. But, apart from the glasses, he couldn't have been more different. His fairish, wavy hair was thinning and his face was round, red and slightly damp. His right eyebrow, as he solemnly came forward to greet me, twitched slightly. His hand, as it shook mine, felt warm and clammy. But in spite of all that, looking back I can feel only affection for him. He eventually changed from being a figure of fun to being my ally and confidant.

Barbara was staying with another family in Volkmarshausen, so we all squeezed into a taxi and set off on the final part of the journey.

We travelled on the right-hand side of the road, of course. It was rather alarming when we passed other cars and the road was extremely bumpy.

We dropped Barbara off first in the centre of the village, where she was staying, and then the taxi climbed a steep, stony path and stopped outside a large, three storey timber-framed house with a tiled roof. I remembered Gudrun had told me that the village school occupied the ground floor and that the family lived on the floors above.

Her parents must have heard the sound of the car, for they were at the door to greet me. Frau Schmidt was a quiet, unassuming woman, her dark hair pulled back in a bun at the nape of her neck. Her kindness and shy smile did a lot to alleviate my inevitable homesickness at the beginning of my visit. Although she spoke no English, we were able to get by with my limited German, supplemented by smiles and gestures. Herr Schmidt came forward and shook my hand. Gudrun had built up a picture of a rather stern, intimidating man, so his amiable, bespectacled face came as a surprise. He led the way into the house and up a flight of stairs. Fritz picked up my case and I could hear him wheezing slightly behind me with the effort of carrying it up.

By this time it was late afternoon and the diary says that the rest of the day was a bit of a blur. I do remember going into the huge living room with its wood burning stove in the centre, various sofas and armchairs on one side, a table and chairs on the other and an upright piano against one wall. After all the travelling, I think I felt a bit sick and all I could manage to eat was a bowl of soup before my head began to nod forwards uncontrollably.

After the meal, Gudrun insisted on taking me for a short walk along the path outside, which led up through the fir woods covering the hill above the house. We came to a clearing and could look back down on to the village and the river running through it.

'The river here in Volkmarshausen is the Weser,' Gudrun told me as if reading from an official guide book. 'It is formed in Hann. Münden, where the rivers Fulda and Werra meet. Tomorrow you will see.'

She also told me that the station was further up the track, that tomorrow we would take the train to school and that there were wild boars in the forest above the railway line. More than anything else, the mention of wild boars made me feel that I was not so much in a foreign country as in another time, an immense distance away from the comforting cocoon I had lived in up till now. I was relieved we went no further. When we got back to the house, Frau Schmidt took one look at me and decided it was time for bed.

I had already been shown the outside toilet, but was surprised to realise there was no bathroom in the house at all and no running hot water. All the rooms in the house seemed huge to me. My room contained two ample beds, a large wardrobe against one wall, a writing desk, chair and large sofa against another – and still managed to look almost under-furnished. Best of all, I thought, was the window seat where I sat briefly that first evening, looking out on to the school playground and to the village and hills beyond. I obviously found my bedding impressive but unusual.

There are no blankets, but a thick eiderdown thing covered with a huge bolster case. It's like dough when you pat it and you can make it go thicker or thinner in certain places. It's not tucked in, but just folded under. It is extremely comfortable and must be lovely and cosy in winter – better than our beds.

I close the diary and put out my light. Downstairs I can hear Ruth telling Geoffrey not to be long. He seems to have got involved in another film, though, because I can hear un-James-Bond-like music seeping out from the sitting room. Although I'm so tired, for a while I find it impossible to sleep. It's as if I've started watching a newsreel of the events in Germany all those years ago and can't tear my eyes away from the screen. As yet the details are still vague, but I know that once I continue reading from my diary, and find the photographs I suspect my mother will have kept, everything will leap into unbearable, sharp-focused close-up.

CHAPTER TWO

PART ONE

Friday 22nd December 1989

I wake before it's light, not quite knowing where I am. At first I can't think why I feel a combination of excitement and trepidation. Then, remembering, I switch on the lamp. It is six o'clock. From across the landing I can hear Geoffrey snoring. At times like this, I'm glad I sleep alone.

I sit up and reach for the diary lying on the bedside table. Before reading any more, though, I decide to find out whether my mother kept the photographs I took in Germany. I get out of bed, put on my dressing-gown and open the door as quietly as possible. When I get downstairs, I see that there's a light on in the kitchen. Ruth is sitting at the table with her back to me, her hands cradling a mug of something hot.

'Ruth,' I whisper, then realise that it would take more than the sound of normal speech to penetrate the noise still coming from upstairs. 'Are you all right?'

'Couldn't sleep, that's all. Shall I make you some tea?'

'No, don't get up. I'll do it.'

When I sit down, neither of us says anything for a while. I have an uneasy feeling I'm intruding.

'I'll take mine upstairs if you like. I really came down to look for some photos.'

'No,' Ruth says, almost urgently, reaching out for my hand. 'If I talk it might clear my mind a bit.'

I wait. I assume Ruth is worried about having to move out of the house. And I'm partly right.

'It's not just that he didn't discuss it with me,' she says at last. 'I have a nasty feeling that once we haven't got the church to occupy us, we'll find that we don't have very much in common any more. Geoffrey is really very keen on going to live in the cottage, you know. After playing the part of the slightly eccentric vicar, I think he's planning that his next role will be country gentleman. Do you think he'll grow his beard again? It ought to be long and straggly and unkempt. I keep trying to imagine what we would do all day. I've got this mental picture of long trudges through the mud walking the dog and Geoffrey swishing brambles and nettles with his hand-whittled stick. Me making jam we never eat, Geoffrey making wine we never drink.'

We become aware of a sudden silence from above and freeze until a particularly loud snort reassures us.

'And endless repeats of James Bond films every evening,' I say.

'I knew you'd make me feel better,' Ruth says, grinning reluctantly. 'I am serious though. I think I'd leave him rather than move to bloody Wales.' She gets up and puts her mug rather too noisily on to the draining board.

'You don't mean that, do you?'

'Yes, I do actually. Even to the extent of making a mental list of the things I wouldn't miss about him.'

'James Bond and the snoring for a start, I suppose.'

'Well, yes, those. But there's the rather superior attitude he takes about what I think of the church. As if it's just a sort of feminine whim and that eventually I'll see the error of my ways. And how I have to drop everything if he wants me to do something – make him a cup of tea, type a letter, visit an old lady.'

It occurs to me that perhaps the banter between her and Geoffrey has never been quite as good-natured as I've always thought it was. 'Come on Ruth, it's not as bad as that. You'd be lost without him, wouldn't you? And I'm sure if he knows how much it would upset you to move away, he'll see it from your point of view. Do you want me to say something to him?'

'Good God, no.'

It's as if our roles have suddenly switched around. I've always had a sneaking suspicion that Ruth still just sees me as her little sister, so I feel rather flattered that she's confiding in me like this. 'Well then, I think you ought to clear all this up with him as soon as possible. Will you promise me you'll discuss it properly? If you don't, you'll have it on your mind all over Christmas.'

Ruth doesn't say anything. It occurs to me I sound like Mother.

'Yes?' I say, trying to catch her eye.

'Yes. I suppose you're right.'

Ruth, in turn, sounds like me, aged fifteen. She grins reluctantly again.

It's beginning to get light. We sit in silence, lost in our own thoughts, listening to the sound of snoring still coming from upstairs. I can't help being fond of Geoffrey, but he has always seemed to me to be playing a part. From what Ruth has just said, the same thought has crossed her mind too. He has a knack of making everyone feel special and over the years I've watched him with the ladies from the church, like Shirley yesterday. He pretends there's some sort of light-hearted conspiracy between them and that they share a secret joke not understood by anyone else. And he's like that with everyone. With me, he likes to pretend he's continually bossed about by

Ruth and his daughters. With his grandsons, he pretends he's on their side against the adult world.

When I first knew him, he was a smart young solicitor, somewhat nattily dressed, a leading light in the Young Conservatives, about to marry the daughter of the local GP. When the girls came along, he slipped into playing the devoted father, started wearing tweeds and woolly jumpers when he wasn't at the office, acquired a bigger house and his first yellow Labrador. Then came what he called his 'crisis of conscience', resulting in genteel poverty, while he trained for the church – and grew his first beard. And then his starring role – the charismatic priest.

'I really came down to look through Mother's photos,' I say at last.

'They're still on the dining room table. I really must get dressed. I've got lots to do today. By the way, the trio are rehearsing here this evening. There's a concert in the church tomorrow night and we're doing a couple of pieces in between the carols. So I've asked Martin and Jonathan to supper. You've never met Jonathan, of course, have you? He's fitted in very well – although of course we still miss Liz.'

Ruth plays cello – rather well, actually – in an amateur piano trio and sings alto in a local choir, just two of the things I know she would miss if she went to live in the country. Liz was their pianist before she moved up to Yorkshire with her husband earlier this year. When they have rehearsals here, Geoffrey always makes a great point of staying in his study, somehow managing to imply that he's far too busy to indulge in the luxury of a hobby of any sort.

'What are you two girls doing up so early?'

We both start, almost guiltily, as Geoffrey shuffles into the kitchen, dressed in old slippers, with his familiar striped dressing-gown over his pyjamas. He switches on the radio and goes over to the kettle. The *Today* programme is in progress and I know Geoffrey will listen to "Thought for the Day", making comments under his breath.

'We're going to do the big food shop today,' Ruth says.

I nod, and pick up the pad and pencil lying on the table, as if to prove that's why I'm here. Ruth, unlike me, is not a natural list-maker, so at Christmas that's one of my first jobs. We both go upstairs to shower and get dressed. I realise I still haven't looked for the photographs, but decide they can wait until later.

After breakfast, Geoffrey goes over to the church, muttering about a 'box job', his rather irreverent way of describing a funeral. Ruth and I settle down at the kitchen table to make the list. By about ten o'clock, later than we had planned of course, we're off. Ruth's driving, to put it kindly, lacks subtlety. Parking, when we eventually arrive at the supermarket, is difficult. I feel worn out already. We fill a trolley each, spend about half an hour in a queue at the checkout, another half an hour packing it all away when we get home before collapsing, shoes off, coffee mugs in hand, on the sofa. Miraculously, we don't seem to have forgotten anything.

'Just the turkey to pick up tomorrow,' says Ruth.

'And the little job of cooking it all,' I add.

Lunch is the remains of yesterday's soup, followed by bread and cheese. At home, food doesn't play much part in my life. Here, we've no sooner finished one meal than it's time to start preparing the next. The most un-Christmassy thing we can think of to have this evening is fish, so we've bought some salmon. As we've got visitors, we decide we ought to have a pudding, so Ruth makes a crumble while I prepare the potatoes. The first opportunity I get to sort through the photos is when some enthusiastic and noisy ladies from the church arrive to discuss the refreshments for tomorrow evening's concert. I make my escape into the dining room and shut the door.

The first box I look into contains the older family photos from before either Ruth or I were born. Our parents, in substantial bathing costumes, disporting themselves in the sea. Groups of great-aunts and uncles in unidentified back gardens, having tea. Wedding photos of long-forgotten friends and relations. Formal portraits of stolid looking children and babies. The photos in the other box chart our childhood. Ruth, wrapped in a thick shawl, in my mother's arms. Ruth, taking her first steps, tottering over the lawn. Ruth, looking nervous and uncomfortable, aged seven, sitting on the sofa, with me as a baby on her lap. Lots of photos of us on the beach, in the garden, at birthday parties. I realise I've spent nearly an hour already and I still haven't found what I'm really looking for.

Then, nearly at the bottom of the box, I find them. They are still in the buff-coloured folder they were in when they were developed, with the negatives on one side and the prints on the other. I decide to look at them later in conjunction with the diary. I take them upstairs and tuck them away safely in my box. Will they confirm the images I already have in my head from all those years ago? I had hardly glanced at them after returning from Germany. I think my parents guessed something had happened, but I had never given the slightest hint and they had never asked.

Downstairs, the noise level reminds me of a school reunion, although when I look into the sitting room there are actually only four ladies there, including, I notice, the faithful Shirley. In the hall, Geoffrey passes me on his way to his study, raises his eyebrows, shrugs and grins at me conspiratorially. In the kitchen, Ruth is making yet more tea and when we carry it in,

I am persuaded to be in charge of an urn tomorrow evening. Geoffrey pokes his head round the door to receive a chorus of greeting, which he seems to relish greatly. I wonder why he wants to give all this up?

I make my escape by saying I'm going to start preparing the supper. In the kitchen I switch on the radio in time for the six o'clock news and hear that in Romania, the riots have spread to Bucharest. In the early hours of this morning, the protesters had stormed the television centre and it appears Ceausescu's twenty-four year long regime is coming to an end. And in Berlin, where sections of the wall have already been removed near the Brandenburg Gate, people from the East are scrambling over it. For over a month now the East Germans have been allowed through the border crossings in the wall to have their first view of capitalism, but this seems by far the most symbolic act up till now. I think once again of my time in Germany, when East Germans were shot and killed by their own countrymen, just for trying to escape to a better life or join their families who were already in the West.

I really can't face the noise and chatter anymore and decide to go upstairs to change before supper. The box sits invitingly on the bed, but I can't actually bring myself to look at the photos yet. I hear the ladies leaving, then the doorbell and more people arriving, voices in the hall. I open my bedroom door.

Then I hear it. The sound of the piano. And what's more, as if it's drifting up through time as well as space, the piece being played is Brahms' "Rhapsody No 2, in G minor". I stop dead. For a moment I think perhaps it's a trick of the mind, somehow triggered by the diary and the photographs and the news from Germany.

Ridiculously, I feel my heart beating wildly, my head spinning. Because that's how it started all those years ago in

Germany; hearing him play those passionate rising chords as I walked into the house that summer evening. I half turn to go back into my room to start searching through the diary. But I know that once I start reading I shall find it impossible to do anything else this evening. Anyway, I feel an illogical, urgent need to find out who is playing now.

Still feeling slightly shaky, I go downstairs, half expecting that it will actually be him. I pause outside the kitchen. Ruth is putting the crumble in the oven. Martin, the violinist from the trio, throws back his head and laughs at something Geoffrey has just said. But I don't join them. I look to my right, towards the sitting room. The only light comes from the tree and the fire. Framed in the doorway, a man is sitting at the piano with his back to me, his head bent slightly over the keys. His dark hair is going a bit grey and curls slightly at the nape of his neck. He is wearing brown corduroy trousers which have seen better days and a slightly worn dark sweater over a check shirt. He is playing from memory and is completely absorbed in the music.

When he has played the final chords, he remains sitting there for a moment, and it's only when he stands up and turns round that he sees me.

'Hello,' he says. 'You must be Margaret.'

'And you must be Jonathan.'

We smile, and that seems enough for the moment.

'We've decided to have a run-through before supper,' calls Ruth from the kitchen. 'Is that okay?'

'Fine,' we both say in unison.

Geoffrey disappears into his study, and while they sort out chairs and music stands, I settle down on the sofa to listen, the dog by my side. Martin has brought a few sets of music with him and they take some time to decide what they are going to play tomorrow. The banter between the three of them is light-hearted and very entertaining in itself, before they've even played a note. I know Martin quite well, as he's been the violinist in the trio from the start. He has a very infectious giggle so that rehearsals quite often become rather disorganised. I fondle Bella's ears. She wags her tail and puts her head on my lap. And I watch Jonathan. I guess he's in his late fifties. His hair is beginning to recede – more on one side than the other. His eyebrows are quite bushy and nearly meet in the middle. When he laughs, the lines round his eyes deepen. Quite often he catches my eye and we smile. I begin to realise he is as aware of my presence as I am of his.

They have decided on Mozart and Schubert for tomorrow evening – nothing too long or heavy. I like the way Jonathan turns slightly, head down, to watch Martin at the start of the Mozart. And how he lifts his hands above the keys before beginning the Schubert, so that he and Ruth, on the cello, both start together. Half way through, I go into the kitchen to put the potatoes on and check on the salmon. There is a sudden burst of laughter from the sitting room and they have another go at a particularly tricky passage. I realise I already recognise Jonathan's voice and find myself listening for it. And I stop and consider what this means. Surely not, I think. This sort of thing doesn't happen to me. I decide I feel slightly drunk, although I've not yet had a drink. And I can't wait to go back in to watch the rest of the rehearsal.

I lean back and let the sound of Schubert's "Notturno" wash over me. This must not happen, I tell myself. It's absolutely ridiculous at my age even to think about getting emotionally entangled with a man I know absolutely nothing about and who is most probably perfectly happily married anyway. For thirty-five years I've avoided getting even remotely involved with anyone. At university I became quite expert at discouraging any young man who seemed to be taking even the most casual interest in me. I settled for a comfortable teaching job in a comfortable girls' school. The only men I know, other than casual acquaintances and my own family, are the husbands of my friends. I have to admit that the phrase "typical middle-aged spinster" must inevitably come to mind when people meet me for the first time. But I like my life. I like my house and I like living alone.

When they've finished their rehearsal, Martin and Jonathan pack up the music and put the stands away. Ruth and I go into the kitchen to lay the table and make the salad. It turns out that Jonathan is not happily married at all – or rather he was, but that his wife died of cancer about seven years ago. By the eagerness with which Ruth tells me this, I begin to suspect she might have plans for me. She's had plans for me numerous times over the years, periodically introducing me to various unsuitable bachelors, with a complete lack of success.

'He's a lovely man,' she says now. 'We knew them a bit when Anna was alive, because she used to sing in the choir. But it was only when Liz left the trio that Martin suggested he might be interested in joining us.'

'How does Martin know him?'

'He's a cardiologist at the hospital.'

I feel an absurd and illogical sense of proprietorial pride.

Ruth despatches me to tell the "chaps" that supper is ready. Geoffrey has emerged from his study and as I go into the sitting room, Martin and Jonathan start a spirited and competitive version of "Chopsticks" on the piano. I have to raise my voice to be heard. As we make our way into the kitchen, Martin grins at me.

'How's Val?' I say.

'She's fine. She's on duty this evening, otherwise she would be here too. She's coming to the concert tomorrow though.'

Martin is an anaesthetist at the hospital and his wife Val works in the casualty department. They married quite late and although they are in their mid-fifties, their only son, Marcus, is still at school and hoping to go to university next year to study medicine.

Supper is a relaxed and genial affair – lots of easy chat and laughter. Martin and Jonathan have both brought bottles of wine and, since no one has to drive anywhere, we manage to get through them with no difficulty at all. Ruth staggers to her feet eventually to get the crumble and make some custard. Geoffrey and Martin clear away the plates. There is a lot of discussion about the best way to stack the dishwasher. Jonathan and I find ourselves sitting at the table by ourselves.

'What made you play the Brahms just now?' I ask eventually.

He pauses. 'I'm not quite sure,' he says. 'It just seemed the right thing to do. Why do you ask?'

'Oh, it's nothing really. It's just that it brings back some memories of hearing it played about thirty-five years ago.'

'Nice memories?'

'Well, let's say mixed,' I reply. 'Perhaps I'll tell you about it one day.' I hope he doesn't think I sound presumptuous. 'But I enjoyed hearing you play it,' I add. 'I'm still very fond of Brahms.'

'I'll play some more for you, if you like, after supper.'

'That would be nice,' I say, and we smile at each other.

After we've finished eating, we take a tray of coffee into the sitting room. Ruth switches on the television in time for the nine o'clock news. There is footage of Ceaucescu, wearing a Russian-style black hat, being heckled while addressing a rally in front of the presidential palace in Bucharest – something unheard of during his twenty-four year regime. Then soldiers shooting indiscriminately into the demonstrators, who are chanting 'Down with Ceaucescu'. Distressing as the violence is, we can't help feeling a sense of excitement, mingled with disbelief, as we watch what must surely be one of the defining moments in history. Later in the bulletin, they show thousands of East and West Berliners mingling at the Brandenburg Gate after the border was opened earlier today. My feeling of optimism is overshadowed by thoughts of the Germany I knew thirty-five years ago, but I don't say anything.

We decide we've eaten far too much and all sink into a rather somnolent state, so that when the phone rings, we all jump. Ruth answers it and it's for Geoffrey, so he goes off into his study again. Martin goes out into the hall to fetch some presents to put under the tree for Helen's boys and Ruth goes upstairs to fetch one for Martin and Val's son, Marcus. Jonathan and I find ourselves slumped comfortably on the sofa together. Without saying anything, he gets up and goes over to the piano. As promised, it's Brahms again, but this time an intermezzo, a perfect miniature, very different from the tempestuous rhapsody he played earlier.

As if from a long way away, I can hear Ruth and Martin talking in the hall and the telephone ringing again. To my consternation, I can feel tears coming to my eyes. It's not just that the music is unbearably beautiful, but that I know Jonathan is playing just for me. When he finishes, neither of us say anything and the spell is only broken when the others come in a few minutes later.

'I hope he likes it,' Ruth is saying to Martin. 'I'll take it back if he doesn't. Anyway, we'll see him on Boxing Day, won't we? What are you doing over Christmas, Jonathan?'

'I'm going to my son's on Christmas Day,' says Jonathan, getting up from the piano. 'But his in-laws have got a big family do the next day. They're all rather overwhelming *en masse*, so I probably won't go.'

'Well then, you must come to us. Martin and Val and Marcus are coming for lunch and one more won't make any difference at all – if you don't mind the racket. Helen's boys will be here too.'

I find myself willing him to say yes.

'That would be very nice. I'd love to come.'

He looks over to me and I feel absurdly happy.

By now it's gone ten o'clock and Martin says he must go.

'Stay and have another drink, Jonathan,' says Geoffrey. 'I expect the girls will be busy in the kitchen for a bit, so I'd like the company.'

Ruth and I look at each other and shrug as we get up.

'Pour the staff one too, will you, please?' says Ruth as we go into the kitchen to make a start on clearing the table. And I think she's only half joking.

'Well, darling?' she says, as she scrapes the plates into the bin.

'Well, what?' I know exactly what she means though.

'He seems very taken with you, anyway.'

'Don't be silly.' But to my utter confusion and embarrassment, I realise that I am actually blushing, something I don't think I've done since, well, my teens I suppose.

'There you are,' says Ruth, grinning. 'Say no more, as they say. Jonathan, you're an angel. A perfect gent,' as he comes in carrying two glasses of red wine. 'Cheers.'

And we watch fascinated, as she swigs hers back in one go.

'I'll have another one, I think,' she says and disappears into the sitting room.

'Is everything all right?' asks Jonathan.

'Yes. Well, no, everything's not all right, actually,' I decide to say. 'Maybe I'll tell you about that later, too.'

We follow Ruth in and find her sitting on the sofa, glass in hand, leaning forward and staring at the fire. Geoffrey is beside her, head slumped slightly to one side. He starts as we come in.

'Sorry, just nodded off then. Jonathan, another drink?'

'No thanks. I must be off. I'll see you tomorrow evening.'

After he's gone, I realise I've already got used to him being around, a fact that bewilders me somewhat. Before going to bed I look at Ruth in what I hope is a meaningful way, trying to convey to her that she ought to say something to Geoffrey about the move. I doubt she'll be capable though with the amount of wine she's had since supper.

Upstairs, the box waits...

PART TWO

Thursday 12th August 1954

...and inside, the photographs. I sit on the bed and take out the folder. The prints are small, about two inches by three, black and white, with a narrow white border. Almost holding my breath, I thumb through them. They are like stills from the film that's been going on in my head since yesterday.

First, a view of the schoolhouse, whitewashed, timber-framed, with the village of Volkmarshausen in the background. Beyond, the hill on the opposite side of the valley is thickly wooded. In front are three figures, standing in a row. Looking straight at the camera is Frau Schmidt, her hair parted in the middle and tightly drawn back. She has high cheekbones and is younger than I remember. She is wearing a shortish, straight skirt and matching dark blouse. Beside her, looking into the middle distance, is Herr Schmidt, bespectacled, casually dressed in white shirt and sweater. On her other side is

Gudrun, her head bent, looking away from the camera, hands clasped in front of her, wearing a full skirt with a patterned border and light coloured top. Yes, I recognise them all. They are just as I remember them. A good start then.

Next, Barbara and I stand on either side of Fritz, the clergyman. We are all arm in arm. He has on the corduroy plus-fours I remember, the tweed jacket and check shirt, both fully buttoned up, the long woollen socks and stout shoes. Barbara and I are wearing blouses, cardigans, full skirts, white ankle socks and quite substantial-looking sandals. We are smiling at the camera, but he is looking anxious and rather embarrassed. Goodness, I can't remember that one being taken. I wonder who took it. Gudrun probably. But once again, it perfectly reinforces what I recollect.

I look through the rest of the photos quickly, because, of course, what I'm really looking for is the photo of him. And it's not here. I am positive there should be one of the two of us. I can remember it being taken. I can remember Barbara taking my camera from me, telling us to smile and insisting that we stand closely side-by-side, his arm round my shoulder. Where is it? Please, where is it?

I get out the rest of the things from the box – the diary, the postcards, the letters. I look inside the envelopes. Nothing. No more photos. Tomorrow, I shall have to sort through the other ones in the box downstairs, in case it's dropped out. Meanwhile, I decide to get the postcards and letters into some sort of order. The postcards all still have their postmarks, from mid to late August, 1954. There are four addressed to my parents and one to my grandmother. Then there are the letters. There appear to be only three, but then I remember. I had kept a sort of "running letter," all the time I was there, adding bits each day until I posted it off and started the next one.

I decide to read the beginning of the first letter and the diary entry for the second day, before going to sleep.

Thursday 12th August

Dear Mummy and Daddy,

This is the first bit of my first long letter. This afternoon we caught the train to Hann. Münden for the official "Welcome to Germany", at the youth club to which most of the girls belong. There were speeches by the mayor and we ate cakes and drank tea with condensed milk in it from tins on the table.

Everyone here shakes hands every time they see each other, even first thing in the morning. For early breakfast they just have bread or cake, but then they have a second breakfast in the middle of the morning. For lunch today we had a sort of fried potato pancake (called a "Puffer", I think). For supper we had bread with sausage, tomato and cheese, eaten from a wooden platter thing. We drank weak tea, without milk, but it was quite nice.

This evening we listened to a concert by the village choir, to which Frau Schmidt belongs. Barbara was there, too, with her family. I will stop now as I am very tired. I will write more tomorrow.

I definitely need more to fill out the day, so I turn to the diary once more.

I was able to sleep late in the morning because I was so tired. I was woken by the sound of the schoolchildren coming out from lessons for their break, all shouting at the tops of their voices, running up the hill or down to the village. As soon as the bell went, they all came tearing back to the playground under my window and filed back in. Gudrun didn't have to

go to school this morning as I was here. Apparently they
normally start at seven o'clock in the morning, but the
students who live out of the town don't start till eight. School
finishes at midday, so they have a lot of free time.

As I read on, it all begins to come back to me. That morning I finished unpacking and after breakfast, while Gudrun helped her mother in the kitchen, I went out into the garden. It surrounded the house and was quite large, with raspberries, blackcurrants and gooseberries round the side and apple and plum trees in the playground area. Coming round the corner to the back of the house I was startled by Max, the family's Alsatian dog. He started to bark hysterically as I went by, leaping at me on the end of his chain. I noted in the diary that I had felt very sorry for him, as I was sure he was a very sweet dog, but that Gudrun had told me I must not try to touch him as he would bite me. I don't think the implication that I could have caught rabies entered my head at that time.

Later, I walked down the path to the village. The houses were mostly quite scattered, but I discovered what appeared to be an inn, and further along the road the post office, where Barbara was staying with Helga. There was no sign of her though, so I posted my duty postcard and turned to go back to the school. A little fair-haired boy aged about four, dressed in short leather trousers, a striped jumper and wellington boots, came out of the house next to the post office and stood, hands in pockets, grinning at me. I was preparing the words to greet him in German when he scuttled back inside.

We had been learning German for about two years, but it was one thing to know the theory, quite another actually to pluck up the courage to speak the language. Barbara was a natural linguist and was fluent already, so she had been sent to a family none of whom could speak English, apart from Helga.

I walked back in time to see the children come streaming out into the playground, all shrieking their heads off again. School was obviously over for the day. At lunch, Gudrun wore a substantial apron over her rather prim, high-necked blouse and full skirt. She told me that the potato pancakes we were eating were one of the family's special dishes and that she herself had made these. I remember detecting a certain smugness and pride in her budding domesticity.

In the afternoon, Gudrun and I walked up through the wood to catch the train into Hann. Münden. There was no road to the station, only the little path which passed the school. As we opened the gate, we saw Barbara and Helga coming up from the village and waited until they caught us up. Helga's family were refugees from the Russian zone and she was the only one of the German girls not to have been to England earlier that summer. They lived next to the post office, which was also the only shop in the village, and we gathered they didn't have much money to spare. Her father worked at the post office in Münden. She smiled shyly at me and I was puzzled that Barbara introduced her as 'Hummel'. I soon learnt that practically everyone in Germany seemed to have a nickname, which didn't necessarily bear any resemblance to what they were really called.

There was no one to issue or collect tickets at the station, which was just cut out of the hillside, with a steep bank opposite and no real platform. The fir wood above us was dark and silent. I couldn't help thinking of the wild boar roaming so close to us and was relieved that, just as we got there, we heard a distant whistle and in less than a minute the train appeared out of a tunnel cut through the hill.

The seats were wooden and not very comfortable, as it was only a local train. A man was already in the carriage to take our money and laboriously wrote on a card where we were going and how much it cost, which took ages.

'He cannot get out of one carriage and into another,' Gudrun explained, somewhat sternly, 'so if he is on another part of the train, you must buy a ticket at the other end.'

The journey was quite short and, when we arrived, we made our way through the narrow streets of timber-framed houses to the *Jugendhaus*. We were greeted by the mayor and various other officials, who made what seemed to be endless speeches in slow, simple German, which was still incomprehensible to most of us. At last we were all able to compare notes about our respective hosts, while we drank our tea and ate our cakes. Many of the girls staying in the town had huge, modern bathrooms with hot water on tap all the time, but others had no bathroom or hot water. In Volkmarshausen, if Barbara and I wanted a bath we had to go to the public baths in Münden. We never did get round to having one the whole three weeks we were there. I can remember even now the feeling of utter bliss when I was able to have a long, luxurious soak in hot water when I got home.

Before we all went to our respective houses again, Miss Harris solemnly presented us with one third of our pocket money, which would have to last for the first week. We were able to manage quite easily on ten marks, or, as it says in the diary, just under a pound. We caught the bus back to Volkmarshausen straight away.

There is no conductor, but when you get on the bus you all queue up to give your money to the driver. As he never knows how many people have got on, I am sure you could easily travel without paying. The roads into Volkmarshausen and, in fact, all round are very bad – terribly bumpy, usually made with cobble stones, so consequently your inside nearly gets shaken out.

It was when we returned to the house that afternoon that I heard the sound of the piano drifting down from the living room above. I stopped to listen, mesmerised, wanting above all to know who was playing. Gudrun was halfway up the stairs in front of me before I spoke.

'Who is that? I didn't know anyone played the piano.'

'That is Peter. He is the son of a friend of my father. On Thursday evening he always visits to our house.'

Gudrun paused. Then the colour rose to her cheeks and she giggled, something I couldn't remember her doing before.

'I think,' she said, 'that my father wants that I marry Peter.'

'Really? You didn't tell me about him. Is he nice?'

'Well, he is beautiful.'

I laughed. 'Beautiful? We don't say that about boys.'

'No? What then?'

'Well,' I said, considering. 'Good-looking, I suppose, or handsome, perhaps.'

She looked down at me and said nothing, then continued up the stairs and opened the sitting room door.

As it turned out, "beautiful" was a completely inadequate description of the Adonis who rose from the piano after a final flourish and looked at me. I realise now that he was the perfect Aryan model – fair hair, blue eyes, long straight nose. And he had the slightly wistful look of someone who is trying to convey to the world that he is a true artist. Regardless of what Gudrun had just said about her father's plans, I was convinced, from that first sight, that I had found the love of my life.

'Oh, please go on playing,' I said. 'That was wonderful. What is it?'

'It is the "Rhapsody G-moll" – I think you say "minor" – of Brahms,' he said.

'Peter will play more later,' said Herr Schmidt. 'Peter, this is our friend Margaret from England. *Gudrun, hilf deiner Mutter, bitte. Ihr seid ein bißchen zu spät angekommen.'*

Gudrun again said nothing, but went into the kitchen to help with the supper.

'Peter was playing the piece he will perform at the concert in Kassel next week,' Herr Schmidt continued. 'Gudrun has perhaps told you that he hopes to become a student next year at the conservatory in Hannover?'

'No, she didn't. How marvellous.'

'Now, I think the meal is nearly ready. You were a little late arriving back.'

He followed his daughter into the kitchen.

At the table I took a seat next to Fritz, the clergyman.

'You play the piano also?' Peter asked me, as he sat down opposite.

'Well, just a little,' I said, wishing I'd persisted in my lessons beyond grade five. 'But not like you.'

'But you like music? What is the music you like?'

'Oh – Tchaikovsky, Chopin, you know, anything romantic. I spend my pocket money buying records, but of course I haven't got a very big collection yet. And books too. Poetry, you know, that sort of thing.'

'You know the poetry of Heine? It is very fine. *"Du bist wie eine Blume, so hold und schön und rein."* He says "You are like a flower, so charming and beautiful and pure". I think like you!'

'Oh gosh,' was all I could say. No one had ever spoken to me in remotely that way before. I blushed, completely overcome. Fritz said nothing. Gudrun came in with the soup and sat down next to Peter, making a great show, I thought, of telling him of her part in cooking it. She ladled his portion out first. I sat silently, just picking at my food. I felt utterly bewildered at what was happening to me. The diary, though, says nothing of what I was feeling.

This evening, Peter, the son of a friend of Herr Schmidt came to supper. He plays the piano very well and is very nice.

And that was all.

The conversation in German carried on around me. They all spoke far too quickly for me to follow what they were saying. Gudrun eventually turned to me.

'On Sunday we will go dancing in the town and Fritz will come with us when he has been to visit his mother.'

They always have anything like dancing on Sundays, not like us who keep Sunday as a rest day. Fancy a clergyman dancing too!

I seemed genuinely shocked at the prospect.

'Peter will not come with us,' she went on, 'as he has to practise for the concert at his school on Monday. We will visit to hear him then. He would, of course, prefer to come dancing with me.'

'What will you play at the concert?' I asked Peter.

'Naturally, he will play the Brahms,' said Gudrun, before Peter could answer. I wondered what she would have said if she knew that Peter had just told me I was like a flower.

'Margaret, this evening at eight o'clock, after the meal, we will go to our local inn,' said Herr Schmidt. 'Our village choir will sing for you, to welcome you to Germany. Perhaps your friend Barbara will also be there. I believe that she also stays in the village.'

'Yes, Herr Schmidt, she is staying with the Altmeyers.'

'The Altmeyers, you know, Margaret, are from the Russian zone of Germany. They must leave their home and their family. Now they wait for their son to come here also. But this is difficult. It is now not allowed. We here in the West believe in freedom, but in the East they do not believe it.'

That was the first time, I suppose, that I had been personally involved in the politics of the Cold War. All I knew was that we were staying in West Germany, which until recently had been under the rule of Britain, France and America, that we were very near the border with the Russian zone and that we would not be allowed to visit it.

After supper Peter had to catch the bus back to Hann. Münden, so Gudrun and I walked down to the village with him. We all sat for a while on a rock down by the river while we waited for the bus to arrive. And then, yes, something that is not in the diary, but that has just come back to me. Gudrun and I were sitting side-by-side and Peter was just behind us. I remember suddenly feeling what I thought was a fly on the back of my neck. I brushed it away, but I soon felt it again. I turned round. Peter was gently tickling my neck with a long piece of grass and smiling at me. I felt flattered and pleased, but at the same time embarrassed and uncomfortable. I don't think I reacted in any way, apart from just getting up and pointing to something over on the other side of the river. The bus arrived shortly afterwards. Peter shook us both by the hand, boarded the bus and was gone.

I can rely on the diary, though, to remind me of what happened later that evening.

At eight o'clock we went to Schaefers, which is really the village pub. Barbara was there with Helga and her parents, who cannot speak any English. The village choir held a special concert in our honour. We felt extremely grand, but a little foolish, for there were such a lot of people in the choir, including Frau Schmidt and Herr Altmeyer, and the audience consisted of only Barbara, Helga, Frau Altmeyer,

Gudrun, Herr Schmidt, Fritz and myself. But they sang quite well and we duly clapped, making a very weak little noise. While they were singing the entire choir kept glancing in our direction, peering over spectacles and from behind music, until we began to feel rather as if we were the ones on show. Then we had to go and sit at a table with some boys, who, by English standards, would have been considered rather spivvy and who weren't very nice. Although we insisted that we wanted nothing to drink, suddenly a schnapps was thrust in front of us, which we had to drink. It is the most ghastly stuff I have ever tasted and burns your throat terrifically, but I managed to get it down somehow.

I can't help smiling to myself as I read this thirty-five years later. The biggest insult I could manage at the time was to describe a boy as "spivvy", implying not that he was of dubious character exactly, but merely that he used Brylcream on his hair. "Nice" boys, boys of our social standing, didn't do that. Peter, of course, was the very reverse of "spivvy". His fair hair flopped over his eyes in the most delectable way, without a trace of hair cream. It might have been the effect of the schnapps or the heat of the duvet but, as I lay in bed, I felt a restlessness and excitement I had never experienced before.

And now, as it did that night, the sound of the Brahms plays endlessly in my head as I finally drop off to sleep...

CHAPTER THREE

PART ONE

Saturday 23rd December 1989

...and is still there the next morning. I vaguely remember waking in the night, aware that the music had become part of a dream. I can hear traffic moving along the road outside the house. Below my window, Bella barks to be let into the kitchen. In the distance a car alarm goes off. When I turn over and look at my watch, I see I've slept till gone nine o'clock.

There is no one about when I get downstairs. *The Times* is still lying on the doormat, so I pick it up and take it into the kitchen. While I wait for the kettle to boil, I sit at the table, reading. "Bloodbath in Bucharest" is the headline. Underneath are three photographs; one shows two jubilant soldiers, their hands in the air; the second is of a grim looking President Ceausescu and his wife Elena; the third shows the helicopter carrying the deposed dictator leaving the central committee building. Inside, is a photo of the smiling president and his wife with the queen on a visit to Britain in 1978 and a report that Ceaucescu has been stripped of the honorary knighthood, which I didn't know he had in the first place. It just shows what can be achieved when a whole country decides it's had enough. I reflect, though, that I'm glad to be living here, where the most we usually do is hand in petitions at Downing Street or hold the odd demonstration in Trafalgar Square.

Then, from the study across the hall comes the sound of Ruth's voice, raised above normal conversational level. I can't hear what she's saying, but guess that she has at last pinned Geoffrey down and made him listen to her. She carries on talking for some considerable time and there is a long silence before Geoffrey says anything. It's then that I realise I've been straining my ears to hear what really is none of my business. So, when I've finished my toast and coffee, I scribble a note and leave it on the table, saying I've decided to take the dog for a walk. As if she's read my mind, Bella follows me out of the room, wagging her tail enthusiastically. She looks pointedly at her lead hanging in the hall.

I close the front door quietly and, as I go down the steps, I see Shirley walking towards the house.

'I'm afraid they've gone out,' I lie.

'Oh dear, how odd. Geoffrey is expecting me.'

'Well, I think it was on the spur of the moment.' It's a good job that the study looks out on to the back garden.

'I should come back a bit later if I were you – say about eleven,' I add. In other words, I think to myself, push off, Shirley. She looks disappointed, but turns back without saying anything.

It's a chilly but fine morning and I decide to walk across the heath and into Greenwich Park. The Brahms rhapsody is still going on in my head and, involuntarily, I try to match my steps to its rhythm, but it's difficult to walk slowly enough. So I speed the music up inside my head, which is just as unsatisfactory. The tempo now is too quick. It's as frustrating as listening to a different recording of a familiar work from the one I'm used to.

I'm glad to be out of the house and in the fresh air. I need time to myself, to take stock of everything that's happened since I arrived on Wednesday. My life has been largely unchanged for several years now and I suppose I've become complacent. I assume I shall go on teaching at the same school until I retire, in about eight years' time. Shortly after becoming deputy head five years ago, I moved from a flat to a small, semi-detached house in a quiet cul-de-sac and enjoy pottering about in my garden. I have a comfortable circle of friends, most of whom also teach at the school. We go to concerts, the cinema and the theatre and often walk on the cliffs or in the country at weekends. I have at least one longish holiday in the summer and go on several short breaks throughout the rest of the year, usually with my friend Frances. And at Christmas, I come here, to my family.

For years now the vicarage has been the focal point for us all, the place we all gravitate to. The first intimation that my cosy world might be crumbling came when my mother died in the autumn. Ruth and I have suddenly been moved up a generation. Inevitably, it will be our turn next. Where will we be next Christmas? How can I not have noticed the apparent rift between Ruth and Geoffrey? And did Ruth not realise that Jane and Philip were growing apart?

When we get to Greenwich Park, I let Bella off the lead. Another thing that's unsettling me, I realise, is the picture I have in my mind's eye of Jonathan sitting at the piano, playing Brahms. Why have I become obsessed with someone I've only just met, and with whom I've exchanged probably no more than a few dozen words? If I'm not careful it will be just like thirty-five years ago and look where that got me. I tell myself that I'm reading far too much into what is really just an odd coincidence. It's not as if I haven't heard the Brahms rhapsody since my visit to Germany, although I must admit I always feel uneasy when I do. I probably wouldn't have given it another thought if he had chosen to play something else instead. But then, inside my head, I hear the sound of his voice above the music.

I'll play some more for you, if you like, after supper, he's saying.

And again I feel tears coming to my eyes. This time they just roll uncontrollably down my cheeks, as if they are overflowing from a reservoir that I've kept sealed up inside me for years. I don't sob or make any noise. I turn my head away from the people walking past me and fumble in my coat pocket for a handkerchief. I continue walking until I reach the Woolf statue, then stand looking down towards Greenwich and the whole of London, spread out in front of me. The river snakes round in a huge loop, before disappearing to my right. Bella pushes her cold nose into my hand and sits down beside me. Now I'm high up, the wind feels icy and I shiver. I blow my nose and surreptitiously wipe my eyes. Ridiculous. Not like me at all. I glance at my watch and see it's nearly eleven o'clock. I decide I've been out long enough.

'I expect I shall get into trouble from your master when we get home,' I tell Bella, who looks up expectantly, eager to please. 'He'll wonder why the faithful Shirley didn't turn up when she said she would.'

When I get back, the house is quiet and there is still no sign of anyone. Perhaps Shirley has been and gone. I go into the kitchen. Bella follows me, goes to her water bowl and takes noisy, messy slurps from it, before climbing into her basket with a contented sigh. Then I glance out of the window and see Ruth standing in the garden, quite still, her back to the house, arms folded, staring ahead of her. She's not wearing a coat and the wind is catching the stray wisps of hair blowing round her face. She makes no attempt to put them behind her ears, as she normally does. Then I hear the door of Geoffrey's study opening and I turn to look into the hall. Shirley is walking towards the front door, then stops.

'I'm so looking forward to it. The Christmas concert is always such a joy,' she's saying.

Geoffrey opens the door and ushers her out.

'Thanks, Shirley, we'll see you this evening.' He shuts the door firmly, then turns and sees me. He grins.

'Ruth's right. She certainly does dither.'

He comes into the kitchen and takes the kettle to the sink.

'Fancy a cup of coffee?'

'That would be nice.'

I know he must have seen Ruth through the window, but he makes no comment, just gets three mugs out of the cupboard. Outside, Ruth turns round abruptly on her heels, as if she's come to a sudden decision. She walks deliberately towards the back door, pausing only to pick up a stray leaf from the grass. She looks up and sees me, grins somewhat ruefully, and comes into the kitchen. Geoffrey pours the coffee and opens the biscuit tin. We all stand round the table for several minutes until Ruth breaks the silence.

'Shirley asked if you could go over to the church to help her set out the cups before the concert – at about five o'clock, if that's all right, Meg. One of her ladies has keeled over with some sort of bug. What did she want to see you about, Geoffrey?'

'We're worried about Mrs Bailey – how she's coping. I noticed she seemed very quiet at the funeral yesterday, as if she was bottling it all up. Shirley says she'll pop round this afternoon and make sure she has somewhere to go on Christmas Day.'

'I think she's got a daughter, hasn't she? She'll probably go there.'

It's as if nothing has happened. I've heard them having conversations like this for years. Did they come to an agreement this morning? And, more to the point, who won? Before we've finished our coffee, the doorbell and the telephone ring almost simultaneously and then later there's a minor crisis when Ruth realises she hasn't collected the turkey yet. It's not until after lunch that things calm down again and I get Ruth to myself. Helen and Ian are due to arrive at about four o'clock, so with any luck we have about an hour. We decide to prepare an easy supper, so we won't be too rushed before the concert, but first we make a cup of tea and take it into the sitting room.

'Well?' I say.

'I suppose you could hear us this morning?'

'Yes, but not what you were actually saying. I shall quite understand if you don't want to discuss it, though.'

'No, no, I want to. It's just that it's more complicated than I thought at first.'

Surely it's not another woman, I think to myself momentarily, but don't say.

'And no, he's not having a mad, passionate affair with the faithful Shirley!'

She knows me too well. We giggle at the thought. She pauses, then takes a deep breath.

'You know how he suddenly "got religion" twenty-odd years ago?' she says finally. 'Well, now he's lost it.'

And I realise I am not surprised.

'He's had long talks with the bishop and they've agreed the best thing to do would be just retire quietly now and not make a big thing about it. He says he's not too keen to go on living near here, though. But I pointed out that he doesn't have to go a couple of hundred miles away. Over the river would do just as well.'

'What on earth made him change his mind after all this time? Don't tell me you finally persuaded him to come round to your way of thinking.'

'I shouldn't think so! When has he ever listened to me? Although, I actually felt quite sorry for him this morning. He does seem genuinely upset. Of course, he used expressions like "a crisis of conscience" and "all the evil in the world now" to try to explain why, but really I think he's lost interest. Just going through the motions, so to speak. Thinking about it, I've noticed lately he's been repeating some of his old sermons from a few years back and he's even started to get a bit tetchy with his "Angels of Mercy". Poor old Shirley will be devastated when she finds out, won't she! He seems relieved I know about it, but I have a feeling he's still not telling me everything. And why he couldn't talk to me before finally making up his mind is something I shall probably never know. But he's agreed to think about the question of where we're going to live. He seems quite shaken, actually. He says he didn't realise I feel so strongly about it. I've made up my mind though. I shall stay near here, regardless of what he does.'

'I'm sure it won't come to that, Ruth. But I was right, wasn't I? It was best to have this out with him before everyone arrives. When are you going to tell them?'

'We thought we'd get Christmas Day over first. Boxing Day perhaps. Then we can tell Martin and Val as well.'

'And Jonathan,' I find myself adding.

'Yes, and Jonathan!' Ruth repeats, looking at me sideways. I pretend not to notice.

Bella suddenly pricks up her ears, gets up and ambles out into the hall, her tail wagging enthusiastically.

'That must be them,' says Ruth. 'They're early.'

I can sense her excitement.

'I haven't seen the boys since half term,' she adds, as she goes to the door. Helen and her family moved to Suffolk last year, when Ian was transferred to the Ipswich branch of his bank. Until then, they lived less than half an hour's drive away, so Ruth and Geoffrey saw them nearly every week.

Above the general hubbub, I hear shouts of 'Grandpa!' followed by shrieks of laughter. Bella, normally a quiet, well-behaved dog, starts barking excitedly. Why am I always surprised by the sheer volume of noise three small boys are capable of generating? It's only for a few days, though. I smile ruefully.

I brace myself and go out to join them. I'm immediately absorbed into an atmosphere of warm, affectionate chaos. But I notice that William, who is nearly thirteen now, is standing awkwardly outside the circle, obviously embarrassed by the exuberance around him. Since I saw him last, he too has moved on to the next stage in his life. He reluctantly allows me to give him a peck on the cheek and mutters something I take to be a greeting. His voice is deeper, the shape of his face is beginning to change, and he has a new, spiky-looking hair cut. Geoffrey and Ian go outside, followed by the two older boys, to bring in the rest of the luggage, and Max lets out a brief howl of protest at his exclusion. Ruth gives Helen another hug.

'I can't tell you how nice it is to have you all here,' she says.

Thinking they might like a moment's peace together, I take Max by the hand. He looks up suspiciously and I realise he probably can't remember me very well. Four months must seem a long time when you're only three. He still has the tender, vulnerable look, which only little boys seem to have.

'Let's go and look at the Christmas tree,' I suggest, hopefully.

In the sitting room he stands quite still, gazing at the lights. William, at that age, would have wanted to examine how the bulbs fitted into the sockets and Jack's first thought would have been to pull them off the tree. But Max seems instinctively to have a sense of wonder. Being the youngest by five years, he is also the most independent and self-contained. Ever since he could stagger about he has lived in his own little world, humming tunes to himself, holding imaginary conversations with his toys and telling them the stories he remembers from his bedtime books.

It's only when Helen and Ruth have taken the boys upstairs to unpack and Geoffrey and Ian have disappeared somewhere together, that I remember the missing photograph of Peter and me in the garden at Volkmarshausen. It's important because I can't remember exactly what he looks like. I know about the fair hair, the aquiline nose, the blue eyes, but I haven't got an image of the whole of his face. So I go into the dining room, intending to have a look through Mother's photos again. I give the cat a quick stroke. As usual when the boys arrive, she has tucked herself away in her favourite bolthole under the sideboard, where she obviously feels safe from the marauding hordes. I look first in the bottom of the box where I had found the other photos yesterday, thinking it might have fallen out. Nothing. Just a school group – my class when I was about fourteen, three years before the trip to Germany. I'm sitting next to Barbara and we both have our hair – hers fair, mine dark – severely drawn back into two long plaits. It must have been the summer term, because we are all wearing ankle socks and sandals, and checked dresses, with neat white collars. I turn the print over and see that I have actually written the names of all the girls on the back, row by row. I'd forgotten how meticulous I was.

'What are you doing Auntie Meg?'

William's voice startles me and I jump, stupidly feeling as if he's caught me out.

'Just looking through Nana's old photos. Look, that's me.'

'You had really black hair then. Who are the others?'

'The girls I was at school with. We were only just a bit older than you are now when it was taken.'

'Do you still know any of them?'

'I went to university with the girl sitting at the end of that row, and I still see her sometimes. Her name's Pamela – Pam Stevens then, but she's called Hartley now. I've lost touch with everyone else.' Even my best friend, Barbara, I add to myself.

Then I remember that the girl sitting next to Pam in the photo, another Barbara, was killed the following year, knocked off her bicycle on her way to school. But I don't tell William. I wonder whether I should. We had all been deeply shocked. It was the first intimation we had that life was arbitrary. I take another photograph at random from the other box.

'Have a look at this one, Will.'

We both examine a sepia photograph of a little boy in a sailor suit.

'That's your great-grandpa – my father – and your granny's, of course.'

'He looks just like Jack, doesn't he?'

'Goodness, I've never noticed that before. Yes, he does. Except, of course, I shouldn't think Jack would appreciate having to dress up in all that!'

We both laugh. We've broken the ice. We look at some more of our relations, most of them long dead, trying to decide whom, if anyone, they resemble.

'That looks a bit like Mum, doesn't it?'

'I know what you mean. It's the dark hair and the shape of her eyebrows. Mine used to be a bit like that, too. I think she may be your great-granny's sister, but I don't know her name. Their father was Italian, you know.'

'That means I'm a bit Italian, too, doesn't it.'

'That's right. Let's see, we need to work it out. Nana was half, I'm a quarter, your mum is an eighth, so you're just a sixteenth!'

When it's time for me to go over to the church hall, William asks if he can stay and look at some more of the photos. Last year he was a little boy, eager to taunt his younger brothers, complaining he was bored. Now it's as if the age gap between the two of us is irrelevant.

Shirley is on her own, making a great fuss over the simple job of setting out the cups and putting some mince pies on to plates. I suddenly realise that I have met her before. I can remember the shocked silence during the interval of last year's concert, when she spectacularly dropped a tray of crockery, as she was carrying it through to the kitchen.

'Sorry I'm late, Shirley. The family have all arrived and I didn't realise the time.'

'They're such lovely boys, aren't they? Geoffrey and Ruth are so lucky. Of course, I'm all by myself now. We were not blessed with children and my dear husband left us three years ago this coming March, you know.'

Left or died? I find myself suppressing a smile. Involuntarily, I echo the tone of her voice.

'I'm so sorry, Shirley. It must be a great comfort that you have your brother and his wife living nearby.'

We fill the urn and I promise to be back in time to switch it on before the concert. As I walk back to the vicarage, I find myself working out how long it will be before I see Jonathan again. Probably less than two hours. Thirty-five years ago, I would have been calculating the exact number of minutes too.

When I get back, they are all sitting round the kitchen table, already eating supper. The boys are starting to get fractious. It's been a long day. Max starts to grizzle and push his food about on his plate. Ian gets up from the table.

'Come on, old chap, let's get you into your bath.'

'No bath, Daddy.'

We can hear their voices as Ian leads his son, still protesting, up the stairs.

I sit down next to Jack. William's right; there's something about the tilt of the head, the look of sturdiness, the fair, slightly wavy hair. I've often wondered why he looks nothing like his brothers, assuming he gets his looks from Ian's family.

'Auntie Meg, Will says I used to wear a sailor suit. I didn't, did I?'

'No, Jack, he's only teasing. We found a photo of your great-grandpa, taken when he was little. He looked a bit like you, that's all.'

'See!' shouts Jack triumphantly.

William lets out a sudden yell.

'Mum, Jack kicked me – really hard!'

'Just grow up boys,' says Helen, wearily. 'Jack, if you don't stop whining, you'll have to go to bed as well. William, go up and change, please, if you've finished eating. And brush your hair.'

After supper, Helen, Ruth and I go upstairs to get ready. Ian has agreed to stay behind with the two younger boys, while William comes to the concert with us. I just hope he stays the course. An hour ago it seemed a good idea; now I'm beginning to have my doubts. But when I go downstairs half an hour later, he has reverted to his more grown-up self and doesn't rise to the bait when Jack comments on his new shirt and the way he has brushed his hair.

Ruth and Geoffrey have gone on ahead, so I walk over to the church with Helen and William.

'Mum, we found a picture of someone just like you. Auntie Meg says she was Italian.'

'You and I have both got the Latin look, haven't we,' says Helen, smiling at me. 'It would be nice to find out a bit more about that side of the family, but it would be difficult to know where to begin.'

'Can we do a family tree, Auntie Meg? We could start tomorrow, couldn't we?'

'That's a great idea, Will. I'm sure between us Granny and I will be able to remember who quite a lot of the people in the photos are. Have you seen them, Helen?'

'Only glanced. It would make a good project for you while you're here, Will. Keep you out of mischief.'

William rolls his eyes at his mother in mock exasperation. I grin at him conspiratorially. I go to switch on the urn, as instructed. When I get into the church, it's already quite full and for a moment I can't see anyone I know. I recognise two of the ladies from yesterday afternoon – one on the door, and another handing out programmes. There is no sign of Jonathan. Then I see Martin's wife, Val, waving to me, as she greets Helen and William, and I go to sit next to them, near the front. Still no sign. I look through the programme for the list of performers – the conductor, the singers, then the trio. His name, I read, is Jacobs. Jonathan Jacobs, piano. Dr Jacobs, cardiologist. Odd, I hadn't wondered about it before.

Geoffrey, in his cassock, appears from the vestry, greets us and says the obligatory prayer. It has become a tradition, over the years, for the concert to start with the choir processing down the church, singing "Once in Royal David's City", with the first verse sung by one of the younger sopranos. As they file in and take their places, I realise that Jonathan has come in and is sitting at the piano. He looks very distinguished in his dinner jacket, I decide. This year, the second carol – "Ding Dong Merrily on High" – is unaccompanied, so all he has to do is play a chord before they start. The choir is not large – probably about twenty-five of them in all – but is of an almost professional standard. The sound of the voices fills the church and I find myself watching Jonathan. In repose, he has deep lines down his cheeks. He looks up and catches my eye. It's only when the carol ends that we look away.

The concert continues, the pattern reassuringly similar each year. One of the altos comes forward and reads from St Luke's gospel – the visit of the Angel Gabriel to Mary. Afterwards, the choir sing an unaccompanied arrangement of an old Basque carol, "Gabriel's Message", with its gentle, lilting rhythm. I watch Ruth, her face radiant with happiness. She mustn't give all this up, I think to myself. I suspect it's what has given her life some sort of meaning, during the years she has been playing the part of vicar's wife. Next comes an audience carol, "Hark the Herald Angels Sing", with Miss Draper playing the organ in her usual determined way. Although I haven't got Ruth's rich alto voice, I enjoy singing on occasions like these. I wonder what Jonathan's voice is like? Bass, I imagine, from the way he speaks.

Then the piano is pushed forward. Chairs and music stands are brought out ready for the trio. They play the Mozart – the Andante Cantabile, the middle movement, from the "Piano Trio in C major", I read in the programme. I watch his hands. Strong, broad hands. Pianist's hands. He plays with a delicate and gentle touch, perfect for Mozart. I feel a sense of uncontrollable happiness.

The first half of the concert ends with "Good King Wenceslas", sung by everyone. I notice that William, beside me, is unsure whether to be the page or the king. By next year though, I think his voice will have settled into a pleasant baritone. I imagine this will delight Ruth and make a mental note to tell her. Before the singing is finished, I get up as discreetly as I can and make my way to the hall to start pouring out coffee and squash. I'm fully occupied until after the second half of the concert has started, which is really rather annoying.

When I come into the church again, the choir is already singing the "Coventry Carol", which is one of my favourites, and I sit at the back until they've finished. I make my way to my seat while everyone is standing ready to sing "While Shepherds Watched". Geoffrey then reads a T. S. Eliot poem –"The Journey of the Magi". I'm always surprised how well he sounds, so unlike the tone he uses for taking services and giving his sermons. I wonder if there's any significance in the fact that this year he has not read a passage from the Bible, as he normally does.

After two more carols, the trio plays the Schubert "Notturno". The piano part has a lot of spread chords, arpeggios and trills. I wonder if at one time Jonathan had considered playing professionally. A question to ask him, I think, with pleasurable anticipation. I become completely absorbed in the music and with watching the interaction between the three of them. For a moment, I can feel my eyes beginning to prick with incipient tears. I pull myself together, sternly. As the sound gently fades away and they finish playing, I'm pleased that there is silence in the church, so the spell remains unbroken for a few seconds, before the applause starts. Then it's "O Come all ye Faithful", and the concert is over for another year. But no, next year won't be the same. I put on my coat and pick up my programme. The choir might be invited back, even though there'll be someone else in charge of the church, but Geoffrey probably won't want to come.

As usual, there's an informal party at the vicarage for the performers, everyone bringing a plate of something to eat and a bottle. For a little while I think Jonathan is not here and move from room to room in search of him, trying not to look too obvious. Ruth has appointed William head waiter and he skilfully manoeuvres himself among everyone, carrying a tray of drinks. I tell him I'm very impressed. Jack has been allowed to stay up and is given a plate of sausage rolls to offer round. I fill a plate with food and make my way to the sitting room. And there is Jonathan, bow tie and jacket discarded, sitting on the sofa, deep in what appears to be an intimate conversation with a soprano from the choir. For the first time in a very long while, I feel an involuntary pang of jealousy. They laugh and Jonathan looks up – and pats the seat beside him.

'Come and sit here, Meg,' he says. I'm disproportionately pleased he has used the name only members of my family call me. Yesterday, it was "Margaret". And even more pleased when the soprano eventually gets up to join a rather good-looking young man on the other side of the room, who puts his arm round her waist. By now the room is crowded and noisy. We finish our food in comfortable silence.

'Come on, Jonathan, we need you!' He gets up and I watch as he sits down at the piano, laughing at Ruth, who is holding out a piece of music. When she lets her hair down, Ruth can be very funny and it's become yet another tradition that she sings something like "Rule Britannia" or a Victorian drawing room ballad in a wonderfully plummy, Clara Butt-like contralto voice at the choir Christmas party. This time it's "Come into the Garden, Maud" and she receives a huge round of enthusiastic applause, as she pulls a rather sheepish-looking Jonathan to his feet to acknowledge it. More people perform their party pieces. I watch Ruth carefully. I suspect that, once again, she has had rather too much wine. She is too flushed, talking too loudly, laughing too heartily. She has the desperate air of someone having one last fling.

It's nearly midnight before everyone has gone and most of the debris has been cleared up. Jonathan went with everyone else, just saying he'd see us all on Boxing Day. Perhaps I'm wrong about him. Perhaps he hasn't given me another thought. In which case, of course, my life will carry on as before. I'm almost relieved, I realise. Much simpler that way. My head is throbbing by the time I eventually get into bed, but in spite of my weariness, I can't resist once again opening the diary...

PART TWO

Friday 13th August 1954

…and starting to read again.

> *I had to get up very early in the morning today – at about*
> *twenty to seven, in fact. After drinking some coffee, Gudrun*
> *and I dashed out of the house to get the train, which leaves*
> *at about half past seven, holding a piece of bread and butter*
> *to eat on the way to the station. We could hear the train*
> *whistling while we were still going up the path and only just*
> *managed to catch it.*

When we got on the train, I realised that Barbara was alone. I
asked her where Helga was.

'They all seemed very worried this morning. I think
they've had some news about Johannes – that's the brother
who's still in East Germany. They've given me a note for the
school, but I don't know what it says.'

I remember trying to put myself in their position. Suppose
the same thing had happened in England after the war? Ruth
was already married at the time of our visit to Germany and
living less than ten miles away. Jane was nearly four and Helen
just two. Suppose they had been forbidden even to visit us. I
could only imagine how devastated my parents would have
been. And now of course, it appears that the division between
East and West is about to be broken down at last. It just
emphasises how absurd it all was.

It seems I had settled into German life without much
difficulty. But I do remember that for the first few days there, I
actually felt quite homesick. It wasn't that I wanted to go home

exactly, but that I felt uprooted and rather bewildered. The school gave us what we would now call a "culture shock". I made a rather prim comment in my diary.

The lessons at the Mittelschule are not so well kept in order as ours and they obviously do not take the same attitude to their work as we do. They almost resent having homework and in the break between lessons they all go completely mad and shout at the tops of their voices. But Anne Owen, whose girl goes to the "Oberschule", said that the atmosphere there was very different – very much like our school. It is equivalent to a grammar school, as it is there that they prepare people for university. There is a girls' Oberschule and one for boys.

Of course, although I don't actually say so in my diary, the biggest shock of all was actually being in a class with boys – at home we didn't even have any men on the teaching staff. We had met some of the teachers from both schools the day before at the *Jugendhaus*. I can't really remember what any of them looked like, so I get out my photos again.

I had written on the back of most of them, in my rather precise, upright handwriting. First, a picture of a man and a woman sitting on a park bench, deep in discussion about something. I turn it over. *Fräulein Braun and Herr Schirrmacher (Herr Rektor)*, it says. I seem to remember that Fräulein Braun was the headmistress of the girls' Oberschule. In the photo, she has dark hair combed back from her face and is looking serious. Herr Schirrmacher was definitely headmaster of the Mittelschule. He is turning away from the camera, gesturing with both hands. He is a thickset, middle-aged man, with thinning, white hair. He wears wide-legged trousers with substantial turn-ups, has a light-coloured raincoat draped over his shoulders and a trilby hat balanced on his knee. The second photo is of a young, pretty woman, with short, fair hair, smiling at the camera, wearing a full-skirted floral dress. *Fräulein Schaefer*, it says. She caused quite a stir, of course. Then there is Herr Schroeder, the English teacher. I smile to myself, remembering. Yes, he obviously fancies himself. He is smartly dressed in a light coloured suit, with a white shirt and a patterned tie. His hair is very dark and brushed back neatly from his high forehead, his complexion quite swarthy, his expression smug.

The first lesson that day was English. Herr Schroeder stood at his desk, trying to bring the class to some sort of order.

'I hate him,' whispered Gudrun. 'We call him Belladonna.'

I learned later that this was because the drug belladonna, made from deadly nightshade, was at one time used by ladies to dilate the pupils of their eyes, in the belief that it enhanced their beauty. Herr Schroeder's eyes were certainly dark and disconcertingly piercing.

A threatening, hissing noise penetrated the general chaos. 'Pssssss.'

This was Herr Schroeder's way of getting attention.

'*Ruhe, ruhe bitte.* We have today our English guest with us. So, we hope she will help us with our English lesson. First we will read a poem. Margaret, please read to us from the book, page twenty.'

I suspected he thought his English accent was rather better than it actually was. Obediently, I opened my book and began to read.

'"*I wandered lonely as a cloud*
That floats on high o'er vales and hills
When all at once I saw a crowd,
A host of golden daffodils,

Beside the lake, beneath the trees
Fluttering and dancing in the breeze.'"

'That was excellent. Thank you. Now, girls and boys, do you know who wrote that? Gudrun?

'Wordsworth, Herr Schroeder.'

'Yes, but you are looking at the book, Gudrun. Before your next lesson with me, you will all translate the poem into German, please. Now, Margaret, do you know any German poems?'

'I know part of one by Heine, Herr Schroeder,' I said, thoughts of Peter uppermost in my mind. 'I think it goes: *"Du bist wie eine Blume, so hold und schön und rein".'*

There was a great shout of laughter from the rest of the class. *'Herr Schroeder ist eine Blume!'* and *'Er ist so schön!'* and *'Ich liebe dich, Belladonna!'* echoed round the room. Then the door opened and Miss Harris came into the room, obviously rather puzzled at the apparent mayhem.

'Excuse me, Herr Schroeder,' she managed to say. 'I'm afraid Margaret must leave the lesson now, as we are going on a trip to Kassel and the coach will be leaving shortly.'

'That is a pity. Thank you, Margaret, for reading to us so well.' I began to see why Gudrun disliked him. His apparent affability hid an underlying sarcasm which at that time we called "smarmy". I was actually relieved to be going.

'Auf wiedersehen, Herr Schroeder. Danke sehr!'

I shut the door behind me and could hear Belladonna trying to quieten his class again, without much success by the sound of it. From behind another door came the sound of singing.

I soon realised that Miss Harris had another reason for getting me out of the class early.

'Margaret. Do you know where Miss Smithson is? I can't find her anywhere and we can't leave without her.'

'I think she went into that classroom with Fräulein Schaefer, Miss Harris. Down the corridor, over there, where they're having a singing lesson.'

Ever since she had taught me elementary science, when I was about twelve, I had never really liked Miss Harris – or Harry, as we all called her. When I chose to go into the arts class, I knew there would be no danger of having her for physics, which was her subject.

'Dear, oh dear, it really is too bad of her.' She strode away and the sound of singing petered out as she opened the door.

'Please, excuse me, Fräulein Schaefer,' I could hear her saying, somewhat acidly. 'Gwen, you really must leave now. You know very well the coach is due to go in fifteen minutes.'

At that time it was very unusual to hear the staff being called by their Christian names. Often we could only surmise what they were, and we had only recently discovered that Miss Smithson was Gwen, and Miss Harris, Irene.

'Oh, sorry, Harry, I really didn't notice the time. Goodbye, Christel, I'll see you tonight.'

As they both came out, I could hear the class starting to sing again.

I began to walk away, along the corridor. By the rather petulant tone of Miss Harris's voice, I realised I was in danger of witnessing some sort of row.

'What do you mean, see her tonight? I thought we were going out for a meal together this evening?'

'Oh, goodness, I'm sorry Harry, I clean forgot. Tomorrow, perhaps. Christel has asked me round to her flat.'

Although I wanted to appear out of earshot, my curiosity got the better of me and I lurked just round a bend in the corridor.

'Well, all I can say is, I think you're treating me very badly,' said Miss Harris, obviously almost close to tears. 'You know very well why I wanted to come with you on this trip. Anyway, come on, or the coach will have to go without us. We're late already.'

The German girls were not coming with us on our trip to Kassel, so we had plenty of room on the coach. Our "second breakfast", we discovered when we unwrapped it, consisted of "Schwarzbrot", or "black bread", sandwiches. I had sausage inside mine and Barbara, to her horror, had raw bacon. We eventually acquired quite a taste for the heavy, dark bread, but never really got used to the rather stringy, indigestible bacon.

Miss Harris and Miss Smithson were now sitting side-by-side several seats in front of us, in what appeared to be stony silence. I told Barbara about the conversation I had overheard between them.

She snorted with laughter and her voice dropped to a conspiratorial whisper.

'Harry's obviously frightfully jealous.'

'Why, what do you mean?'

'Oh, come on, Mags, you are so innocent. I can't believe you sometimes. You must know Harry has a huge crush on Miss Smithson. That's why she wanted to come on the trip. They really wanted Mrs Williams to come – she can at least speak a bit of German. Harry can't speak a word.'

Although some of the staff at our school shared houses and were what we would now call "an item", Miss Harris, who was actually considerably older than Miss Smithson, lived with her elderly mother. By chance, I met Miss Smithson, years later, at a teachers' conference of some sort and was surprised to learn that she had got married quite soon after I left school. It seems strange that we didn't see the implications of the numerous crushes we had on the all-female teaching staff and, sometimes, on fellow pupils. I don't think I even knew the word "lesbian" then, and I certainly didn't think there would be any lasting effect on any of us once we left school.

At the time of our visit, remarkably little had been done to rebuild Kassel, even though the war had ended over nine years before. I don't think we were prepared by any of our teachers beforehand for what we would see, or ever discussed it when we got back home. Perhaps they decided to leave us to see for ourselves and draw our own conclusions.

Kassel was one of the most badly bombed towns in Germany and it is rather depressing to walk round there because nearly everything is still flat. They are only just beginning to build it up again and the buildings that were not bombed very badly are being pulled down because they are not safe. I suppose as a modern town it will be quite nice when it is finished. After walking round the town for a bit, we went to the museum. We looked round various rooms and saw some extremely beautiful pictures, including a very famous one by Rembrandt, of which I bought a postcard. There were also some statues, most of them either without heads or just heads without bodies.

Now I remember. I had been acutely aware during the previous few months that Barbara and I were beginning to grow apart. I still considered her my best friend and we continued to go out together and visit each others' houses. But she had begun to show what I considered to be an alarming development. She would often insist we spent time hanging about outside the boys' grammar school on our way home, and had even gone a few times to a local coffee shop with the brother of one of the girls at school. I was more shocked than I cared to admit. In the museum, she was examining the statues with interest.

'I say, Mags, they really do go into detail, don't they? Look at this chap. It's very small, though, isn't it? P'raps he's lost a bit. Still, no-one will recognise him, because he hasn't got a head, poor thing.'

'Really, Barbara, you shouldn't say things like that.' I couldn't help sniggering, though, in spite of myself. 'Anyway, I've seen other statues of naked men, and he looks about the same to me.'

'But then, you haven't seen the real thing, have you?' she said over her shoulder, as she walked on into the next room.

'And look at this one,' she continued, when I joined her again. 'I should think it was painful when she lost that bit, wouldn't you?'

I decided to ignore her and we soon caught up with the others.

After that I began to feel unwell. I had the beginnings of a sore throat and felt hot and shivery at the same time. At first I didn't say anything, but then Miss Smithson must have noticed, because she took me into a chemist's shop near the museum and bought me some pills, which I said were like little yellow beads and took two of them in the shop.

I don't know whether my temperature was ever really explained – homesickness, or even lovesickness perhaps! Looking back, I realise it may have been the beginnings of the severe bout of glandular fever I developed when I returned to England. We got back on to the coach again and were taken up to a hill above the town to the Herkules Monument. I thumb through my photos again. Yes, there he stands, in front of some kind of large, white painted gazebo, across a lake, on which swim some very artistically placed swans. When I turn it over, though, I see the photograph was taken by another of our party, Jennifer Parsons, who obviously had a better eye for a picture than I had.

The others walked down to visit a castle, but as I wasn't well, I stayed on the bus to go down the hill. There was just me, sitting at the back, and the driver sitting in the front. The road was terrifically bumpy and my ears went funny and I couldn't hear properly. At the bottom the driver parked the coach and we got out and sat in some gardens with lawns and trees and beautiful flowers and hot houses. He asked me about England and I told him about Ruth and my parents and our school. He told me about his family and showed me a photo of his wife and little boy. He had been in the war and had got to know several English officers. He now goes gliding at weekends and it took me about five minutes to find out what he meant, but my German must be better than I thought it was because I could understand most of what he said. Soon we could see the others coming back. Barbara, of course, accused me of "getting off" with the driver. I said this was nonsense, as he was old enough to be my father and that, as I wasn't feeling well, we hadn't said very much, to which she said that words weren't necessary. But really he was very kind to me and was rather sweet – not a bit like a bus driver.

Did I really write that? I obviously didn't know about the dangers of stereotyping!

On the way back from Kassel, I had the most awful sore throat and I think my temperature was up again. When we got back to Volkmarshausen I went straight to bed. Frau Schmidt, who had been a nurse before she married, took my temperature, which was not very high, and made me gargle with some horrid stuff, which nevertheless helped. I went to sleep in the evening, while Gudrun and her parents went to

*a promenade concert in Münden, I think, so I was extremely
cross to have missed it.*

I wonder how much I had told my parents about not being
well, so I get out the letter again. I had written it the following
day.

> *Saturday 14th August*
> *Yesterday we went to Kassel, which is very bomb-damaged
> – they are just beginning to build it up again – and visited
> a picture gallery, which had some lovely pictures and
> sculpture in it. I'm afraid I wasn't very well – just a chill I
> think – but am better now.*

There was more in the letter about what happened on
Saturday, but, as I can scarcely keep my eyes open now, I
decide to take just one day at a time. It seems strange that,
apart from a very cursory mention, I didn't say anything about
Peter in the diary. I seem to remember, though, that he was
constantly in my thoughts from the first meeting.

It's nearly one o'clock by now. I turn out the light…

CHAPTER FOUR

PART ONE

Sunday 24ᵗʰ December 1989

…and next morning, I realise I must have immediately fallen into a deep, apparently dreamless, sleep. All three boys are sharing the room next to mine and I can hear them shouting to one another, even though they must be only a few feet apart. It's not seven o'clock yet, so I decide it's still too early to launch myself into the hurly burly outside. Although I've only had about six hours' sleep, I have a feeling of anticipation – excitement even – which I find surprising. I usually need a strong coffee and a shower before I'm ready to start the day.

Through the wall I can hear one of the boys bouncing up and down on his bed. Then a yell and a crash, followed by silence. As I'm leaping up, scenes of mayhem flashing through my mind, I hear shrieks of hysterical laughter from next door. Ian, Ruth and I all arrive together, to be met by the sight of a forlorn and bewildered Max, sitting on the collapsed heap of his folding bed. Will and Jack are rolling around the floor in glee.

When they lived nearer, Helen and her family would usually just arrive on Christmas Eve and go home on Boxing Day. This time they're staying until the New Year, so that I fear this visit will be something of an endurance test for us all. Calm, of a sort, is restored at breakfast. Geoffrey goes off to take the early service. Plans for the day are tentatively made and revised. We will all come together this afternoon to decorate the tree. Some of us will go to the midnight service in the church. No one has yet heard when Jane will be arriving. We assume tomorrow, but we don't know if she will decide to stay the night. When Geoffrey returns, he and Ian are persuaded to take the boys out to play football on the heath – or anything to get rid of surplus energy – while we stay and stuff the turkey. Will says he'd rather start on his family tree. His enthusiasm for football is mostly passive and academic.

'Helen and I can manage the turkey between us,' Ruth says to me. 'You go and help Will.'

Ruth looks weary this morning – not exactly the "morning after", but quite pale and drawn. She's always been very close to her younger daughter and a quiet morning together will probably do her the world of good. I suspect she is planning to tell Helen about the move, before anyone else knows.

By the time the two younger boys come in, flushed and grubby, from their outing, Will and I have made a good start on the genealogical project.

'We need to ask you some questions, Grandpa,' Will says to Geoffrey, who, I am rather startled to see, is wearing an old striped rugby shirt, baggy shorts and bright red socks.

'Aren't you rather chilly in those?' I ask.

'He won't admit it, but his knees turned a very nasty shade of blue while we were on the heath,' says Ian.

'Nonsense. Just suitably dressed. What do you want to know, old chap?'

'We need the names of your grandparents. And Auntie Meg thinks your father was called Sidney and your mother was Gladys. Is that right?'

'Correct. Sidney Charles and Gladys Emily, to be precise. Let's have a look and see what you've done so far.'

I leave them, heads together, bending over the table, and follow the others into the kitchen. Ruth is looking more relaxed already and is listening to Jack's blow-by-blow account of the football match. Geoffrey obviously threw himself – literally – into the part of goalkeeper, but failed to save "loads and loads" of goals.

'Come on, you two,' says Ian. 'Let's go upstairs and hose you both down.'

Good old Ian, I think, almost guiltily. We all take him for granted. I know Ruth secretly thought he was a bit dull when she first met him. A bespectacled bank clerk was obviously not what she had in mind for her daughter. But I've always got on well with him. He tends to retire into the background at family gatherings and we've often found ourselves sitting together, just observing what's going on around us. Then he'll come out with an apt, often witty, sometimes acerbic comment, which makes me laugh out loud. And in his quiet way, he's done just as well as the high-flying, more ebullient and charming Philip. Ruth was initially much more enthusiastic when he and Jane got married. I reflect, ruefully, that it's just as well they didn't have children, in spite of being married for over ten years. If his efforts at playing the role of favourite uncle are anything to go by, he would have been the sort of father who would over-excite his children one minute and completely ignore them the next. So it was often something of a relief when he and Jane just made a duty pre-Christmas visit, before going off somewhere exotic, leaving a trail of chocolates, vintage wine and expensive presents.

'Mum's told me the news,' says Helen, going up to Ruth and giving her a hug. 'Actually, I'm not surprised. It just takes a bit of getting used to. I think sorting out Jane will be far more difficult.'

'Helen knew there was something up a couple of months ago,' says Ruth.

'Yes, I'm sorry, Mum. She made me promise not to say anything. It put me in rather a difficult position. Anyway, it's out in the open now.'

Even as a child, Jane kept what I can only describe as a protective shell round herself. She seemed impervious to any physical or mental knocks she received and was always disparaging about any weaknesses in those around her – including her younger sister. She had always been phenomenally bright and had no difficulty getting a place to read politics and economics at Oxford.

'Helen says she seemed genuinely upset,' says Ruth. 'When she told me, though, it was almost as if Philip was going away on a business trip, not pushing off for good.'

'I think it's the only time she's admitted to me she might conceivably have a problem – and, what's more, that she actually needs my help.'

'Oh, darling, I think that's being a bit hard.'

'No, Mum. You probably don't realise how horrible she could be sometimes when we were small. She used to say some really awful things to me. She always had this need to be superior, to be the best. She could never admit that she could possibly come second. Well, now she knows what it feels like.'

'I hope you didn't say that to her.'

'No, of course not. But you ought to know what I think. She always thought Philip was so marvellous. That she'd made such a wonderful catch. But we all knew about his flings – I think he would even have tried it on with me given half a chance, would you believe! And Jane always just went on pretending nothing was happening.'

'I can see we're going to have a jolly time tomorrow,' I say. They both laugh.

'It's all right, Meg. Now I've got all that out of my system, I shall be a model of the loving, sympathetic sister.'

Even so, I hope Jane doesn't spoil Christmas for everyone else. Ruth is on edge enough as it is, without coping with anyone else's problems. I can hear the two younger boys clattering down the stairs towards us, demanding yet more food. Why is getting a meal for eight people so complicated? It's partly, of course, because two of the boys want baked beans, one wants tinned spaghetti, whilst the rest of us are going to use up the leftovers from last night. When it's ready, Geoffrey is missing, so Will is sent to look for him and by the time he gets back, his beans have got cold.

'I thought we were going to decorate the tree,' says Jack, rather petulantly, immediately after he's finished his spaghetti hoops. That's another thing. The boys can never understand why we don't leap up from the table immediately we've finished eating, but just sit around talking and drinking coffee.

'Why don't you all go into the sitting-room and start taking the decorations out of the boxes?' suggests Ruth. 'Carefully!' she adds, as all three of them stampede off.

'Is that a good idea?' I'm thinking of Mother's fragile tree ornaments. 'Shall I go and keep an eye on them?'

But when I go in, Will has already taken on the role of supervisor.

'It's all right, Auntie Meg, I'll make sure they don't break anything.'

'Will there be chocolate?'

'I expect so, Max. We'll have to ask Granny.'

The ceremony of decorating the tree goes back as far as I can remember. We never vary it. Before we begin, we have to make sure everybody has something to hang up. Then we go up, one by one, in turn, youngest first. After that, things get much more casual. By the time everything has been hung up and tinsel draped over the branches, the tree often has a rather lopsided look.

Until Ruth found them, I had assumed that all the decorations I remember from my childhood had long ago been thrown away. As well as coloured glass balls, there are little imitation parcels tied up with ribbon and a whole collection of miniature straw animals. As we get them out of the box now, we can see why they were gradually replaced over the years. The balls have lost their lustre, the parcels have become squashed, their brown paper torn off, the ribbons missing and most of the animals have come apart, so it's difficult to see what they are meant to be. But the feeling of nostalgia they evoke almost takes my breath away. And there, right at the bottom of the box, is the angel. To me, as a child, it was a magical apparition, dressed in pure white, with shining silver wings and a crown, smiling down at me from the top of the tree. Now though, it seems much smaller than I remember, its gown discoloured and tattered, its wings and crown tarnished and its expression actually rather glum – grumpy even. We decide to perk it up by giving it a new tinsel crown, and hang it under the star at the top of the tree.

It's dark by the time we've finished. For a moment, even the boys are silent.

'I hope Mother would have been pleased,' Ruth says eventually, smiling at me.

'I'm sure she would. It's just a shame we didn't know she'd kept them all. She would love to know the boys have been able to see everything.'

Geoffrey goes out of the room saying he has to make a phone call, Jack decides he wants the television on, Will goes back to his family tree and the rest of us go into the kitchen and switch on the radio, to catch the end of the carols from King's College.

I've been so caught up in the family today I've hardly given anything else a thought. Now I find myself wondering what

Jonathan is doing, whether he's listening too, then tell myself not to be so stupid. What do I know about him? Very little. Do I know what he thinks about me? No. And what did I know about Peter all those years ago? Not a lot. Certainly not enough to decide, within a few minutes of meeting him, that I had found my soul mate. After we had returned from Germany, while I lay in bed recovering from glandular fever, I had resolved that I would never, ever, make that mistake again. That I would learn to become a rational, unemotional, self-sufficient person. Which I did. Now look at me. Ridiculous.

After the boys have had their tea, we are all caught up in another Christmas ritual – the "hanging up of the stockings". Max suddenly panics, when he thinks Father Christmas won't know he's here.

'You wrote to him last week, didn't you, Mum?' says Jack, obviously delighted to be joining in the adult conspiracy.

'I certainly did, darling. He knows you're staying here, Max, with your granny and grandpa. So you need to go to sleep as soon as possible, because he won't come if he knows you're still awake.'

We're all upstairs, watching the boys hang their stockings on the end of their beds, when the door bell rings. Ruth sighs.

'Go and see who it is, William, there's a dear. Tell whoever it is we're busy.'

We hear him opening the door and greeting someone.

'It's Auntie Jane!' he calls out.

Although, of course, we're expecting her to arrive at some time, we are all obviously a bit taken aback that she's here already. There is a moment's silence, before Ruth hurries out.

'Hello, darling,' we hear her say. 'What a lovely surprise. We weren't expecting you yet.'

Helen and I exchange glances, but say nothing. When we get downstairs, Ruth and Jane are sitting at the kitchen table, clutching mugs of tea. Ian, Geoffrey and William, who this year is being allowed to stay up for a grown-up Christmas Eve supper, are nowhere to be seen. At a quick glance, Jane seems not to have altered. She wears a smart black trouser suit and fashionable shoes. Her short, dark hair is still stylishly cut and her makeup meticulously applied. But since I last saw her, which was at my mother's funeral, she seems to have lost her healthy bloom; her face looks drawn, she is less assured, frailer somehow, and when she gets up to give me a brief embrace, I can tell she has lost weight. Will anyone broach the subject of Philip? Apparently not, at least not yet.

'I'll make up your bed after supper. I hope you don't mind being in one of the top rooms. We can't really rearrange rooms now, I'm afraid. Actually, we weren't sure whether you'd be staying, so I haven't made up your bed yet.'

'Don't fuss, Mother. Just leave the things out and I'll do it when I go upstairs.'

I'm obviously not alone in hearing a note of impatience in Jane's reply, because Helen catches my eye and makes a barely perceptible grimace. The vicarage has no fewer than ten bedrooms, some of them up in the attic, where any waifs and strays stay from time to time. The boys have been put in Jane's old bedroom.

As usual on Christmas Eve, supper is just omelette and salad, followed by cheese and fruit. William goes up to bed and we take coffee into the sitting room to watch the nine o'clock news. By now, everyone is caught up in the developments in Eastern Europe, and we watch in silence and disbelief. It seems the Romanian revolt has been successful and that Ceaucescu and his wife have fled the country. Albania is now about the only hard-line communist state remaining.

Ruth is staying with the boys and not going to the midnight service. The rest of us will be going over to the church at half past eleven, but until then we all disperse to do our separate things. I go upstairs, thinking once again of Helga and her family all those years ago, waiting in the village for news of Johannes. I try to picture them, and rummage around in the box until I find a group photo, which includes Helga. Then another one, of her little brother, running through the wood towards the camera. But there isn't one of her parents. I can, though, remember quite vividly what Johannes looked like, but only because of the framed photograph, which stood on the mantelpiece in their tiny house in Volkmarshausen. So, I remember him as a thoughtful-looking young man in his early twenties. He is standing on a beach, sand dunes behind him, his dark hair blowing in the wind, dressed casually in a jacket over a thick sweater, a scarf round his neck, looking straight into the camera. The image is burnt irrevocably into my mind, as clear today as it was thirty-five years ago. Why, if I can remember so clearly what Johannes looked like just from remembering a photograph, is Peter still an indistinct blur, just a list of parts, not a recognisable whole?

And as I stand in my room now, another image comes to me. A mental picture of me, tearing a photograph into tiny pieces, tears running down my cheeks. That's why I can't find the one I know I had, of Peter and me in the garden. And then I realise there is somewhere else to look – in the folder, in the opposite pocket from the prints, are all the negatives. I hold them up to the light in turn. Then, when I'm just about to give up hope, there we unmistakably are, standing side-by-side, the trees behind us bleached of colour, the sky midnight-black, our hair white, as if in shock, our faces eerily dark, our eyes and mouths clown-like, unrecognisable parodies of ourselves, grimacing at the camera, not smiling as we undoubtedly were. Now I just need to get the negative printed. The more I look, the more desperate I become to restore the positive likeness I now know is within my grasp. But there is nothing I can do over Christmas, so I'll just have to be content with what I have for now.

My high temperature, I'm sure, didn't last long. I think that by the morning after the trip to Kassel, I was feeling much better and that Peter turned up unexpectedly at the school…

PART TWO

Saturday 14th August 1954

…while I was by myself. I quickly thumb through my diary entry for that day. Yes, I'm right, but it tells only the skeleton of what happened.

> *I stayed at home today. This morning Peter came to visit and we went for a walk.*

I had woken late that morning, feeling light-headed, my fever gone. When I got up, still slightly shaky, I realised I was alone in the house. There was a note on the floor outside my door. "Home at twelve hours," it said. It was now nearly nine-thirty. I had forgotten that Saturday was just another normal school day. Gudrun, Helga and Barbara would have caught the train into Münden as usual. Herr Schmidt and Fritz would be taking lessons in the school downstairs. Perhaps Frau Schmidt had gone shopping. In the kitchen, I found bread and cold sausage and managed to make myself some coffee. I suddenly felt ravenous. I decided to take my breakfast downstairs into the garden with a book to read and sit in the sun. I was happy to be by myself for a bit.

'Good morning, Margaret!'

His voice made me jump violently. I could feel a flush spreading down to my neck and I jumped to my feet. In my confusion, my plate and book slid on to the grass and my cup dropped from my grasp, splashing warm coffee on to my feet. He was quickly kneeling beside me, mopping me up with his handkerchief, as I fumbled around to pick everything up. Not an auspicious start.

He took my arm and led me to the seat under the apple tree. From inside the school came the sound of the children shouting. At the back of the house, the dog started to bark. What did we talk about as we sat side-by-side in the sunshine? I can't remember, nor can I remember whether he explained why he had come so early in the morning. Was it an excuse to see me alone, when he knew everyone else would be out? I don't think that had occurred to me at the time, but thinking about it now, it probably was.

Then, to my delight and confusion, he suddenly leant closer to me.

'You will now walk with me? I will take you to the river. In Münden, the Werra and Fulda meet and there become one. So here in Volkmarshausen, we have the Weser.'

'Oh, I say, yes, thank you. I'd like that very much. Gudrun told me the other day about the river.'

As we opened the gate and began walking slowly, side-by-side, down the steep, stony path to the village, I wondered what Gudrun would have thought if she had known what I was doing. At first, Peter was silent. It wasn't quite clear whether this was because he couldn't think of anything to say, or because that was how romantically inclined young men behaved.

'We're going to the Edersee on Monday,' I said eventually. 'Do you know it?'

'But yes! You will think it is beautiful. The mountains are all round the lake. I think to look at them is very romantic. To feel that one is alone with nature.'

He stopped and looked down over the valley. I waited patiently beside him, gazing too.

'Our poet, Goethe,' he continued, 'believes that the mountains bring peace to the soul.' He paused, turned and looked up to the wooded slopes behind us. '"*Über allen Gipfeln ist Ruh, in allen Wipfeln spürest du kaum einem Hauch: die Vögelein schweigen im Walde. Warte nur! Balde ruhest du auch.*" Do you understand?'

I felt bewildered. I could understand a bit, but before I could say anything, he went on.

'He says: "Peace is over all the mountain tops and you can feel scarcely a breath in the treetops. The little birds are silent in the wood. Wait, soon you also will be at rest."'

I immediately persuaded myself that I, too, had always felt the need for the peace of the mountains. I didn't admit to myself that I hadn't thought much about solitude before.

'Oh, that's really beautiful. I do wish you were coming with us, so I could look at the mountains with you. But I'll think of you all the time I'm there.'

He said nothing, just looked at me, then continued walking down the hill. I remember thinking that perhaps I'd gone too far. When I caught up with him, he just talked about his piano studies and how he was really very good and hoped to make a career as a famous concert pianist – with, perhaps, I gathered, a sideline as a Romantic poet. I was disappointed at first that there was no more gazing into my eyes or saying I was like a flower. But when we reached the river and stood together looking down at the swiftly moving water, he suddenly took my hand and told me my hair was as black as the night and my eyes like stars – which, of course, I believed with every ounce of my young, romantic soul. I was lost, I thought, forever. Suddenly, he bent down and kissed me lightly on the lips. I was speechless – and not a little embarrassed. My face, I knew, was flushed, my heart was racing and my palms were sweaty. I didn't know whether he was expecting any response and could think of nothing to say anyway. By now the sun had gone in, and I suddenly shivered.

'But you are cold. We must return to the school, as it will soon rain.'

Behind us, dark clouds were rapidly approaching, blown by a strong breeze. Peter seized my hand and almost dragged me up the hill. The first drops of rain were starting to fall, as we went through the gate into the garden. To my surprise, he left me at the door, saying he had to catch the bus back to practise the music he was playing in the concert on Monday. Before I could protest, he was gone. I half thought I must have imagined the whole thing. As I climbed the stairs, trying to regain my breath, I could hear voices. It appeared that while I was out, everyone had returned. Gudrun, Herr and Frau Schmidt and Fritz all stopped talking abruptly and stared at me as I went into the living room.

'Ah, Margaret, you have returned,' said Herr Schmidt.

'It's raining,' was all I could say, as if that explained my absence in the first place. I remember thinking that if they didn't know that Peter had made his apparently unplanned visit, I was not going to tell them.

'We worried because you are not well,' explained Gudrun, which of course immediately made me feel guilty.

'I feel better now, thank you.'

'However, we think it best you stay here this afternoon, as it is now cold and wet. We have to visit my aunt in Münden. But Fritz will remain here.'

I have to refer to the diary again to remind myself what happened after they left.

This afternoon, Heinrich – another clergyman – came to visit Fritz. He is quite short and very thickset – not really fat – and has dark, curly hair. They talked together for a little, then invited me to play rummy with them. It was rather muddling, because the rules are different from the English version. We played for pfennigs. I won. When Heinrich was dealing the cards, Fritz twitched as each one went down on to the table. He often twitches, just above one eyebrow. And when he laughs, he wheezes terrifically and chuckles afterwards to himself. We then had coffee and cakes and while we were eating, Barbara arrived.

Fritz immediately leapt to his feet to fetch another cup and plate. I had thought, until now, that he was a solemn, humourless young man. Perhaps he had wanted to make a good impression on Herr Schmidt while he was a guest in his house, and teaching in his school. But I soon realised he could be very good company. It was that afternoon that he and Barbara started the charade that developed as the holiday progressed.

'You must be our butler,' she said, when he returned from the kitchen with fresh coffee and more cakes. 'We shall call you James. All butlers in England are called James.'

I was at first appalled at her flirtatious tone. But to my surprise, Fritz seemed delighted. I suppose the concept of the butler fitted his image of the typical Englishman.

'What can I do for you, *gnädiges Fräulein?*'

'You may hand me another cake, James. And you must call me "m'lady".'

'Is there anything else, m'lady?'

'That will be all for the time being, James.'

And so "James" he became.

Soon afterwards, Heinrich left and Fritz went to his room. Barbara and I looked at each other and giggled.

'What I really came about, Mags, was to bring you a message. Helga's parents have asked you to come down and visit us this evening, after supper – and Gudrun too, of course. They haven't said anything more about Johannes today, so I suppose it was a false alarm yesterday.'

'I'd like that. I don't think there's anything else happening this evening. They're all out at the moment, but they should be back soon.'

So far, Barbara didn't know anything about Peter. I hadn't even mentioned his existence. But after my walk today, I couldn't resist telling her all about him, and what had happened that morning. On reflection, it was probably a mistake. I might have known she wouldn't be content until she'd wrung every last detail from me.

'I expect he'll lure you up to the woods next, and have his wicked way.'

'Oh, shut up, don't be silly. He's not like that. It's just a spiritual relationship.' Even as I said it, I knew it would be met with scorn.

'Don't you believe it, girl. He's probably just lulling you into a false sense of security. Anyway, he sounds a bit wet to me. All that stuff about nature! Very boring.'

Did I detect a slight hint of jealousy? At the time, probably not.

'Don't tell a soul, will you? Especially not Gudrun.'

'No, no, all right.' But by her dismissive manner, I already knew her promise wouldn't stop her making some sort of barbed comment, if it suited her.

In the letter to my parents, I reveal even less than in my diary entries.

*This morning I went for a walk down to the river and this
afternoon I met a friend of Fritz, the clergyman. This evening
Gudrun and I are going to meet Helga's parents.*

I must have written that part of the letter late in the afternoon.
That evening, after the usual supper of bread, cold meat, cheese
and tomatoes, I walked down to the village. Gudrun said she
would follow when she had helped to clear away the supper
dishes. I offered to stay and help.

'No, Margaret, you are on holiday. You must not work.'

That, of course, made me feel guilty again, especially
bearing in mind she still didn't even know about Peter's visit,
let alone our romantic walk together.

I was glad to be in the fresh air. The clouds had lifted and
it was now a clear, warm evening. A little flaxen-haired boy
answered when I knocked on the door. I realised I'd seen him
before – on my first walk down to the village. He grinned shyly
at me and then scuttled away down the narrow hall. Helga
came out of the room to my right, smiling a welcome. She was
a fresh faced, rosy, plumpish girl, her fair hair pulled back into
one thick plait.

'Good evening, Margaret,' she said, holding out her hand
to me. Although she had only started to learn English when
she came to the West, she was already quite fluent. 'Please,
come in and meet my parents.'

They both rose from their chairs as I went in and both
shook me by hand.

'*Guten Abend, Margaret,*' Frau Altmeyer said. '*Willkommen
in Deutschland. Helga, komm mit mir.*'

Helga followed her mother out of the room and I could
hear cups rattling, and a kettle beginning to boil. Herr
Altmeyer and I smiled at each other, but my German deserted
me and I knew he didn't speak or understand English. I

noticed the framed photograph on the mantelpiece and went up to look at it.

'*Mein Sohn, Johannes,*' said Herr Altmeyer, proudly.

I was relieved when Barbara came into the room, holding Helga's little brother by the hand.

'Hello, Mags. *Heiko, hier ist meine Freundin, Margaret.*'

He peeped at me from behind Barbara, but said nothing.

When Helga and her mother returned, we all sat round looking shyly at one another, sipping weak, black tea and eating yet more cake. By the time we had finished, Gudrun arrived. She sat down beside Frau Altmeyer and had obviously brought a message from her mother. I didn't really understand what she was saying, but I think she began to tell her about a village choir rehearsal. Frau Altmeyer got up, took Heiko by the hand and said something quietly in his ear. He came over to me.

'*Gut' Nacht,*' he whispered, holding out his hand.

'*Gute Nacht, Heiko,*' I said, smiling at the little boy and taking his hand. '*Schlaf gut.*'

He went round to everyone in turn, before going upstairs with his mother.

Herr Altmeyer sat quietly by himself in his armchair beside the fireplace. Helga got out an album of photographs from a drawer in the desk and settled beside Barbara and me on the sofa.

'When we are coming to the West, we are not bringing many things. Only what we could carry. But we are bringing our photographs, so we remember. This is our house. It is near the sea, in the north of Germany. But we are now unable to return. Sometimes I have sickness for my home.' She turned the pages. 'That is Heiko when he was a baby, with my grandmother, who remains in the East. And here is my brother, Johannes, with me in our garden. We dig the ground and grow potatoes and tomatoes.'

She paused and, glancing up at the photograph above the fireplace, lowered her voice.

'We hope that my brother will soon be here from the East. He did not come with us when we left our home. Now he works on a farm. He will escape over the border, through the woods, but it will be very dangerous. It is possible that the Russian soldiers will shoot him. This happens many times. But, please, you must say nothing of this.'

She was near to tears, and I didn't know what to say.

'No, of course not. It must be awful for you. Do you know when he'll be able to escape?'

'No, but my mother and father hope soon. But he cannot send messages, so we don't know.'

'Nein, Helga. Nein.'

Herr Altmeyer's voice was suddenly raised in protest. In spite of his lack of English, he had obviously understood the gist of what his daughter was saying, because he became extremely agitated. Helga said nothing, closed the album and got up to put it away in its drawer. As she did so, she lightly touched a guitar, which was leaning against the wall, beside the desk. The strings made a soft, eerie, perfectly tuned chord.

'Yes,' she said, when she returned to her seat beside me. 'I also am carrying my brother's guitar. It is waiting for him to return.'

The only sound in the room was the ticking of the clock on the mantelpiece. The silence was only broken when Frau Altmeyer came downstairs, unaware of the tension in the room. Gudrun and Helga started talking, almost too enthusiastically, about school and their mutual dislike of Herr Schroeder. We laughed, almost too loudly, when Helga described how Elke Meyer had seen him standing in front of a mirror, combing his hair, turning his head from side to side to admire his profile, and how he had quickly turned away and pocketed his comb when he realised he was being observed.

I had already got used to the way the Germans all shook each other by the hand at every possible opportunity, even first thing in the morning and last thing at night. But I was not prepared for the intensity of Herr Altmeyer's almost iron-like grip as he took my hands in his, or the stifling effect of Frau Altmeyer's sudden embrace, as I got up to leave.

Now, thirty-five years later, it seems amazing how quickly we had all realigned. In less than ten years, the "baddies" of my childhood had become the "goodies" of my adolescence. Most of the time I was in Germany, by a tacit, mutual agreement we didn't mention the war, or the Jews, or the concentration camps. It was as if two other, mythical, forces had been involved. A new "them and us" had been formed. Although the Berlin Wall was yet to be built, Churchill had already spoken about the "Iron Curtain" descending over Europe and we were united against our new common enemy – the Communists and Soviet Russia in particular.

Now, I find myself standing quite still, as if I've only just been released from physical restraint, the presence of Helga and her family almost tangible. I'm only brought back to England and the present when I hear Helen's and Ian's voices outside my door, less real to me than the echoes of the German voices in my head. I realise it is almost time to go over to the church. I put the photographs and the diary back in their box...

CHAPTER FIVE

PART ONE

Monday 25th December 1989

…and go downstairs to join my family. In half an hour, it will be another Christmas Day. The last Christmas here. The last Christmas Geoffrey will lead the way down the steps, while we follow, huddled up in hats and scarves against the midnight cold. The last Christmas Ruth will stand in the doorway, waving to us, before going in and shutting the door. Is she collapsing on to the sofa, a drink in her hand, relieved to be alone for a while? Or is she venting her feelings of frustration, as I've often heard her do when she thinks she's alone, by walking round the house, muttering to herself under her breath? In spite of our apparent closeness over the years, I can never guess what she's feeling, or predict what she'll do next.

I was still at school, of course, when she first met Geoffrey. She had just completed her first year at university, but she wasn't enjoying life there, and told my parents she was thinking of giving up. She spent that summer playing tennis and going to parties. She joined the Young Conservatives, not out of political conviction but because they were, as I remember her saying, "a jolly crowd". And there she found Geoffrey, who was beginning to think he ought to settle down. Marrying him meant she didn't have to make any more decisions about what to do with her life. Looking back, I wonder, perhaps rather unkindly, whether he was just a convenient excuse. But she seemed, to me at least, very happy. She had become the wife of a young professional man, apparently without a backward glance at what she might have become. Before she was twenty-one – after a respectable interval, in spite of my mother's original suspicions – she was pregnant. Jane wasn't quite two when Helen was born. She remained supremely confident – and I still envied her, especially her ability to take everything in her stride. I adored my two nieces, but couldn't imagine myself ever coping with the broken sleep and the constant chaos involved in caring for tiny children. It was at this time that Ruth joined a local choral society and started to play her cello again – the only intimation that perhaps she needed more to occupy her time than domesticity. Even then, Geoffrey used to dismiss this side of her life as "Ruth's little hobbies". Later, while he was training for the ministry, she got a job just round the corner at the doctor's surgery. I remember her saying, with a hint of bitterness I thought, that someone had to support the family now and it looked as if it would have to be her. But actually, I think she was glad to be out of the house and meeting other people.

Although the girls were becoming more independent – they must have been about fourteen and twelve by then – they spent a lot of their time with my parents. My father had retired and I was teaching, but still living at home. One particular incident, trivial in itself, seems to epitomise the shifting relationships within the family. Ruth and the girls had come round for supper. It was a warm evening in early summer and we decided to eat outside. My father opened a bottle of wine and poured a small glass for each of the girls. We were all relaxed, happy in each others' company, laughing at the slightest thing. But then Geoffrey arrived. We were obviously not expecting him, because we hadn't kept any food for him, and there was no wine left. My mother went into the house to find him something to eat, Ruth stood up and gave Geoffrey a perfunctory kiss on the cheek and the girls abruptly stopped giggling. The atmosphere immediately became almost formal, as if an intruder had infiltrated our closed, cosy circle.

In spite of the ever more visible rift between Geoffrey and the rest of us, Ruth seemed to be happier during this period than she'd ever been. It all came to an abrupt halt when Geoffrey got his first job in the church – as curate in Hackney and, later, after a period in the country, as vicar in Blackheath. Ruth missed our parents and they missed her and their granddaughters. She had to get used to living in London after being in Dorset and the girls took some time to settle into their new schools. But, Ruth being Ruth, she soon immersed herself in her new life, cheerfully coping with whatever was asked of her. There were no more signs of disagreement between Ruth and Geoffrey that I could see – until now, that is.

But all this time she was playing a part, albeit extremely well, giving a very convincing imitation of a vicar's wife.

When we reach the church, Shirley is at the door to meet us and hustles Geoffrey away. Helen turns to me, grinning.

'Do I see an Angel of Mercy?'

'A fairly new recruit,' I say and we laugh.

The church is full. Geoffrey's Christmas midnight service is one of the highlights of the year. When we find a seat, I'm rather startled to see that Jane immediately bends forward, leans on the seat in front of her, and rests her head on her arms, her eyes closed. Until now, she has always had the same attitude to the church as Ruth. 'Mother and I are both devout Atheists,' she would say. And although she and Philip always came with us to the midnight service when they were staying for Christmas, they made it quite obvious that they were only there out of a sense of duty, to support Geoffrey. They used to make a striking couple, both in dark overcoats, Philip with a silk scarf at his neck and Jane with a fashionable Russian-style black fur hat pulled down low over her forehead. Surely, she can't actually be praying, can she? She soon straightens up and sits staring ahead of her, her face devoid of make-up, pale and drawn.

I'm suddenly aware that someone is sitting down beside me.

'Hello,' says Jonathan.

I don't know why, but it hasn't crossed my mind that he might be here. Has he come hoping to see me? Ridiculous thought, of course. All I can do is mutter something inarticulate, before it's time for the service to start. Now I know that Geoffrey no longer believes in what he's doing, it's as if I'm watching a television sketch, in which he's doing a very good turn as a vicar. I want to share this thought with Jonathan, and so store it away in my mind to bring out at a more suitable moment. I'm not really taking much notice of what's going on, aware only that he is beside me and that there's something about the curve of his nose that makes me want to reach out and trace its outline with my finger. And I'm sure his face would feel slightly bristly against mine, if I were to lean over and put my cheek to his. When we stand up, I realise he's probably nearly a foot taller than me. He has to bend down and lean over to find the right place for me in the hymn book.

'You haven't been paying attention!'

'My mind's been on other things,' I say, somewhat ambiguously, wondering whether he realises what I really mean.

The service is actually quite brief, but Geoffrey has a knack of making it appear supremely significant. There are special prayers, as usual, for Terry Waite and his family. Before he was taken hostage, he worked as a captain in the church army, which has its headquarters in Blackheath, and regularly came to the services here. I can see now that his wife is sitting a few rows in front of us.

Before we know it, it's Christmas Day and we have left the light and warmth of the church behind us and are heading back to the vicarage.

'We don't usually see you here, Jonathan,' says Geoffrey, when he catches us up. 'Why don't you come in for a minute? Ruth will have heated up some mulled wine while we've been out, I expect.'

Ruth has indeed heated up some wine. She gives me what Mother would have called "an old-fashioned look" as we go into the kitchen and gets out an extra glass.

'Hello, Jonathan,' she says. 'This is a pleasant surprise.'

'Well, I'm not on duty tonight, so I thought it would be a nice start to the holiday. I won't stay long, though.'

So perhaps he actually did come specially to see me? I try to picture myself, to see myself through his eyes. Shortish hair, going a bit grey. Not overweight. Neck not too wrinkled. Jaw line not too jowly. Altogether, not too bad for my age, I suppose, but surely not the sort of person to be the object of anyone's desire.

We stand around in the kitchen, our faces glowing from the cold after our brief walk, our chilly fingers clutching the comfortingly warm glasses of spicy wine. Ruth's face is flushed and I suspect she's already sampled some before we arrived back.

'Well,' she says, 'I think we ought to drink to something. I suggest the future.'

It's a strange little ceremony. We're all standing round the kitchen table, but no one catches anyone else's eye. We dutifully raise our glasses.

'The future,' we mutter, with a mixture of amusement and embarrassment. Geoffrey doesn't join in the toast and I wonder who else has noticed.

'Anyway,' Ruth continues, 'I can hardly keep my eyes open, so if you'll excuse me, everyone, I'm off to bed.'

We finish our drinks in silence and all follow her out of the kitchen. I find myself standing with Jonathan at the front door.

'Sorry about that. I promise you'll know what it's all about on Boxing Day, when Martin and Val are here too.'

'Right. Just as long as I'm not intruding.'

'Of course not.'

'See you tomorrow, then. About half past twelve?'

'Earlier, if you like.'

And he's gone. As I go upstairs to bed, I feel vaguely unsettled, as if I've let an opportunity slip away, but an opportunity to do or say what? I want to tell him about my feeling of overwhelming happiness as I watched him playing the Schubert "Notturno" at the concert, two days ago. I want to tell him about the first time I heard the Brahms rhapsody in Germany thirty-five years ago. I want to know where he was and what he was doing at that time. And I want to tell him how much I think about him when he isn't with me.

Next morning I'm awoken early – how early I'm not quite sure – by predictable whoops and exclamations from the boys in the next room. It all seems fairly amicable, though. I can see the faint outline of the window beginning to appear. I suddenly remember one particular Christmas morning – I must have been about five or six, I suppose. I had woken in the half-light then, too. At the end of my bed, I could see the outline of my stocking. Sticking out of the top of the stocking was a head of some sort. I could wait no longer. A golliwog – now politically incorrect, but then most desirable – made of black felt, its mouth embroidered in bright red silk, its woollen hair sticking up on end. When I got it out, I saw it was dressed in smart striped trousers, a red waistcoat and, round its neck, a pale blue satin bow. But the material was familiar. How had Father Christmas managed to make my new golliwog's clothes out of my old cotton frock and my outgrown nightdress? And how had he managed to get hold of one of my hair ribbons? Then I remembered seeing scraps of material on the sitting-room floor a few days earlier, beside my mother's favourite chair. Suddenly, everything clicked into place. My worries about how Father Christmas could possibly get round to all the children in the world in one night were resolved. But something – a wish not to spoil the day for my parents, perhaps – prevented me from saying anything about my discovery to anyone. It wasn't until the following year that I decided I could no longer keep my secret to myself and confided my momentous knowledge to Ruth.

'Is it morning time yet?' comes the plaintive voice of Max from outside my door.

'Nearly!' I say, sleepily enough, I hope, to postpone the moment of invasion. Knowing they will not get an enthusiastic welcome from their parents or grandparents this early, they make me the traditional first port of call at Christmas, and I'm secretly quite flattered. Suddenly, the door bursts open and my room becomes the centre of activity. Max and Jack, carrying a selection from their stockings, launch themselves on to my bed. They are followed more slowly by William, who stands rather awkwardly by the door, grinning somewhat sheepishly, as if not quite sure whether someone of such mature years should be seen in a lady's bedroom.

'Look at this, Auntie Meg!' Max pushes some sort of book up far too close to my face and I sit up to take a proper look.

'That's very good, Max, did you colour that in all by yourself?' I give him a hug. He climbs in under the bedclothes and snuggles up beside me, thumb in mouth. His bare feet are cold against my leg. His hair feels unbelievably silky as I place a quick kiss on the top of his head.

'And look what Father Christmas brought me, Auntie Meg,' says Jack, giving me what he obviously hopes is an unobtrusive wink, holding out three Matchbox model cars, still in their boxes.

'I wonder how he knew you collected those, Jack?' I say, with exaggerated surprise.

'We all wrote to him last week, didn't we, Max?'

'Are there more presents?'

'I have a feeling there may be some more under the tree, Max, because these are from Father Christmas. I know I put one there for you, and I expect Mummy and Daddy and Granny and Grandpa will have left some, too.'

'And Auntie Jane?'

'I don't know, darling, I expect so.'

'Isn't Uncle Philip coming for Christmas? His presents are always well good.' I suppress my teacher's instinct to comment on William's phraseology and say that I don't think he can manage to come this year.

'Yeah, and he always makes us laugh,' shouts Jack, leaping off the bed, waving his arms about and sticking out his tongue.

'Right,' I say firmly, 'out you go. I'm going to get dressed. It's nearly breakfast time.'

Enough is enough. Besides, I really don't want to get involved in complicated explanations about Jane's marital problems.

By the time I'm dressed, I can hear them all downstairs in the kitchen with Ruth. I feel exhausted already. And there's a turkey to cook yet. Christmas Day always has a sort of inevitability about it. The morning is taken up with preparing lunch while Geoffrey goes over to the church. When he comes back, it's time to open the presents left under the tree. After lunch, to prevent utter somnolence setting in, we go for a brisk walk. The children are given some tea and are sent off to bed fairly early, before they get too fractious. No one really wants any more to eat, but we always have cold turkey sandwiches and a bottle of wine and then collapse, far too full of food and drink, in front of half-watched programmes on television, trying not to nod off. As far as the structure of the day is concerned, the familiar pattern has never changed.

But, of course, the details are always different. Today, nine of us will sit round the table for lunch. In previous years we've had as many as fifteen or more and once, I seem to remember, we were down to four. The important thing is to have a set of rules, with Ruth as the boss. In the kitchen, we support the "too many cooks" school of thought, rather than the "many hands" principle.

Now, it's just gone ten o'clock. Ruth, Helen and I are in the kitchen, preparing the vegetables. Earlier, Jane appeared briefly to make a cup of black coffee and has now disappeared again. We decide to count her out of the duty roster. The turkey is already in the oven. Geoffrey has gone to the church for the morning service, taking Ian and the boys with him as the token family representatives. When they come back, they will lay the table and get out the drinks.

'I've been thinking, Mum,' Helen says, carrying on peeling and chopping carrots. 'Next year, it'll be my turn to organise all this.'

'Nonsense, darling, I love having you all here.' Ruth pauses, realising her mistake. 'Well, perhaps not actually here. But by next year we should be settled into wherever it is we're going to be.'

Helen's right, of course. In the evolving roles we all play within the family, it is her turn next, especially as Ruth and I have both moved up a generation from last year. Ruth must have had the same thought.

'And don't imagine that Meg and I will be sitting in the corner, nodding off by the fire quite yet.' She turns her back on us and goes to the sink to fill a saucepan with water. 'Have I done enough potatoes, do you think?'

The subject is obviously closed as far as she's concerned. Helen looks at me and shrugs her shoulders.

'We won't get any more in the oven, will we?' she says. 'Anyway, we've got plenty of time to think about next year.'

I continue with my allotted task – preparing what feels to me like several hundred sprouts.

We all turn towards the door, as Jane comes into the room again.

'Anything I can do?' By the tone of her voice, she obviously hopes there isn't.

'Not really, darling. We seem to have everything under control.'

'I think I'll go for a walk, then. I'll take Bella, if that's all right.'

At the word "walk", Bella pricks up her ears, gets out of her basket, and, with only a cursory sniff at the oven, follows Jane out into the hall.

'That must be a first,' comments Helen, acidly.

'Come on, darling, that's unfair. It's not like you to crow. She needs all the support we can give her.'

'OK, Mum. Sorry. I promise I won't say another word.'

I decide not to join in the little spat between them, but am inclined to agree with Helen. Jane has often given the impression it's beneath her dignity to join in the ordinary, everyday goings-on of the family. So, even taking the dog for a walk seems out of character.

There's nothing much more we can do for a while. We make yet another cup of coffee and, because the kitchen is beginning to get rather hot and steamy, take it into the sitting room. Before we know it, the church party has returned. It's absurd, but I can't help feeling a sense of excitement at the prospect of opening my presents, even though I know what half of them are going to be, having exchanged lists with Ruth, who acts as a sort of clearing agent for the whole family. Soon, the noise level has risen by several decibels and the room is full of wrapping paper. I'm pleased that my presents to the boys – the science encyclopedia William asked for, a kite for Jack and a Batman dressing-up outfit complete with mask for Max – have been approved. Philip's "well good" presents have been replaced, I notice, by envelopes containing, I suspect, generous cheques. And I've got the books I asked for and some more besides.

As usual, I'm amazed that, by one o'clock or near enough, everything has finished cooking more or less simultaneously. The vegetables are done to a turn, the bird isn't tough or dry and we haven't forgotten the gravy or the bread sauce. So here we are, sitting round the table looking expectantly at Geoffrey, who has the carving knife poised for the first incision into the turkey. I think, for a moment, that he's going to start without saying grace. But he turns to William, who has obviously been coached in his new role.

'Thank you, Lord, for our good food,' he says, turning rather pink and looking down at the table, embarrassed.

'Well done, old chap,' says Ian quietly, patting him on the shoulder. He lifts his glass. 'To Ruth.'

'Not just me,' she protests, passing plates of turkey down the table. 'Meg and Helen, too.'

'Yes, but you organised it all, Mum. We only carried out orders.'

'And I laid the table,' shouts Jack.

'And put all the knives and forks in the wrong places,' puts in William.

'No I didn't! Anyway, you dropped a glass, so there.'

'And I laid too, Mummy,' says Max.

'Did you, darling? Well done.'

We laugh and relax. There is silence as we all start to eat. For a while, any underlying tensions between us seem to be forgotten. I have to admit that I often wonder to myself whether all the work that goes into this one day is worth the effort. One of my friends at school just stays at home with a good book and cooks herself an omelette; another colleague and her husband fly to somewhere warm, specifically to avoid having to visit her mother. Now, I look round the table and feel a surge of affection for them all. My family. And of course we don't go through all this ceremonial for the sake of the food, or the presents, or even the church services. We celebrate Christmas because it gives our lives some sort of structure, an opportunity to pause and reflect and start again. We gather together because not to do so would be breaking the rules of the family, laid down generations ago. Helen will no doubt eventually take over from Ruth, who took over from our mother, who in turn took over from hers, as the centre of the family.

Jack has cleared his plate already.

'Can I have some more, Granny?'

'Wait a bit, Jack. We haven't finished yet. And leave room for the pudding, won't you?'

'Have you put some money in it?'

Nothing changes. I can remember asking the same thing when I was his age. Then, it was sixpence. Now, it's twenty pence.

I notice that Jane, sitting beside me, has already put her knife and fork down, with her plate still half full. In her twenties, especially before she married Philip, she always seemed to be on some sort of diet, even though she had never been overweight – the very reverse usually. She had gone through a vegetarian period – it might even have been vegan, now I come to think of it – then a phase when she refused to eat any carbohydrates. Another diet seemed to consist entirely of grapefruit, then there was a strange one when she could eat practically anything, but only in the right order. So it's never been unusual to see her picking at her food, especially at Christmas.

The pudding comes and goes. In order to have at least a show of impartiality, we are served in order of age – youngest first. In spite of this, Ruth somehow manages, as usual, to work it so that the three boys get a twenty pence piece each, and we all pretend to be amazed and indignant.

It's beginning to get dark by the time everyone is ready for the walk on the heath. Jane says she's been out once today and has no intention of trailing about in the half-light. So when I go back quickly into the house a few moments later for a forgotten pair of gloves, I'm surprised to hear the sound of stifled sobbing coming from the sitting room. I can't make up my mind what to do. She obviously hasn't heard me come in again. Should I make a great show of opening the door again, loudly this time, to give her the opportunity to stop? Or should I creep out again and pretend I haven't heard anything? Before I can make up my mind, she turns and sees me, as I stand indecisively in the hall. The last time I can remember seeing her looking so upset, so vulnerable, she was about seven.

'Oh dear, you've caught me, Meg. It's just that for the first time in my life, I don't know what to do.' Her voice, normally tinged with irony, is low, almost expressionless.

'Would it help to talk?'

'I think it would. It might get things sorted out in my mind. Don't worry, I've got it out of my system now. I shall be my usual self when you come back. You'd better go and catch them

up now though, or they'll begin to wonder what's happened.'
Almost as an afterthought, she calls after me as I open the front
door. 'Don't say anything to anyone else, will you?'

'Of course not, darling. We'll find a time later on –
tomorrow morning perhaps.'

As I walk down the drive again to catch the others up, it
occurs to me that the one weak spot in Jane's otherwise
impregnable shell is her dignity. While Philip's affairs over the
years were kept on a comparatively clandestine basis, her status
could be maintained. I have a sneaking suspicion that she's so
upset now not because she misses Philip, but because she's
worried that her colleagues, friends and family might actually
pity her. Accepting sympathy would mean admitting she is no
longer the best, something she hasn't had to do for a long time.

We don't go far and when we get back it's almost
completely dark. Jane is still sitting where I left her, but there's
no sign she's been crying. She's turned on the television and is
watching the end of *The Sound of Music*. She gets up.

'I've put the kettle on,' she says. 'I'll make some tea.'

Helen opens her mouth to say something, but obviously
thinks better of it. Ruth and I exchange glances and follow Jane
into the kitchen. On the television, Julie Andrews is about to
make her escape to wherever it was she was going.

Later, as Ruth and I are clearing away the tea things, we
switch on the radio for the six o'clock news and are stunned to
hear that Ceaucescu and his wife have actually been shot by a
firing squad a few hours ago, after what must surely have been
a travesty of a trial. I find, rather to my surprise, that although
I'm pleased Ceaucescu has got what he deserved, I am actually
shocked that the people took such a momentous decision so
quickly, without going to a proper court. Back in the sitting
room, the chaps are all watching *Crocodile Dundee*, which
almost seems more realistic than the events in Romania.

By half past eight, the two younger boys are in bed. Max fell asleep over his tea and was carried upstairs to bed by six o'clock, but Jack somehow persuaded Helen to let him watch the end of the film. William has been allowed to stay up later and is engrossed in a book about football. Geoffrey and Ian are half-watching *Miss Marple's Caribbean Mystery*, and discussing whether to stay up and watch *Raiders of the Lost Ark*, which doesn't finish until nearly half past one. Helen and Ruth are in the kitchen, making some sandwiches for supper. They are talking and laughing together and I'm surprised to hear Jane's voice, too, sounding quite cheerful. I go into the dining room to fetch the wine left over from lunch. I decide to have another quick look through the photos. I want to make sure I've found all the ones taken at about the time of the trip to Germany. I manage to find the box under the sideboard and when I lift it out, I see the cat's anxious face peering at me. She sniffs my hand, but doesn't move.

'It's all right, Sam, they're in bed now.'

She eventually crawls out and makes her way cautiously towards the kitchen.

I find a few more school group photos, to add to the one I found the other day. And there are some of Ruth and me on the beach, one of my father and me flying the old box-kite, and another, obviously taken at one of my birthday parties, of me and about a dozen other little girls, standing in a row, all in our party frocks. No more from Germany. Another trawl through the negatives after supper might be a good idea. But now I can hear footsteps in the hall, the rattle of cutlery, the clink of glasses. Obviously supper is ready. I put away the photos and pick up the bottles of wine.

It's another couple of hours before I'm upstairs in my room, ready for my nightly instalment of what I'm beginning to think of as "My Life in Germany"...

PART TWO

Sunday 15th August 1954

...and once again, opening my box of memories.

I'm quite disappointed to find that the negative of Peter and me is the only one I can't match with a print. But then I presumably hadn't destroyed any of the other photographs after I returned to England all those years ago.

I didn't see Peter that Sunday, because it was the day we went dancing. He had told us he couldn't come with us as he had to practise for his concert the following day. But thoughts of him began to fill every moment. I was becoming obsessed. Hardly surprising, really. It was the first time in my life a young man had kissed me – let alone on the lips.

My letter to my parents, as usual, says very little.

> *Sunday 15th August*
> *Yesterday evening I met the family Barbara is staying with. They are from Eastern Germany. This morning Gudrun and I went for a walk in the woods above the house and in the afternoon we went dancing in Münden.*

So, once again I resort to my diary, which isn't very helpful either.

> *This morning I felt completely better. After breakfast, Gudrun and I decided to go for a walk in the woods. We found some funny mushrooms, which looked more like toadstools, but which Gudrun insisted we could take back to eat. It was really quite alarming, but we're still here!*

I remember feeling slightly uneasy during that morning's walk. I was more accustomed to the deciduous woods near my home, where the dappled sunlight was filtered through the leaves. Here, the tall pine trees completely shut out the sun. I was used to having grass to walk on and to hearing the sound of birds singing above me. Here, there were just soft, dead pine needles underfoot, and complete silence overhead. I remember thinking it would be a different matter if I were with Peter. We would be walking hand in hand and he would again be quoting Goethe to me, before taking me in his arms and giving me the gentlest of kisses.

Gudrun strode on in front, so I had difficulty keeping up. I was feeling increasingly uncomfortable in her presence. In England, she had been polite, shy, sometimes awkward. Here, on her home territory, she was confident, almost bossy. And, of course, she was now my potential rival. Ahead was a grassy clearing in the wood and I could see she had stopped and was bending down to look at something on the ground. When I came up to her, she had already picked some small, dark mushrooms and was putting them in the pocket of her dress. Involuntarily, I gasped and took a step back.

'You can't eat those, surely?'

'But yes, of course. They are very good.'

She seemed surprised at my revulsion and gave me a handful.

'You have pockets?'

I took them gingerly and reluctantly stowed them away.

When we got back, Frau Schmidt was in the kitchen preparing chicken for the midday meal. She seemed delighted with our find and tossed them into the gravy. At lunch I tried to leave them, as unobtrusively as possible, on the side of my plate, but Frau Schmidt insisted I ate them and Gudrun implied that she would be most offended if I didn't. I noticed

I had been given more than anyone else, presumably because I was the guest, but remember being relieved that the others were eating some too: I would not die alone. I don't think I was even aware of the existence of a psychedelic variety then. I turn the page of the diary.

> *After lunch, we caught the train to Münden and met two boys from the village who were coming dancing with us. We were going to walk round the town for a bit, but when we arrived it was pouring with rain, so we went straight to the Bergschlößchen, which is really a hotel.*

There was quite a gathering of people from the village waiting to catch the train when we got to the station, including Barbara and Helga and several other boys, in addition to the two I mentioned in my diary. There was a party atmosphere already. Fritz was going to visit his mother and brother in Münden, before joining us later. When the train arrived, we all piled into the same carriage and Helga went to sit with two other girls from school. Barbara, Gudrun and I sat with Fritz, and the two boys were a few seats away.

'*Komm mal her,*' one of them called out to us. '*Bist du Engländerin? Wir gehen tanzen. Kommst du mit?*'

'Ignore them, Barbara,' I muttered nervously. 'They look a bit spivvy to me.'

But Barbara waved and smiled at these potential abductors, then giggled.

'Oh, come on, Mags, don't be a spoilsport. *Ja! Wir sind Englisch!* We are going dancing in Münden! I'm going over.'

'They are Werner and Helmut,' laughed Gudrun. 'They live in our village. They are nice boys. I shall go to sit with them also. '*Tag Werner. Wie geht's deiner Mutter?*'

Fritz looked at me curiously.

'I think perhaps you don't like boys, yes?'

As usual, I could feel a deep blush spreading over my face.

'Oh, no, well, yes, I mean. I like some boys. I like Peter, for example.'

'Ah, yes,' he replied, smiling. 'I thought on Friday that you liked him. You know, during the war, when he was a little boy, he lived with the Schmidts at their school. I also stayed with them then for a short time, and I remember that Peter was so shy that he said only *"Guten Morgen"* and *"Gute Nacht"*.'

I began to feel I had an ally. I was eager to find out more.

'Why did he live with them? Did his mother stay there too?'

'Peter's mother is dead. It is very sad. She died when Peter was born, so he did not know her. And during the war, Peter's father was an officer in the army. He is a good friend of Gudrun's father.'

'You know, you're the first person who's actually mentioned the war since I've been here.'

'I think that the German people want to forget the war. We are not proud of that time. Peter's father never talks about it. I believe now he wants to make as if it did not happen.'

'But I thought all the German officers were put on trial? I remember my father telling me about it.'

'It was just the generals and the SS officers who were condemned, I believe. There were many people who were afraid to speak against the authorities at that time. Now Peter's father says he was always unhappy about what he had to do. I do not know if he was involved in – in – the cruelties of those times. So, please, you will not speak to them of this.'

'No, of course not. Wasn't Herr Schmidt in the war?'

'No, he remained here, as a teacher. He was not a strong man at that time, so he was lucky.'

The war had ended a mere nine years before, but to me it was only a vague memory by then.

'I was too young during the war to know much about it and I'm glad I didn't. But even where we live – not near London or anything – I remember hearing the air raid siren and the sound of bombs dropping really quite nearby. Did you have to go into the army, Fritz?'

'Only at the very end.' He paused, as if deciding whether to go on. 'I was in the Hitler Youth – we all had to be – and we were trained to fight, so that when they needed more soldiers, we were ready. I will perhaps tell you more another time. But we did not know of the terrible things that were happening to the Jews. And when we heard, we did not believe, at first. I think that is why I wished to become a pastor. But now, we are here, in Münden, and we will talk of better things. I will go now to visit my mother and then see you later at the dancing.'

'Yes. Bye, Fritz – and thank you.'

Barbara came bouncing up to me and I could see she was curious. She could never bear to feel she'd been left out.

'What were you thanking him for?'

'Oh, we were just talking. I think he's a nice man, Barbara. It's just a pity he's got such a red face and is so plump and wheezy! So, I don't want to make fun of him anymore.'

'My God, Mags, you're developing into a real bore. Do you know that? It's that awful boy isn't it? He takes himself far too seriously.'

Sometimes I felt that I really disliked Barbara. We had been friends ever since we were in the first form at school, and, not for the first time lately, I felt that perhaps it was time to move on. We took our A levels the following year and I planned to go to university. Barbara was talking about going into nursing.

'Oh, yes,' Barbara went on. 'Helmut and Werner say they've got a friend who will do nicely for you, who may be at the dance. Come on, hurry, it's beginning to rain.'

We sheltered from the rain for a while under a large tree, then again in an alleyway. Then, with much giggling, we decided to go straight to the dance. To my extreme embarrassment, the boys insisted we take their arms as we hurried through the streets. I hoped I wouldn't be seen by any of our English party.

The Bergschlößchen was a large, imposing hotel in the town. We went to sit at one of the tables round the edge of the long room and watched the youth of Münden trying to dance in the cramped space in the centre, to a small dance band. I couldn't get over the fact that they were holding a dance on a Sunday. In England, everything still came to a halt. My parents were not regular churchgoers, but I knew they thought that going to the cinema, which was shut on a Sunday anyway, let alone dancing, was unthinkable. Barbara was having the time of her life.

'Come on, Mags, let yourself go! I think Helmut's really smashing. You really should have danced with him. He must think you're so rude.'

Helmut had asked me to dance, but I'd been so embarrassed that I had refused point-blank. He had shrugged his shoulders and immediately turned to Barbara. Now she had come back to the table, slightly out of breath and glowing after being clasped in the arms of the dishy Helmut.

'You know I don't like boys who put grease on their hair,' I said, primly. 'Just leave me alone. I'm quite happy sitting here just watching.'

'You're determined to be grumpy, aren't you! Just because lover boy isn't here. He sounds a real bore if he doesn't want a bit of fun now and again. Do you really think he's practising the piano? I expect he's really seeing someone else. He's probably got a whole string of lovelorn maidens all pining after him already.'

I could cheerfully have hit her, but in fact decided the best course of action was to ignore her. I was imagining what it would have been like if Peter had been with us. In my mind's eye, I could see him sweeping me up into his arms and twirling me round in the middle of a suddenly deserted dance floor. Gudrun, I was delighted to see, was dancing with Werner, the more serious of the two boys. Perhaps she didn't care too much for Peter, after all. I look to my diary again.

Actually, Werner is a bit nicer than Helmut – not so 'spivvy'. He looks a bit peculiar, though, because he was hit with a snowball when he was little and his nose is a funny shape.

Barbara suddenly gave a shriek.

'Oh look, there's Fritz! Doesn't he look amazing? All red and grinny. Fancy a clergyman dancing – and on a Sunday too! He's seen us.'

He looked so incongruous, advancing towards us across the dance floor, that I found it impossible to suppress my giggles in spite of what I'd said earlier.

'Fritz – or James, I should say,' said Barbara, with mock solemnity, when he stopped by our table. 'You may kiss my hand if you like.'

'*Gnädiges Fräulein,*' said Fritz, bowing low and taking Barbara's hand in his. 'First, I will do my duty as your butler and fetch coffee for you and your beautiful friend. Wait here, please.'

Soon he was weaving his way precariously back, between the dancers, carrying three cups of coffee.

'*Danke schön, James.*'

'*Bitte sehr, Gnädiges Fräulein,*' he replied, clicking his heels together.

'Now, *mein schönes Gretchen,*' he added, turning to me, 'I will be very happy if you will dance with me.'

Over his shoulder, I could see Barbara grinning and nodding.

'Well, I don't know, I'm not very good. And why do you call me Gretchen?'

'That is because your name is Margaret. It is a small name.'

'A nickname, we say,' interrupted Barbara. I could see she was a bit put out. 'What is my nickname, James?'

'I cannot give my Gnädiges Fräulein a nickname. You will be Fräulein von – what is your family name?'

'Hill.'

'Ah, then you will always be Fräulein von Hügel to me. When one has "von" before the name, it means you are aristocratic.'

'Well, that's certainly me, isn't it, Mags? Now, I want to see you two dancing. I should think it'll be fascinating. Go on, off you go.'

Once again, I felt acutely embarrassed, especially when one of my fellow English students spotted us and waved to me enthusiastically. Fritz had a unique dancing style – I described it in my diary as "sort of jazzing up and down." Because the floor was so crowded, we stayed in practically the same spot for the whole of the dance. Fritz held me far too tightly and his hands got clammier and his breathing heavier and noisier in my ear, as we shuffled around. We didn't say a word to each other.

The room was becoming unbearably stuffy and a little later Fritz took Barbara and me outside on to the terrace, which overlooked the town. It had stopped raining and the air was clear and refreshing. On the hill opposite was a tower, which, he told us, was a monument to Wallenstein who, I understood, had something to do with the Thirty Years' War. He pointed out his church and his old school, of which he was obviously very proud.

'We will go there tomorrow,' he said. 'It is the school your friend Peter attends and where he will play in the concert.'

'You didn't tell me about that, Mags,' said Barbara, indignantly.

I said nothing. I certainly wasn't going to ask her to come along.

We went back inside to look for Gudrun, as it was almost time for us to go home. I suppose the last traces of my homesickness had disappeared and at last I was looking forward to the rest of the holiday. And I had no reservations when Gudrun suggested, as there was no bus or train due to leave for over an hour and the stars had come out by this time, that we could walk back to Volkmarshausen. In England, the thought of going along an unfamiliar road, through unknown countryside, in utter darkness and, what's more, with two young men I'd only just met, would have filled me with absolute horror and dread. But when Gudrun took Werner's arm, almost without hesitation or embarrassment, I took his other. I could imagine what bliss it would have been to have taken Peter's arm and strolled with him under the stars, while he quoted the appropriate German poetry to me. Barbara set off in front, between Helmut and Fritz. She told me later that halfway back Fritz had taken her hand and given it a very friendly squeeze, but even then I wasn't quite sure whether she was exaggerating. Someone produced sandwiches, which we ate as we went along – another thing that, back in England, was definitely not the thing to do. I believe at one point we even burst into song. I remember suddenly feeling very happy; no complications, simply happy that the rest of the holiday was to come and that the next day we were going to hear Peter play in his concert.

Now, as I climb into bed at the end of this Christmas Day, the same feeling of complete happiness and expectation overwhelms me. Whether or not Jonathan feels the same seems immaterial. I'm just glad he exists; it doesn't seem to matter whether or not we have any future together. It's enough, for the time being at least, that the possibility remains. That when I wake up tomorrow…

CHAPTER SIX

PART ONE

Tuesday 26ᵗʰ December 1989

…I know that in less than six hours, I shall see him again. But first, there's my promised session with Jane, which I must admit, I'm not looking forward to. The more I think about it, the more surprised I am that she seems eager to confide in me – or anyone else, for that matter. Even when she was little, the only person taken into her confidence about anything was her grandmother. As I stand in the shower, I try to imagine what I will say to her.

The opportunity to be alone with her comes sooner than I think. It's still not yet eight o'clock when I go downstairs. Jane is already in the kitchen, sitting at the table, no makeup on, her hair somewhat dishevelled, a cup of coffee in front of her. She looks up as I go in.

'Nana never pretended she liked Philip much, even from the start. I was quite upset about that, actually. But she was right after all, wasn't she? I miss her a lot, you know, Meg.'

'We all do, darling. But I know she always had a particularly "soft spot" for you, as she would have said.'

Jane says nothing, as if not sure whether to continue. I sit down opposite her at the table. I decide to wait till she's ready. Then, suddenly, it all pours out. She speaks quietly and quickly, perhaps afraid that, if she pauses, she won't be able to start again.

'She knew all about his affairs. She also knew that I had an abortion. A year after we were married. I made her promise not to tell anyone, and I don't think she ever did – not even Mum. It was Philip's all right – I've never been unfaithful to him, not once. I'd just got a new job and Philip had just been promoted. It meant he had to travel a lot, if you remember. So we both decided to "put our careers first", as they say. Such a bloody silly thing to do, wasn't it? Later – it must have been at least five years – we decided a baby might be a nice idea. I realise now we would have made lousy parents. But anyway, nothing happened. At first I didn't mind and Philip seemed quite relieved. I found out later he was actually in the middle of one of his affairs at the time – I can't remember which one it was now. It made it much worse, of course, when after a couple of years, Helen calmly announced she was pregnant yet again. No trouble at all.'

'I had no idea you felt like that, Jane. You always seemed to have everything you wanted.'

'I put on a good show, don't I? Rather like Mum. We saw a lot of what went on between her and Dad, you know. Oh, nothing dramatic. Just that Dad always had to be the one in charge – without appearing to be, of course. Everyone thinks he's so easy going, don't they? Sometimes I felt Mum put up with it for a quiet life. Just like me with Philip. Not that Dad had affairs, of course!'

We both smile at the thought, which breaks the tension for a moment. It appears that Jane doesn't yet know about Geoffrey's latest decision, so I must make sure I don't say anything about it. I'm beginning to realise it's very difficult to know at the moment who knows what about whom.

'And now, of course, Philip's actually going to be a daddy!' Jane's usual ironic tone has returned and I can hear real bitterness in her voice. 'Not that I think he'll make a particularly good one – once the novelty's worn off.'

From upstairs comes the sound of activity. I get up, and put some bread in the toaster. It soon becomes obvious we won't be able to carry on talking here. Jack comes hurtling down the stairs and into the kitchen, followed more cautiously by Max, both still in their pyjamas, both demanding breakfast. I get out bowls, cereal and milk. I look at Jane. There is obviously still something on her mind.

'How about coming for a quick walk after breakfast? Bella will need to go out anyway. That is, if you want to.'

'Well, there is something else I want to get off my chest. If that's all right.'

I try to imagine what else it can possibly be. It seems I'm beginning to take on my mother's old role as confidante for the whole family and I'm not sure I'm ready for it.

It's cold outside, so we walk at a brisk pace. Bella trots beside us, heading into the wind, pausing occasionally for a quick sniff at an interesting clump of grass. When Jane eventually speaks, it's almost as if she's been rehearsing what to say.

'I don't think I ever really loved him, or even liked him much. I enjoyed being seen with him of course, especially when people used to turn and look at us. He'd had lots of girlfriends before me and it boosted my ego no end to be envied as the one he had eventually chosen. But we were never really affectionate towards each other, even at first. We sort of behaved as if being together and then being married was some sort of sophisticated joke. In fact, I don't think we ever actually once said we loved each other. And now he's gone, I feel I ought to mind much more than I actually do. I don't feel in the least devastated.'

She pauses and I wonder why, if she feels as she does, she seemed so upset yesterday.

'What really worries me, though' she says finally, 'is I don't think I'm capable of loving any one properly, Meg, which can't be right, can it? I just don't understand when people say they're "in love". And I don't understand about feeling jealous. You all probably thought either I didn't know about Philip's affairs, or if I did, I just pretended I didn't mind. But I didn't really feel anything much. It never really interfered with my life, because his behaviour towards me never changed, whether he was in the middle of a fling or not. Do you know, I've never in my life been obsessed with another person. And everyone says that's the real test of what love is, don't they?'

I'm not sure what to say – or indeed if Jane is expecting me to say anything. I think of Peter. I was certainly obsessed with him – and knew what it was like to be jealous. And now there's Jonathan. But obsession can be dangerous. It can obscure reality.

'Some people might say you've been lucky not to know what it feels like.'

She turns towards me, her curiosity aroused.

'You're a dark horse, Meg. It may seem ridiculous, but it's never occurred to me you might ever have been in love.'

'It was a long time ago. I was certainly obsessed, I don't know about in love. Let's just say the experience rather put me off the idea.'

'But you don't regret not marrying?'

'Sometimes I think I've missed out on a lot – especially by not having children. But then I think of all the marriages I know that have gone wrong.'

'Including mine!'

We both walk on in silence for a while.

'This girl that Philip's got involved with,' Jane says eventually. 'I've only met her once – at some office do of Philip's. I didn't give her a second glance then. She seemed immature – childish, really. Long blond hair, short skirt, little girl voice. Not his type at all. She's only twenty-two, you know.'

'And presumably pleased about the baby?'

'I suppose so, yes. Anyway, she's hooked Philip. She's managed to do something I couldn't do. I'm not used to failing.'

'You haven't failed, darling. It's not your fault. Was that why you were so upset yesterday?'

'Partly. If I'm honest, though, I suppose my pride's been hurt more than anything else. I was more shocked than upset when it happened. And I've been so busy putting on an act recently – especially at work. On the one hand, pretending I don't mind about the baby, and on the other, pretending I miss Philip, whereas really it's the other way round! Do you know, before I could pluck up the courage to tell Mum and Dad, I even went to see Helen and poured it all out? She was very sympathetic, of course, but I could tell she was secretly crowing – delighted that for the first time ever her big sister was actually asking for help. Even when I arrived here on Christmas Eve, I couldn't bring myself to say what I really felt. It was just such a relief to be home, so nice to see everyone, yet all I could do was snap at Mum. Then in the church I was suddenly afraid I was going to start blubbing. It was more like crying at a happy ending of a film, rather than at the sad bits, I suppose. You know, like the last scene in *The Railway Children* when their father comes home. I could hardly believe it when I could feel tears just rolling down my face yet again, after you'd all gone out yesterday. And then what was on the television? Only the end of *The Sound of Music*, so I was in serious danger of starting all over again!'

We look at each other and start to laugh. We've done a circuit of the heath and are now nearly back at the vicarage. As we walk across the grass in front of the house, she pauses for a moment, bends down to take off Bella's lead, then stands and faces me.

'There's the chance I could be offered a job in the New York office for a couple of years. If it comes up, I think I'll take it. What do you think, Meg?'

'I think it would be just what you need, darling.'

As we go in, I glance at my watch. Just over two hours to go. I can actually feel my stomach beginning to churn with nerves. How stupid. Indoors, noise seems to be coming from every direction. From the sitting room, cartoon voices blaring out of the television. From the kitchen, the sound of a Mozart symphony playing on the radio, and competing with it, from upstairs, some kind of pop music, complete with what sounds like a full percussion section. As we take our coats off, Jane and I exchange grins.

'Better now?' I ask.

'Much.' She actually gives me a hug. Not just a polite gesture, but a proper hug, something she hasn't done since she was tiny.

'And I promise not to whinge any more today. The last thing I want to be accused of is self-pity. Actually, I'm quite looking forward to the party.'

I seem to have found out more about Jane this morning than in the last twenty or so years.

'I'll go upstairs I think,' she says. 'I need to make myself presentable. Put on my face. Shame Philip won't be here to see how I'm coping very well, thank you very much, without Mr Wonderful.'

At least she's not lost her old acerbity. In the kitchen, Mozart has finished and been replaced by a soprano, with too much vibrato, singing something I can't identify. Ruth is alone, emptying the dishwasher. She switches off the radio.

'Where is everyone?' I ask.

'Well, Helen's just gone upstairs to see if she can prise William out of bed. He's obviously awake, judging by the noise! Jack's busy in the dining room, making name cards for everyone and Ian's watching a cartoon version of *Robin Hood* with Max. I've no idea where Geoffrey is. Did you and Jane enjoy your walk?'

Her casual tone doesn't disguise the fact she obviously can't wait to hear what we talked about. I'm not sure how much to tell. Not about the abortion. Or her admission about her real feelings – or lack of them – for Philip. Or even about the possible job. I decide to be as non-committal as possible.

'Mmm. It was quite cold though. What can I do?'

'The table needs laying. I'll put Jack's cards round when he's finished them. I've worked out there will be thirteen of us, now Jonathan's coming too. Mother wouldn't have been happy with that, would she? Perhaps we should invite someone in off the street. I'm sure Geoffrey would be delighted to welcome another down-and-out. What did Jane want?'

'Just a bit of a chat, really. I think she's exhausted, but doesn't like to admit it. But she did say how nice it was to be home. By the way, I presume you haven't yet told her about Geoffrey's latest bombshell, so I didn't say anything. She'll be all right though, I'm sure. She made some pretty caustic remarks about various things – including Philip and his new woman. I'll make a start on the table. Will we have enough chairs?'

'I think so, if we bring the ones in from Geoffrey's study and a couple from upstairs. I have to say, I'm glad Philip's not here. He could never exactly fade into the background, could he?'

'Look, Auntie Meg!' shouts Jack, as I go into the dining room. As usual, he seems to find it impossible to speak in a normal, conversational way, even at close quarters. He has painstakingly copied all the names, from a list beside him, on to the cards.

'I've done a picture for everyone. There's yours.'

I have a flower. William has a football, Max a balloon. The more I look, the more it is apparent that Ruth has had a considerable hand in suggesting suitable images. She herself has a star. Geoffrey, I see, has a church, complete with steeple.

'They're really great, Jack. What have you drawn for yourself?'

'A kite, like you gave me for Christmas. Look!'

'Perhaps if it's fine this afternoon, we could go and try it out?' I suggest, delighted my present seems to have gone down so well.

'Yeah, can we?' he shrieks in my ear.

Lunch today will be mainly cold, apart from some jacket potatoes, so we can set most of it out on the table well before anyone is due to arrive. By the time we've finished, it's getting on for twelve o'clock. I leave Ruth putting round Jack's cards.

Upstairs in my room, I stand in front of the wardrobe, undecided about what to wear. Nothing I've brought with me seems quite right. Certainly not the skirt and jumper I've got on now – far too dowdy. Perhaps the deep red blouse with my navy skirt. When I've changed, I look in the mirror and catch myself looking rather flushed and anxious – certainly not the impression I want to make. Before I can dither about any more, though, I hear the doorbell. That will have to do. If he doesn't like me the way I am, there's nothing I can do about it. As I open my door, I can hear Martin's unmistakable laugh and then realise that everyone has arrived together, because I can also pick out Jonathan's voice from the general chatter coming from below.

Thirty-five years ago, I probably would have pictured myself floating down the stairs into the arms of my beloved, dressed in some sort of trailing frock, accompanied by music played on massed violins. Now I'm quite happy that I can make my entrance carrying the tray of nibbles Ruth puts into my hands as I pass the kitchen door. I see that Geoffrey is doing his genial host act, dispensing drinks with considerable panache. He is wearing a red bobble hat and a tartan bow tie. I'm glad to see Jonathan is not.

The mood in the room is festive, without the slightest sign of the underlying tension I know to be there. Jane has changed into black trousers and a silky top and once again looks her usual immaculate self. I find it difficult to believe that a couple of hours ago she was pouring her heart out to me, like a diffident adolescent. She smiles at me and continues talking animatedly to Martin and Val. I'm pleased to see that their son, Marcus, is deep in conversation with William. I was afraid that, with his newfound adult status, William would feel rather left out today. Marcus certainly makes a good role model; serious, without being too solemn, intelligent without being too intense. The two younger boys are under the piano with Bella, and I suspect, by the tail wagging that's going on, they are feeding her with forbidden crisps.

Ian, Helen and Jonathan are standing over by the window, surveying the scene. I take a glass of red wine from Geoffrey and go to join them. The sharp pine smell from the tree suddenly reminds me of the forest above Volkmarshausen and I have an involuntary, momentary feeling of dread. I tell myself not to be so silly. Before I can say anything to Jonathan, I notice Ruth has come in from the kitchen, glass in hand, and has gone over to stand next to Geoffrey. She claps her hands and I realise immediately what she's going to do.

'Can we have some hush for a moment.' She has raised her voice and now pauses to let the chatter die down.

'Geoffrey has something special he wants to say to you all.'

Geoffrey looks far from happy and mutters something to her under his breath.

'Well, you'll have to now, won't you,' she says, quietly, but audibly.

'Well,' he begins, apparently at a loss to know how to start. He looks at Ruth, as if for help. She remains impassive, surveying the expectant faces of her friends and relations, a fixed smile on her face, refusing to look at him. His red hat now looks incongruous and faintly ludicrous.

'Ruth and I are not getting any younger, so we've decided it's about time I retired,' he begins. 'We're both really looking forward to taking life a bit easier. I shan't be leaving here till the summer, though, so we've got plenty of time to talk about where we're going to live.'

He beams at us all.

'That's not absolutely accurate, though, is it darling?'

There is silence in the room, the discomfort almost tangible. Ruth pours herself some more wine, and takes a generous sip.

'Because,' she continues, 'as I'm sure you all know, Geoffrey's a great one for springing surprises on his nearest and dearest.'

She waits for the responding murmur to die down.

'So I want to let you all know where I stand, and then we won't talk about it anymore today. I wasn't actually consulted at all about any of this, so it came as rather a surprise to me too. I just want to say that I have absolutely no intention of taking life more easily. Neither have I any intention of living in Wales or Outer Mongolia or wherever else it is Geoffrey has decided is to be his new spiritual home. But I expect I'll survive, just as I've survived all the other crises in my married life. Now, you must be starving after all this excitement. Why don't you all drink up and go into the dining room. I'll be with you in a minute.'

And, looking somewhat flushed, she strides from the room. Helen follows her out. Jack and Max crawl out from under the piano.

'Come on, chaps, let's go and get your hands washed.' Ian seizes his sons as they rush past us and marches them out of the room. I see that Geoffrey has regained his composure remarkably quickly, considering the ferocity of Ruth's onslaught. He strolls over, glass in hand, to talk to Martin and Val as if nothing untoward has happened, perhaps oblivious that he's still wearing his silly hat. Jane, I notice, walks pointedly away from him as he approaches.

'Well,' says Jonathan. 'You said I would know what it was all about today. Ruth is certainly not happy, to put it mildly!'

'It's not as if it's the first time he's just gone ahead and done something without consulting her first. Did you know he was a solicitor when they were first married? When he "found God", as he puts it, she had to go along with that too. And what he didn't say just now was that he's "lost God" again, and that's the real reason he feels he must leave the church now. Although, actually, Ruth suspects there may be even more he's still not telling her.' I wonder if I've said too much. 'That's not official, so don't say anything, will you?'

'Of course not. I'm very pleased you told me though. Come on, let's go and sit down.'

As we walk out into the hall, he smiles down at me and gently touches me on the shoulder. So perhaps he really does feel I'm someone special. I'm aware that Ruth is coming out of the kitchen carrying a dish of steaming jacket potatoes and is following us into the dining room. No doubt she will make some sort of knowing remark to me later. I'm not surprised that she appears once more to be her usual cheerful self and says something to Geoffrey as if nothing untoward has happened.

'Before we start, we must congratulate Jack for making such wonderful cards, so we all know where to sit,' she calls out as she puts the dish on the table. My card, with its flower, has been put next to Jonathan's. I see his has a drawing of a heart and guess Ruth has chosen the image for reasons not entirely due to his profession – the crafty old so-and-so.

'Yes, well done, old chap,' cries Geoffrey, beaming round at us all. 'Would you like to say grace again Will, please?'

William looks surprised, but stands up, looking a little uncomfortable.

'Thank you, God, for our food.'

'Start passing the potatoes round down your end of the table, will you please Geoffrey,' Ruth says, with only a hint of impatience in her voice.

Eventually everyone has a plateful of food. Crackers have been pulled, jokes read out, and paper hats put on. The wine is passed round the table; I notice that both William and Marcus have poured themselves some and have already taken a quick slurp each. Jonathan lifts his glass and clinks it against mine.

'Prost!' he says.

'Prost!' I reply.

'What does that mean, Auntie Meg?' asks William, from across the table.

'It's what they say instead of "cheers", in Germany. I went there when I was seventeen.'

'Cool,' says William, and turns away to continue his conversation with Marcus.

'And I was born there,' says Jonathan, unexpectedly.

'Were you? I didn't realise. You sound so English.'

'That's because I left before I was three.'

'What about your parents? Were they German?'

'My father was. He never really lost his accent. My mother was born here, although her parents were originally German, too. She's still going strong at nearly a hundred, actually. She's spending Christmas with my sister. You must meet her – you'd like her. Anyway, it's a complicated story. We must add it to the list of all the things we have to tell each other.'

So he hasn't forgotten. But do I really want to tell him about what happened thirty-five years ago? He would be the first person I've ever told.

'Yes, we must,' I find myself saying.

He turns away in response to something Jane says to him. I'm still acutely aware of his presence beside me – hearing his voice, feeling his arm occasionally touch mine. And I feel immensely happy.

'Do you think they really will move away?' asks Martin, who is sitting on my other side.

'Not if Ruth has anything to do with it!'

'I gathered that. I don't blame her for feeling rather peeved. I can just imagine what Val would say if I made a decision like that without consulting her.'

'Val's very lucky to have you. And may I say what a nice young man Marcus has turned out to be. A real credit to you both!'

'Well, though I do say it myself… ' He laughs, then lowers his voice. 'And while I think, Jonathan was asking all about you the day after the rehearsal the other night. You've made a bit of a hit there!'

'I can't imagine why,' I mutter. The conversation seems to have taken a very personal turn. I feel extremely embarrassed, but at the same time immensely pleased. It's as if I've suddenly lost control over the direction my life may be about to take, and I'm not sure whether I like the feeling. I find myself just looking at the food on my plate, not eating, in a bit of a daze. I'm relieved when everyone's finished and I can get up from the table to help Ruth and Val clear away the plates and bring in the pudding. Perhaps now I can recover my composure a little, but I'm not helped by the knowing grin Ruth gives me as we go into the kitchen. I pretend to ignore her, but I know it's a sign that she'll want a "blow-by-blow account", as she often says, after everyone's gone.

'We're all going out to fly my kite!' yells Jack, when we return to the dining room. 'Like you said, Auntie Meg!'

'I'm afraid that's all my fault,' I say to Jonathan. 'I gave it to him for Christmas.'

'I'm rather good with kites,' he replies.

Jack insists that we all – including Bella – come out and watch. By the time everyone is eventually rounded up after lunch, it's nearly half past three and the light is already fading. It soon becomes obvious that kite flying is considered a masculine sport. We girls stand on the sidelines, as the men and boys mill around, gesticulating, discussing, getting tangled in string and failing to get the kite off the ground. It turns out that Jonathan is indeed good with kites. He takes charge. The knack, apparently, is for someone – in this case William – to keep the kite on the ground, while someone else – Marcus – runs backwards for about fifty yards, holding on to the string. William then releases the kite and it immediately soars up into the sky. We all cheer. Bella barks.

'It's my kite!' Jack wails.

Jonathan takes the string from Marcus.

'Come on Jack, help me hold on. I'll show you what it can do.'

The kite in fact has two strings, one on each side, which enables it to swirl and swoop, one moment coming to within a few feet of the ground, the next spectacularly rising up, making a fierce whirring sound, until it's silhouetted against the reddening sky for a moment, before plunging down again. Max comes over to stand beside Helen and slips his hand into hers. She bends down and places a light kiss on his cheek. He watches the whirling red and yellow kite, as if mesmerised. At the age of three, he will be storing up his first memories. Will this be one of them? This and the lights on the Christmas tree? It would be nice to think so.

I watch Jonathan. It's the first time I've seen him from a distance. I see he has a grace of movement as he manipulates the kite high above him. And broad, strong shoulders. No hint of middle age stoutness. The spell is broken when the kite suddenly plunges to the ground. It's almost dark by now, so we decide to go inside and have another go tomorrow.

'You must come and help us again, Uncle Jonathan,' insists Jack.

'Sorry, Jack, I've got to work tomorrow. Another day, maybe.'

'You'll have to do it then, Grandpa.'

'I should think we'll be able to manage that, old chap, now we know what to do.'

Tomorrow he won't be here. I may never see him again. The thought, repeating itself involuntarily inside my mind, over and over again, is what I can only describe as devastating. It mustn't happen. Like it or not, he has become an indelible part of me. I am, I reluctantly concede, obsessed. But, as we all troop back to the house, he comes and walks beside me.

'Do you think they could spare you tomorrow evening? I thought it might be nice to start catching up on all those things we said we'd talk about. There's a rather nice Italian restaurant in Greenwich. I'll book a table if you like.'

'That would be nice.' I'm aware I must sound rather banal, but I'm unable to find the words I really want to say.

'Good. I'll come and collect you about half past seven, if that's all right.'

Yes, yes, yes, I want to say. Perfect. Unbelievable. Fantastic. All the superlative words there are.

'What are you smirking about?' Ruth asks. We are once again in the kitchen, making what seems like countless cups of tea. I take a deep breath.

'He wants to take me out to supper tomorrow. And please, Ruth, don't make a great big thing about it. I just need to come to terms with the idea.'

'I knew you'd like each other. I'm so pleased, darling. Seriously, I promise I won't make any more silly comments or anything. It's just nice to see you looking so happy.'

She gives me a quick hug. I look at her.

'And you?'

'Oh, I'll be all right. I always am, aren't I?'

She turns away to get milk from the fridge. The kitchen is soon filled with people and noise and we say no more.

'I want juice, Granny. And biscuits. I don't like tea.'

'I know you don't, Jack. Look, I've already put juice on the tray for you and Max. And I've got something to show you afterwards.'

'What? Tell me what it is!'

'Just wait and see.'

It turns out to be an old, brown leather suitcase filled with all the dressing up paraphernalia Mother had kept squirrelled away in her spare room. Ruth pulls it out of the cupboard under the stairs and drags it into the sitting room. We all gather round as she opens the lid, to reveal the jumble of hats, scarves, waistcoats, dresses, trousers, wigs and false beards accumulated over fifty years or more. Jonathan comes and stands beside me. We give each other a quick smile, which I find churns me up inside somewhat.

Soon we're all raking through the case almost feverishly, putting things on, posing in front of the mirror and each other, dressing ourselves more and more ludicrously. Perhaps it's the release of built up tensions, perhaps just because we're all feeling relaxed, but we all soon become convulsed with hysterical laughter. Ruth produces her camera and props it up on a pile of books on the coffee table, to take a remote controlled photo of everyone. She arranges us all – some on the sofa, the rest either standing behind or sitting in front on the floor – and we wait for the flash, while she manages to dash back to her place just in time.

'One more and then I think that will be the film finished.'

But as she comes back for a second time, the camera begins to slide off the books and tilts forward so it's almost pointing to the ground. We all involuntarily bend down lower and lower to remain in line with the lens until the flash goes off for a second time.

We slowly start putting everything back into the suitcase, almost shamefacedly returning to normal adulthood. Jack, Max and Bella fall in a heap together on the floor. William takes Marcus upstairs to listen to his music and we soon hear a steady beat coming down the stairs. Later, when the younger boys are in bed, we open a bottle of wine and all find it difficult not to nod off, until it's time for the news on television, which is much later than usual. We watch in silence. Comment seems superfluous. There are pictures of the trial of Ceaucescu and his wife, Elena, while a list of their crimes is read out. Then, distressing images of them lying dead, slumped against a wall. It's hard to believe this has actually happened now, within a few hours flying time of where we are sitting in civilised comfort; that it's not some sort of television drama depicting events from the distant past.

And suddenly, the evening is over. Arrangements are being made. William is going to spend tomorrow morning with Marcus and be taught the rudiments of playing the guitar. Ruth and I arrange to meet Val for coffee on Thursday morning, as she has a day off. In a sort of euphoric state, I can only smile at Jonathan when he quietly confirms he'll see me tomorrow evening.

Now I'm alone in my room. Tomorrow I shall offer to take the film to be developed. I shall take the negative of Peter and me in Germany to be printed at the same time. Today the photograph has become of secondary importance, but important nevertheless. If I'm to build up a complete picture of what happened – especially as it seems that I'm about to share my memories with Jonathan – I need all the evidence I can find. So, late as it now is, I once again open the diary…

PART TWO

Monday 16th August 1954

…and turn the pages.

We went to the Edersee today. The German girls did not come with us, so Gudrun and Helga left early to catch the train and go to school. Barbara and I decided to go into Münden by bus. We waited for ages at the bus stop, but we didn't worry, as German buses are always late. But eventually a bus came the other way and the driver leaned out and asked us if we were waiting for the bus. Apparently they had just changed the timetable, so our bus had gone ages ago. I knew there were some bicycles at the school, so we dashed back so we could ride into Münden. Fritz insisted on coming with us, too. Barbara tried to get on her bicycle by scooting first and thought it wouldn't work. Fritz then told us that the brake is put on by peddling backwards, but we kept on forgetting and suddenly stopping halfway down a hill. We set off on the left hand side of the road, so Fritz had to keep on shouting 'Rechts! Rechts!' Halfway there he decided to go on ahead and tell the others to wait for us, as the coach was due to leave shortly. He gave us strict

instructions not to ride on the left, to go in single file, to be
careful in the town, watch for policemen and ride slowly.
Then he was off, peddling furiously.

I had forgotten about that incident. Now I can remember that
Barbara and I could hardly ride we were laughing so much as
he disappeared into the distance, coat tails flapping, still
gesticulating wildly. I notice that I wrote more about the bicycle
ride than about the trip to the Edersee itself.

The Edersee is very beautiful and is really a reservoir,
surrounded by mountains. We were able to walk near the
dam and then had lunch at Schloß Waldeck, which overlooks
the lake.

No mention of the fact that all the time I was there, I was
thinking of Peter, remembering his quote about the peace of
the mountains and wishing he were with us. I thumb through
the photographs again. Yes, the Edersee is very beautiful. I had
taken four pictures – one from the dam, with the castle in the
distance, one from above overlooking the dam and two from
the castle overlooking the reservoir. There is another one of
several of us sitting at a table, talking, gesticulating, eating and
drinking, mountains stretching away into the distance behind
us. Even now, I can almost taste the wonderful German cakes
we rapidly became addicted to. In the austerity of post-war
Britain, where we still had rationing, we had nothing to match
them. They were more like an elaborate flan, topped with fruit
and piled high with whipped cream. On the seat beside me is
something I've completely forgotten about, but which, together
with the duffle coat, was just the thing to have at that time – a
bucket bag. Mine, I remember, was made of stiffened cream
fabric, so that it remained open at the top, with brown leather

trimming. I have a feeling that Barbara had an identical one, bought on one of our Saturday morning shopping expeditions.

Among the collection of postcards were two of the Edersee – one showing Schloß Waldeck in the snow, looking just like a fairytale castle. The other shows the reservoir and the surrounding thickly-wooded mountains. I turn it over. Even with my somewhat rusty German I can understand that it gives all the statistical details of the reservoir itself – length, breadth, depth and the fact that its dam is one of the largest in Europe. During its construction, three villages were completely submerged under the water. Was it, I wonder now, one of the dams destroyed during the raids on Germany during the war? I make a mental note to find out; I don't think anyone even mentioned the destruction of the dams while we were there. I had sent this card to my parents.

> *It is really beautiful here. On the way up the mountains we stopped at a spa – "Bad" something or other – and had some of the water to drink, which was ghastly. Miss Smithson said it was like "Bath" water and we took it the wrong way! Love from Margaret.*

I do vaguely remember the spa and its foul water. Now I come to think about it, I also remember that Miss Smithson and Miss Harris appeared to have made up after their tiff on Friday.

According to Barbara, who seemed miraculously to know about such things, it had all been a lot of fuss about nothing. We were sitting on the coach, on the way back from the Edersee. She lowered her voice conspiratorially once again.

'Apparently, Miss Smithson's intimate supper with the lovely Fräulein Schaefer on Friday turned out to be nothing of the sort.'

'How do you know that?'

'Well, Anne Simmonds is staying with that girl with the very short hair – you know, Ursula something or other – and her parents know Fräulein Schaefer. Anyway, it was actually a party, and Harry was invited as well. And practically the whole school staff and their friends and relations were there, including – wait for it – Christel Schaefer's fiancé! Who is – well, guess.'

'I've no idea. How could I?'

'Only Herr Schroeder – otherwise known as Belladonna with the beautiful eyes!'

'Really?'

Even I was intrigued, in spite of my professed dismissal of gossip.

'Can you imagine it,' she went on. 'I thought the only person he fancied was himself. He makes me squirm, just to look at him. As for more intimate contact, if you know what I mean… '

She looked at me in a knowing sort of way and giggled, before continuing.

'So, Gwen and Irene presumably had their intimate supper on Saturday and now everything's all hunky-dory again. Mind you, the thought of becoming intimate with Harry is rather a ghastly idea, too!'

'Barbara, I wish you wouldn't say things like that. It's not very nice.'

'Not very nice!' she repeated mockingly.

She had an infuriatingly smug look on her face, knowing that her teasing had had the desired effect, but said nothing more. To my chagrin, I could feel tears beginning to prick my eyes. I turned away and looked out of the window, upset and angry, but determined not to be drawn into an argument. The one consoling thought was that in a few hours I would see Peter again, when I went to hear him playing at his concert that evening. And I was more determined than ever that Barbara would not come with us, although I supposed it was inevitable that she would meet him eventually. I bitterly regretted telling her about him in the first place. When we arrived back in Volkmarshausen and got off the bus, I hoped she would have forgotten about the concert. She hadn't, of course.

'Give my love to the gorgeous Peter! Enjoy yourself – and be good!' she called out as we parted.

I was too excited to eat much supper. As the time came for us to leave to catch the train into Münden, I felt flushed and almost feverish.

I hoped no one would notice; the last thing I wanted was to be left behind because they thought I was ill again. By the time we arrived at Peter's school, I was in a bemused daze. Herr Schmidt, smartly dressed in jacket and tie rather than his usual sweater, went up to an elderly, frail looking man and shook him warmly by the hand.

'That is Peter's father,' said Gudrun. 'Come, you shall meet him.'

He kissed her on both cheeks.

'*Hier ist meine Freundin Margaret aus England,*' Gudrun said. 'Margaret, this is Herr Köhler.'

She looked at me smugly. I realised, as I shook his hand, that I had not previously known Peter's full name. It was only when I actually said the name out loud, that it dawned on me how odd it sounded to English ears.

'*Guten Abend, Herr Köhler,*' I found myself saying. In spite of my nervousness, I found myself smiling at the sound of his name. I imagined what Barbara would say when – and if – I told her.

'*Hair Curler? What is he? A hairdresser? You can't have a serious relationship with a hairdresser!*'

The hall was crowded and hot. For one awful moment I

thought I was going to faint. When we sat down, Gudrun was on one side of me, and Fritz on the other. By the time the concert started, I had calmed down a little and began to look around. And there, in the front row, sat Peter. I immediately recognised the back of his head, his fair hair just skimming his collar in the most delicious way. He turned and saw us and smiled. My inside gave a sort of lurch and I felt slightly sick. Gudrun smiled back and waved enthusiastically.

Had I kept the programme? I doubt it, considering that I had destroyed the only copy of Peter's photograph. I rummage through my box and, finally, among my old school reports and music certificates, there it is. It is typed and duplicated, the paper yellowing and fragile. I open it gingerly, quickly skimming down the faded, Gothic script looking for Peter's name. He was playing twice – a movement from a Mozart sonata in the first half and the Brahms rhapsody towards the end of the second.

As far as I can remember, most of the concert was much the same as every school concert I have been to. The orchestra, with slightly out of tune strings and over-enthusiastic percussion, playing pieces which were rather too ambitious for their capabilities. The choir, singing, in a far more gutsy way than English school children ever have, folk song arrangements and excerpts from Brahms' Requiem. Solos from a succession of nervous young students. A young boy, hands glued to his sides, reciting Goethe's "Mignon" – 'Kennst du das Land, wo die Zitronen Blühn?'. Peter, though, stood out over and above everyone else and got the loudest and longest applause of the evening. After the final flourish at the end of the Brahms, he rose to his feet, a slight smile on his face, and bowed deeply. Gudrun, clapping enthusiastically, hands high above her head, beamed round proprietarily.

After the concert we found Peter holding court, surrounded by his enthusiastic admirers, receiving their congratulations as if he had been doing so all his life. He was even signing programmes for a group of excited young girls. Did he sign mine? I seem to remember he did. And there is his signature on the front cover, written, I remember now, with the professional, illegible flourish of the famous.

I didn't think for a moment that we would have any time alone together that evening. But then we all started to move into another room where refreshments were to be served and he suddenly took my hand and squeezed it.

'You know, Margaret,' he said softly in my ear, 'it was good for me while I played that you were listening.'

'I was so pleased I was able to come,' I managed to whisper, trying to ignore the fact that my heart seemed to be beating unnaturally loudly. 'You played so well, Peter – much better that any of the others. I expect that's why you played nearly last.'

'Yes, I think so also.'

At the time I saw no irony in his remark.

'Now, I will fetch a glass for you. You must stay here.'

I could see Gudrun in front of us, obviously looking for Peter, who had gone off in the other direction. He was soon back, carrying a glass of what looked, and tasted, a bit like weak blackcurrant syrup.

'I think you enjoyed your visit to Edersee today?'

'Yes, you were right, it's very beautiful.'

We were back on the Romantic poets again, apparently, for he suddenly turned to me.

'*O Täler weit, O Höhen, O schöner, grüner Wald, Du meiner Lust und Wehen Andächt'ger Aufenthalt!* Do you understand?'

'No, but it sounds lovely.'

This time, he didn't translate.

'And you saw Kassel?'

'Yes. On Friday. I was surprised that it is still damaged and not yet repaired. I think it is very sad we fought each other.'

'You do not hate us?'

'No, of course not.' This was getting difficult. 'Everyone has been so nice and friendly since we've been here.'

'That is very good. And now, I think, we will become very good friends.'

That was better.

'You will go to school tomorrow?'

'Yes. In the afternoon we will be going on a tour of the town.'

'That is good. I will meet you outside the school. We will go to the café nearby before you go for your tour.'

I wasn't quite sure whether he was inviting me by myself, or whether this was a pre-arranged meeting with Gudrun as well. But before I could work out a way of asking him, he once again took my hand and led me back to the others. He said nothing more to me until we were about to go home. He gazed into my eyes.

'Until tomorrow.'

I had thought that, at best, I would see him again during his visit to the house on Thursday. But the chance that tomorrow he might once again hold my hand, recite poetry to me – kiss me even – was more than I dared to hope. That night, of course, I couldn't sleep. While I tossed and turned under my steamy duvet, my imagination worked overtime. My life as the devoted wife of a famous concert pianist seemed assured and by the morning, I had planned my future in minute detail.

Now I turn out my light and start thinking about the events of today. I resolve not to repeat the mistakes of thirty-five years ago. But the last thing I remember, before falling asleep, is feeling a mixture of excitement and apprehension until…

CHAPTER SEVEN

PART ONE

Wednesday 27ᵗʰ December 1989

…in the middle of the night, I suddenly wake up from a vivid dream. And not just any dream. I've been visiting familiar territory. I've been to my other house. In my dream I always recognise this house as mine, although, of course, it bears no resemblance to my real house, my safe, secure house. Because this house is always falling apart. Sometimes I find that the only way in is through a window, high above me and I have to climb up the wall, which suddenly begins to tilt outwards. Sometimes I'm inside and realise that the walls are becoming thinner and thinner, as if they are made of rapidly melting ice. In others, I'm high up, on the roof perhaps, and there is no way down without negotiating steep, precarious, crumbling steps. I seem to have these dreams whenever I'm at a turning point in my life or whenever I'm feeling insecure in some way. And I always wake up, as is the way with dreams, before I come to any real harm. They started when I returned from Germany with glandular fever and formed part of the accompanying delirium.

Now, I lie here, trying to capture the dream before the details fade. This time I'm inside the house, which is huge. There are rooms I've never seen before, behind doors with flaking paint and broken handles. There are staircases with missing steps and collapsing banisters. As I make my way down a long, dark corridor, I can hear people shrieking and laughing and the sound of breaking glass. I'm angry. I burst through the door and shout at them to get out. They have dropped food, spilt drink and covered the floor with rubbish. They stare at me, as if I'm the intruder. I don't recognise any of them. They turn away, ignoring me.

Goodness, that must all mean something extremely significant. I turn over and look at my clock. Half past three. The unease caused by my dream has stayed with me and I lie awake for some considerable time, unable to prevent random thoughts and memories from churning around in my head.

Am I really sure that I would want my life to change in the dramatic way it inevitably will, if I get involved with Jonathan? The phrase "be careful what you wish for" comes into my head. Remember Germany. And then the maxim "*Carpe Diem*" pops unbidden into my mind. Seizing the day is not something that comes naturally to me. I'm a natural ditherer, preferring to weigh up the pros and cons of any situation before making up my mind. But perhaps I've done too much of that over the last thirty-five years. Perhaps it's about time I did something unplanned for once. And, in spite of myself, I begin to feel a real sense of excitement. I suspect I've gone past the point of being able to control my feelings and I hope Jonathan feels the same. But the same as what? What do I feel? Physical attraction? I remember looking at his profile in the church and wanting to touch him; remember the feeling of pleasure when he put his hand on my shoulder and his arm brushed mine. But would I have felt like this if he hadn't been playing the Brahms when I first saw him? Perhaps not. Above all, though, I just feel that I've been waiting to meet him for a long time. It's as if I thought, "oh, there you are then," when I came down the stairs and saw him for the first time – just five days ago. I begin to imagine what will happen this evening. Once again I'm playing the very unwise game of inventing a script, not only for myself, which is bad enough, but for someone else as well.

I've not set my alarm and by the time I wake up again, it's gone nine o'clock. Downstairs, the day is well under way. Marcus has obviously already arrived for the promised guitar lesson, because I can hear the sound of Will's tentative efforts coming from the sitting room. Otherwise, it's unusually quiet. I find Helen alone in the kitchen, reading the paper.

'Where is everybody?'

'Dad and Ian have gone out to fly the kite again with Jack and Max. Mum's popped out to the shops.'

'Do you know where she's put the film she finished yesterday? I thought I'd take it to be developed. I've got something I want to take in too.'

'I think she took it with her.'

'Actually, I might need a proper photographic shop. I want to get a print from an old negative.'

'You'll have to ask Mum. I would imagine there's one in somewhere Blackheath.'

I make myself a mug of coffee and some toast, then join Helen at the table.

'It says here in the paper that several hundred soldiers volunteered to shoot the Ceausescus. They said they wanted to die together, which would be quite touching if they hadn't been such terrible people.'

We sit side-by-side reading in silence for a while. The trial lasted a mere two hours, before they were led outside and shot.

'It seems almost ghoulish to show the whole thing on television, doesn't it? You can't imagine that happening here.'

I feel sluggish from my disturbed night, but restless at the same time and decide some fresh air will do me good. I go upstairs to fetch my precious negative. It suddenly seems imperative to get it printed as soon as possible, as if I need to get as full a picture as I can of the past, before I embark on the future. I can see the kite-flying party in the distance on the heath as I come down the steps and turn towards the village.

I find the shop quite easily and even manage to persuade the rather lugubrious owner to have it ready for collection by late afternoon. Although whether I shall actually want to show it to Jonathan is another matter. Outside, I feel as if a weight has suddenly been lifted from my shoulders – the sort of feeling of relief and happiness you get when you manage to find something you thought had been lost forever. I don't feel like going back just yet. A little way down the hill is a rather expensive-looking boutique and I go and look in the window. I decide it might be nice to buy something a bit special to wear this evening. It's not like me to actually feel like buying clothes; it's a chore I put off for as long as possible, usually coming back from one of my infrequent trips, tired, irritable and having bought nothing at all. Today my eye is caught by a deep red dress and jacket in the window and I go inside, just to see whether they have it in my size. They have and it's only when I've tried it on and, much to my surprise, find I look rather nice in it, that I think to ask how much it costs. It's more than I've ever spent on one garment in my life. I feel an illogical sense of guilt at even contemplating buying it. What the hell, it's my money after all. I try to remember the last time I spent so much just on impulse.

'I'll take it,' I find myself saying.

Spurred on by my daring, I decide just to have a look in the shoe shop over the road. After all, the shoes I've brought with me have definitely seen better days and are far too dowdy for my nice new outfit. Half an hour later, I'm opening the front door of the vicarage almost furtively, carrying my two rather posh-looking carrier bags and hoping to slip upstairs unnoticed, feeling somewhat embarrassed by my extravagance.

'There you are darling!' calls Ruth from the kitchen. 'I was wondering where you were.'

'Just been to the shops,' I say, as casually as possible, starting to go upstairs. But Ruth has obviously seen my bags.

'Come on, show me what you've bought.'

She takes the bag from me and peers inside.

'It looks very smart. Just right for this evening, I should say. And shoes too!'

She's reverted once again to her big sister role. I give her a despairing look.

'Sorry darling, I promise I won't make a fuss. Go upstairs and try it on. I'm dying to see what it's like. I'll be up in a minute.'

I'm expecting, as usual, to be disappointed with what the outfit looks like now I've got it home. But it feels right, and actually makes me look taller – and more elegant – than I know I really am.

Ruth, when she comes in, doesn't say anything at first. She just stands in the doorway and looks at me, head on one side, smiling. I grin back.

'Yes, darling, I think you'll do,' she says at last, and gives me a kiss on the cheek. 'That colour really suits you.'

'Do you think so? I'm not quite so sure now. You don't think it's too bright?'

'Of course not, don't be silly. You look really nice. You'll have a lovely time.'

As Ruth leaves the room and goes back downstairs, I take off the dress and carefully hang it up. It occurs to me that I'm making far too much of this evening. Jonathan is probably not giving me a second thought today and he certainly won't have dashed out to buy new clothes. He'll most likely turn up casually dressed in the old jumper he was wearing when I first saw him, and there I shall be, dressed up to the nines, looking completely out of place. It's a good job I didn't go the whole hog and get my hair done as well. He wouldn't have recognised me at all. I resolve not to think any more about it for the rest of the day.

In fact, events overtake me, so I don't have time to brood. As I'm going down the stairs, the doorbell rings and I go to answer it. At first, I don't recognise the youngish man standing there, looking distraught and somewhat dishevelled.

'Hello, Philip,' I say after a moment. 'This is a surprise.'

'Hello, Meg,' is all he appears to be able to say.

'Come in. I'm not sure where Jane is, I haven't seen her today. She might have gone to work.'

Before he can answer, Jane emerges from the sitting room. I don't quite know what to do, so I turn to go into the kitchen.

'No, Meg, don't go. Philip won't be staying long, will you Philip? I'm sure he's needed elsewhere.'

'Well, no, actually. I've left Debbie.'

'Good gracious! I didn't expect you'd get tired of her as quickly as all that.'

'You might as well all know, I suppose,' Philip says, somewhat dramatically. 'I've just found out that the baby isn't actually mine.'

He looks so pathetic, I feel quite sorry for him. But Jane actually bursts out laughing.

'I'm sorry, Philip, I can't help it. You mean you weren't able to manage it after all?'

'Don't be like that, Jane.'

He seems genuinely surprised and hurt at her reaction. She takes a deep breath and continues.

'I suppose you think you can come running back to me now, like you always do after one of your little flings? Well, actually, this time, the answer is no, you can't. I've just about had enough of being taken for granted. Anyway, I shall be out of the country for a couple of years – in New York – so it wouldn't be convenient.'

There is silence for a moment. Philip, for once, appears at a loss for words. Then, quite suddenly, he begins to sob. Ruth and Helen both come out of the kitchen. For a moment we all stand looking at him, embarrassed, astonished, not knowing what to do. Ruth eventually steps forward.

'Come and sit down, Philip. Can you put the kettle on Meg, please. I think we all need reviving a bit.'

She takes him by the arm and leads him into the sitting room. I go into the kitchen, as instructed. Almost immediately, Jane follows me in. She goes to a cupboard and gets out a glass.

'He's decided he'd like a whisky and ginger instead, would you believe. I think we all need the coffee though, don't you? I cannot believe he's got the nerve to come here and make such an exhibition of himself. If he thinks he can get my sympathy that way, he's very much mistaken, I'm afraid. I'm really sorry, Meg, that you've all had to get involved like this.'

She bursts out laughing again, although I can't help thinking it's more of a nervous reaction than genuine mirth.

'I think Mum is about to tell him it'll be all right in the morning and that she'll kiss it better. She seems to be coping with him remarkably well, though. I suppose it's her experience with tiresome parishioners.'

She goes through to the dining room and I can hear the clanking of bottles and the fizz of the ginger before she goes back into the sitting room.

'Quite like old times, isn't it?' I can hear her saying. She's certainly going overboard with the sarcasm and I suspect she's actually beginning to enjoy herself.

By the time I've made the coffee, Philip seems to have pulled himself together and is sitting in front of the fire, sipping his drink, looking quietly pleased to be the centre of attention. We all turn expectantly as we hear the front door opening. Jack comes bounding into the room, with Max trotting along behind.

'Uncle Philip!' he yells. 'We've been out flying my new kite, haven't we Max? Auntie Meg gave it to me for Christmas. Uncle Jonathan taught us how to fly it yesterday.'

Ian has followed the boys in and almost does a classic comic double take when he notices his brother-in-law. He glances at Helen for guidance, but she just shrugs her shoulders slightly and grins.

'Have some lunch before you go, Philip,' says Ruth. If he had been hoping to stay on, he must by now realise, in spite of the apparent thickness of his skin, that he won't be welcome much longer.

'If it's not too much trouble, Ruth, that would be great.'

We all seem only too eager to leave him to finish his drink, but Jane remains standing by the mantelpiece, hands on her hips.

'Well now,' we can hear her saying as we go out into the hall. 'How did you find out that your precious Debbie had not been telling you the entire truth?'

'I'd better go and warn Geoffrey,' says Ruth. 'I suppose he's in his study.'

'No, he's gone to the church,' says Ian. 'Said he had something to do before lunch.'

'We'll get the food if you want to go and tell him, Mum,' says Helen. 'I'll fill Ian in about this morning's rather melodramatic developments.'

And I shall have more of the family saga to tell Jonathan this evening.

By this time, William and Marcus have finished the guitar lesson and we can hear the usual steady beat coming from upstairs. Jack is sent up to fetch them down, but Marcus says he has to go home and will see Will later this afternoon to cycle into Greenwich. Lunch is largely silent, not only because of Philip's presence but because Ruth and Geoffrey, having returned from the church, appear to have had some sort of disagreement. Ruth looks particularly grim and Geoffrey merely uncomfortable. Oh dear, not more drama, surely. It's all rather too much for one day. Even the boys are subdued and they don't say much, as if they sense any exuberance on their part would be out of place.

By the time we've finished the meal, Philip has regained his self-assurance and has almost become his old, arrogant self. He's gone out in the garden to kick a football with Jack and is now careering round the lawn with Max on his shoulders. Jane and I stand in the kitchen, watching them.

'He's really enjoying himself, isn't he,' she says, almost affectionately. 'But it's a novelty for him. I'm sure if they were his kids he'd soon get bored. Shame, really. Anyway, I've agreed he can go back to the flat for a couple of days, and that he can use it while I'm in New York. I haven't told Mum yet, but I've definitely decided to take the job if it's still available. Best to make a clean break, I think. By the way, he said that he's found out that the lovely Debbie is actually still seeing her baby's father, who is unemployed at the moment apparently. He got her to admit it couldn't possibly be his. She was actually pregnant before she started her fling with Philip. He thinks she just thought he was a better bet.'

In spite of herself, I can tell she's really rather enjoying his comeuppance, as I'm beginning to think of it. His farewells, when he finally decides it's time to go, are enthusiastic, as if we are all trying to persuade him to stay longer. Ruth, Helen and I all get hugs and kisses on both cheeks, although he does have the grace to draw the line at doing anything more than giving Jane a tentative touch on her shoulder. He even gives Bella a firm pat on the back. The two younger boys dance around him as he goes down the drive. Marcus is just arriving and Philip greets him enthusiastically, stopping to inspect his bicycle. As is usual when he's gone, the house seems uncannily quiet and peaceful. We all stand in the hall for a moment, uncertain what to do next.

It's only later in the afternoon that I learn from Ruth what happened in the church. Geoffrey had gone in to tidy up some things and had found Shirley arranging the flowers. He had decided that it might be a good opportunity to tell her about his departure. By the time Ruth came in, Shirley was in tears and had become hysterical, saying how Geoffrey was her life and that she didn't know what she would do without him.

'She told me I didn't deserve such a wonderful man and accused me of dragging Geoffrey away from all he held sacred. He obviously didn't tell her why he's going, so she doesn't know that he's managed to lose his faith without any help at all from me. But what actually made me angry was that he didn't say a word to support me. Just muttered soothing words to her, patted her on the shoulder and offered her his handkerchief. When she calmed down a bit, all she could say was that she would pray for me. I was furious at the time, but now I'm beginning to see how ludicrous it all is. What am I going to do with him, Meg? I really despair sometimes, but I know he'll never change. Anyway, by now, I expect it'll be all round the parish. If you want to let everyone know something, you just have to tell one of the Angels of Mercy.'

'Poor old Shirley. How long has she been coming to the church?'

'She and her husband moved here about three years ago. They used to live in Lewisham before he retired. They bought quite a big house opposite the heath. He was a bank manager, I think. He died soon afterwards, though. Had a heart attack. It was then that Shirley got involved with the church. She'd always been very much the "little woman", I should think. Geoffrey helped her sort out various financial things she didn't have a clue about, so she got more and more reliant on him. Although that's a joke, of course. As you know, Geoffrey has absolutely no idea how to deal with his own money, let alone someone else's. She's always "just popping in for a moment" as she always says. She sings in the choir, helps with the flowers – that sort of thing. I've always got the impression, long before today's outburst, that she thinks I'm not good enough to be a vicar's wife – that she would be far better, which is absolute nonsense, of course. She's so disorganised she wouldn't last more than a week.'

It's dark outside by now and I suddenly realise that if I'm going to collect the print before the shop shuts, I'd better get a move on.

'Won't be long,' I mutter. I haven't told Ruth about the photo and it seems too complicated to explain now. I get to the shop just in time.

'It hasn't printed out very well,' complains the same mournful looking man, as if I've hurt his pride by not providing him with something better to work on.

'That doesn't matter.'

Now I stand outside the shop, not actually daring to look at the photo. I need to wait till I'm by myself. I put it in my handbag. And I realise I can't remember precisely what Jonathan looks like either. I need a photo of him too. Two and a half hours to go before he comes to collect me. I'm beginning to feel nervous. Stupid. I'm startled and surprised that my feelings have become so – well, I suppose the right word would be "intense".

I manage to slip into the house without anyone seeing me and go upstairs to my room. My hands are actually trembling. Ridiculous. I get out the photo. I don't quite know what I'm expecting to see. Certainly not the image of the rather unassuming, fair-haired young man, standing with his arm round the shoulder of the slight, dark-haired girl, just about recognisable as me. Over the years, my mind's eye has created an idealised version of reality. I've put together the aquiline nose, the fair hair, the blue eyes, the romantic aura and made someone who didn't exist, who could never exist. And yet the memory of this person has coloured the whole of my life ever since; has made me wary of developing feelings for anyone, because of the fear of being let down; has denied me the possibility of a mature relationship, which might have led to marriage and the possibility of having children of my own. How absolutely ludicrous.

I put the photo in my handbag again, just in case I want to show it to Jonathan. I glance at my watch and realise it's getting late. I still need to shower, wash my hair and change, so I start to panic. Inevitably, I find that in the end I am ready far too early. When the doorbell goes, I've been trying to fill in time in my room, for over half an hour.

'Hello, Jonathan,' I can hear Ruth say. 'Meg's still upstairs I think. Meg!'

When I go down, Ruth has tactfully gone back into the kitchen and Jonathan is standing in the hall, smiling at me. For a moment we are both slightly embarrassed, not knowing what to say. I'm relieved, though, to find that my doubts about my new dress are not justified. He looks really rather smart. He's wearing grey flannels, a blue and white striped shirt, a navy blazer and a red tie, with some sort of pattern on it. As I get nearer, I see that what I first of all took for spots are in fact musical notes – crotchets, quavers and semi-quavers in what appears to be a random pattern, not based on any real melodic line.

'I like the dress,' he says. 'It suits you.'

'And I like the tie,' I say. He laughs.

'Do you really? It's a Christmas present, chosen, I think, by my daughter-in-law. It's not too ostentatious?'

'No, it's actually quite discreet!'

'I did bring a more conventional one, just in case you didn't like it.'

He rather sheepishly gets out a plain, dark blue tie out of his pocket.

'Which?'

I point to the musical one. We grin at one another and he puts the other tie back in his pocket. I decide it's a good start after all. I'm going to enjoy myself. The tone of our conversation as we drive into Greenwich remains light-hearted – jocular even, with undertones of irony.

In the restaurant, Jonathan is greeted enthusiastically.

'Very nice to see you, Mr Jacobs. I trust your usual table will be satisfactory?'

'That will do very nicely, thank you, Roberto.'

We are shown to a table over by the window. The atmosphere is friendly, the menu varied – not just pasta and pizza – and the other tables are nearly all full, quite a lot of them occupied by lively Italian families. I wonder, with a sudden pang of jealousy, who else he has brought here. Then tell myself not to be so stupid, that it's none of my business.

'I come here for supper quite often if I can't be bothered to cook myself anything,' he explains, as if I have conveyed my thoughts to him somehow. 'They do very good pasta dishes, but I thought tonight we might have something a bit more special. The fish is always very good.'

We both get out our spectacles and study the menu in silence for a while.

'What's the fish today, Christina?' he asks the waitress who is in charge of our table.

'Sea bass, Mr Jacobs, baked with dill. I think you will like it.'

'Does that sound good to you, Meg?'

'It sounds wonderful.'

'And first some antipasti?' enquires Christina.

'Definitely. I'll have the asparagus. What do you fancy, Meg?'

'Goodness, they all sound delicious. I'll have the same, I think.'

'Right. That's two asparagus and two sea bass, please, Christina. And a carafe of the house white to be going on with. Is that all right, Meg?'

'Just right,' I say, feeling in rather a daze, but suddenly very happy.

'Christina always looks after me very well, don't you?' Jonathan says. 'Usually knows what I want before I know myself.' His tone is humorous, slightly flirtatious even. He seems very much at home here.

'Roberto is my father-in-law,' Christina tells me, laughing. She is, I guess, in her thirties, dark, plump, pretty. Her accent is pronounced, her English excellent. 'It is a family restaurant. My husband is the chef, and my mother-in-law sees to the accounts and orders the ingredients and generally manages everything.'

'And stands for no nonsense from any of them,' adds Jonathan.

We settle back, relaxed, easy in each other's company already. We sip our wine, nibble some garlic bread.

'Any more startling developments back at the vicarage?'

'Only Philip arriving, to say his fling is over and the baby is not his after all!'

'I haven't actually met Philip, only had various hints about his somewhat dubious reputation – with the ladies, that is, not his financial dealings, as far as I know.'

'I've never really liked him, actually,' I say, trying to think of a concrete reason. 'I've never really analysed why before. I suppose he's just too over-the-top in everything he does – too ostentatiously generous, embraces everyone too enthusiastically. But underneath you feel he's weighing you up all the time, and finding you wanting.'

'And Ruth?'

'She's coping, I think. There was a bit of a scene in the church today, though, when Shirley... you know Shirley?'

'She's the rather dithery one, with the short grey hair and glasses, isn't she?'

'That's right. Anyway, she practically had hysterics when she found out Geoffrey's leaving. I think she's just got a crush on him – or whatever it is they say now. I can't imagine it's more serious than that. Although, come to think of it and I know I shouldn't say it... '

'You never can tell, with Geoffrey. I've not known him well for very long, of course, but he seems to have an air of abstraction about him, somehow. And I've noticed that he sometimes contradicts himself, depending on who he's talking to at the time.'

'Well, he's always playing a part; husband, father, grandfather, provincial solicitor, vicar – and soon, well, who knows what.'

I wonder whether I'm saying too much. I've never discussed my brother-in-law with anyone like this – apart from my friend, Frances. But then Frances doesn't know him and probably never will, so it somehow doesn't seem to matter, doesn't feel like a betrayal.

'And what about you?' Jonathan looks at me, smiling, his head slightly on one side.

'I seem to have become the family's confidante,' I say, after a pause. 'That used to be my mother's role, until she died in September. I'm not sure I'm the right person to take it on, though.'

'I should think you'll be perfect for the job,' Jonathan said, as if he had already given the matter some thought. 'You seem to have an instinctive feel for what makes people tick – and you're a good listener.'

I laugh, embarrassed. 'You don't know me well enough yet to know that!'

'I think I do. I feel as if I have known you for a long time already.'

We are both silent for a minute or so, as if trying to take in the implications of what he has just said. Between us, the things on the table – the glasses, the carafe of wine, the napkins, the cutlery, the plate of bread – all seem to take on a special significance. I know the picture of them will stay in my mind's eye for a long time; will be something I shall be able to recall when I'm alone. I look up and see he is watching me.

Christina arrives with our starters.

'Silvio asks me to say hello to you both and he hopes you enjoy your food.'

'Tell Silvio, please, that I'm sure we shall, as always.'

And it is indeed delicious. I realise how hungry I am. Everything is beginning to feel slightly unreal, as if the action of eating is something I'm imagining, just part of the script I've been writing for myself during the day. I put it down to the effects of the wine. I don't often drink, but when I do, it always goes straight to my head. Jonathan tops up our glasses.

'What was it Ruth drank to the other night? The future? Well, I think we should do the same.'

We solemnly touch glasses and smile at each other. Our food arrives. This time Christina says nothing, as if not wanting to intrude on what must seem to her an intimate moment. The sea bass is cooked to perfection, as are the vegetables.

'Tell me about the Brahms,' says Jonathan after a while, not looking at me, concentrating on his fish. 'I don't want to pry, though, if you'd rather not.'

I wonder how to begin.

'I've just found out that my mother kept the diary I wrote while I was on a school exchange visit to Germany in 1954. Reading it has made the things that happened then seem very vivid. But I haven't got to the end yet and I'm not sure I actually want to. You'll be the first person I've told about what happened. If nothing else, I think it will be very cathartic. '

'Well,' he says, looking up now, grinning, 'I am a doctor!'

I wonder whether I should presume that I shall see him again before I go home. Because before I tell him everything, I need to have finished reading the diary, to have come to the end of the story.

'You could start, anyway. Then perhaps tell me the rest another day.'

'I need to fill you in a bit first – about the sort of person I was then. It's as if it all happened to someone else entirely.'

He says nothing, waiting for me to continue.

'I mean, I like to think of myself now as a grown-up, rational, practical person. But then, I was the very opposite – emotional, innocent, naive even.'

I pause, not quite knowing how to go on. We continue eating in silence for some time.

'I was staying at the village school. We came back from a trip one day and I could hear someone playing the Brahms rhapsody. So when I heard you, it was as if the sound was coming directly from my past – almost uncanny, really.'

'Who was playing it all those years ago?'

'A boy called Peter. I remember him as the most romantic person I had ever met – fair, aquiline nose, faraway look in his eyes. He played well, but I suspect now not as well as he thought he did. He kept quoting German Romantic poetry at me too – Heine, Goethe and poets I'd never even heard of until then. And of course, as is the way with innocent young girls, I thought I had found the one true love of my life.'

'But you hadn't.'

'No. Far from it. But all this while, I've been picturing in my mind's eye what I thought he looked like. You see, when I returned from Germany, I tore up the only photograph I had of him. I did keep the negative though and today I managed to get it printed out. The irony is he was really quite ordinary, nothing special at all. Look.'

I bend down to pick up my handbag, get out the photo and pass it to Jonathan.

'And that's you with him?'

'Yes. See what I mean? I look so different now, don't I?'

'Oh, I don't know. I recognise the cheekbones and the eyes, the smile, the way you are standing. But I agree, there's nothing very special about Peter.'

'He flattered me, flirted with me I suppose and no one had ever done that before, so I took it all very seriously. But, as they say, it all ended in tears. Is that enough to be going on with do you think?'

He nods.

'Now,' I say, relieved to be changing the subject. 'Tell me how you came to be born in Germany.'

'Well, more to the point, is why I was brought up here. My father's family were all doctors, but Jewish doctors, so that when Hitler began his persecution of the Jews, my father lost his job at the hospital. My mother's family, though, lived in

England – in South London. My grandfather was director of a chemical company. We managed to get out of Germany in 1936 and for a while lived with my mother's parents in Wimbledon. I was only two at the time and so I learnt to speak only English. My father had to retrain in order to be allowed to practise here, and was actually interned for a while on the Isle of Man during the war. His father had been a doctor too before he retired. I can't remember either of my grandparents, because they stayed behind in Germany and landed up in Auschwitz. We never saw them again.'

Once again, we sit in silence for a while. I look at Jonathan while he finishes his meal. His face is already becoming familiar to me. With his dark hair and brown eyes, he is the very antithesis of Peter. And it occurs to me that Peter's father could very well have played a part in Jonathan's grandparents' extermination.

'When the time came for me to decide what to do when I left school,' continues Jonathan eventually, 'I thought at one time I would go to music college to study the piano. But I decided to keep the family tradition going and become a doctor. In a way, I suppose, I felt I owed it to my grandfather – that I would somehow be betraying him if I didn't.'

I don't know what to say. It's actually a relief when Christina comes to clear our plates away and asks if we would like to see the menu again.

'I'm not sure I can manage anymore,' I say.

'An ice cream, perhaps?' suggests Christina.

'You really ought to try one,' says Jonathan. 'They are out of this world.'

'Why not,' I say.

'I think that's probably enough catching up for one day,' says Jonathan. He reaches across the table, and lightly touches my hand. 'Incidentally, I've got tomorrow afternoon off, so I thought it might be nice to go for a walk, if it's fine. You can tell me the next instalment of your life so far then – if you want to, that is.'

'That would be very nice indeed.'

'As long as you haven't got any more family dramas to sort out!'

'They'll have to manage without me, won't they?'

This is all happening so quickly. I feel extremely happy, but at the same time bewildered, as if my life is being taken out of my hands. I actually feel I want a moment to myself.

'I think I'll just pop to the ladies, if you don't mind – before the ice cream arrives.'

I examine myself in the mirror, as if I need to confirm I still look the same. I half believe I won't recognise myself. But apart from looking rather flushed I don't appear to have changed at all.

'You're being courted,' I say quietly to my reflection, then smile to myself at my use of the ridiculous, old-fashioned expression. 'And it appears you quite like the experience.'

Christina is just bringing our ice creams when I get back to the table.

'Shall we have coffee, Meg? I'm rather partial to espresso, but maybe that's rather strong for you.'

'No, that's fine. I like it myself.'

Jonathan leans back, his hands behind his head.

'Well now,' he says. 'I think this has been very nice.'

'I've enjoyed myself a lot,' I reply, and we smile at each other. 'Thank you for a lovely meal.'

It's as if we have mutually agreed that it's not necessary to say any more at this stage.

It's very cold when we get outside. Jonathan takes my arm.

'I've got an early start in the morning, so I think I'll take you straight back to the vicarage. I'll give you a ring when I get home tomorrow – it will be after lunch.'

As I'm getting out of the car, he leans over and gives me a light kiss on the lips.

'Night-night. Sleep well.'

'You too,' I say.

I'm conscious that he's watching me as I go up the steps to the front door. I turn and wave as he drives away.

Inside, I stand in the hall, trying to come to terms with the implications of his fleeting goodnight kiss. I am inevitably reminded of that first kiss Peter gave me on our walk in Germany. But Peter's lips then were cool; Jonathan's tonight were warm. I decide that what I mustn't do is to read too much into one kiss. I mustn't take it for granted that it will lead on to anything else; mustn't plan out my future on the strength of it.

'I thought I heard the door,' says Ruth, from the kitchen. 'You didn't ask him in then?'

'He's got an early start,' I say.

'But you had a nice time?'

'Yes, I did. We went to an Italian restaurant in Greenwich. The food was good and we seemed to get on really well. And I think I've had a little bit too much wine!'

'That's supposed to be my trick,' says Ruth, laughing. 'I'm not going to pry, so don't worry.'

'We are going for a walk tomorrow, though.'

'There you are, you see. I knew it would work out.'

'I'm just going to take one step at a time. And if you don't mind, I think I'll go up now – the world seems to be reeling about out of my control.'

'I shall go to bed myself soon. I feel exhausted. Helen and Jane have gone already. We'll leave the chaps to it, shall we?'

We climb the stairs, to the sound of gunfire, accompanied by full orchestra, coming from the television. Outside my door, Ruth gives me a hug, but doesn't say any more. Inside, in spite of my good intentions, I feel excited. I have enjoyed the evening immensely and snippets of our conversation are going on inside my head.

I seem to have known you for a long time already. And I see the glasses, the carafe of wine, the napkins, the cutlery, the plate of bread, just as I knew I would.

What was it Ruth drank to the other night? The future? Well, I think we should do the same. I hear the clink of our glasses. *I thought it might be nice to go for a walk, if it's fine.* And I feel the light touch of his hand. *Night-night. Sleep well.* And the warmth of his lips on mine.

I glance at my watch and am surprised to find that it's only half past ten. Time for the next instalment of the German story. So first, I get out the photo of Peter and me again and stare at it…

PART TWO

Tuesday 17th August 1954

…trying to recall my feelings thirty-five years ago. Nothing. The two figures could be two strangers standing there, side-by-side, half smiling at the camera, looking slightly embarrassed. How is it that such intense feelings can completely evaporate?

If I'm to make sense of what happened in Germany, I still need to try to re-live what I went through. Only then, perhaps, can I completely come to terms with the past. So I get out my diary and once again start to read the next instalment.

We went to school in the morning, but instead of going by train, we went by bus with Herr and Frau Schmidt, who were going out for the day. The bus was terribly crowded. It seems they never refuse anyone as long as there is room for them to put one foot on the ground. We had to cling on to the seats to prevent ourselves from falling over. We had the driver we went to Kassel with, but he didn't see me because there were so many people and we didn't get on at the front.

No mention of Peter. Yet I know that, being obsessed by now, I must have been thinking about him practically all the time.

The first lesson this morning was German. They were reading a translation of Twelfth Night *or* Was ihr wollt. *Their teacher, "Poseidon", made Barbara and me read out the passage they had reached in the original English – the "Make me a willow cabin at your gate" bit.*

Another example of an unexplained nickname. I have no idea what his real name was, or if I ever knew.

He is very nice, although he is rather ugly because he was kicked by a horse during the war and his nose is crooked. His speech was also affected a bit, so it is rather difficult to understand what he says.

That reminds me of an odd thing about several of the people I met while I was there. Helmut, at the dancing on Sunday, also had a crooked nose, in his case blamed on a snowball. It must have been a pretty hefty snowball. More likely it had something more offensive in the middle of it. Later, I noticed that another teacher had a long scar down his cheek – part of some kind of initiation ceremony, perhaps.

Miss Harris and Miss Smithson came to the next lesson, which was English, together with about half a dozen more

English girls. It must have been for our benefit that
Belladonna suddenly stood up in front of the class and
started to sing very lustily and we were all expected to join
in. We sang all sorts of English songs, some of which I have
never heard of. We kept catching each other's eyes and it was
as much as we could do not to burst out laughing.

I think we usually went back to Volkmarshausen for our
midday meal, so presumably I had to make an excuse for
staying behind that day. Did I write about the planned meeting
with Peter, which must have occupied my thoughts far more
than the pompous Belladonna? I skim quickly down the page.

After school, I went to the café near the bus stop, before we
all went on a tour of the town.

So, again, no mention of Peter at all. But I do remember
vividly what happened. I waited outside the school gates, as
arranged. Once everyone else had gone and I was just
beginning to think that he had forgotten, he was suddenly
there beside me. Had he been lurking round the corner until
the coast was clear perhaps? I didn't ask. I was immediately
completely tongue-tied and could only follow him down the
road, into the Café Obst, which was near to the bus stop, and
sit down opposite him at a table by the window. Further down
the road, I could see Barbara and Gudrun still waiting for the
bus, which only emphasised the clandestine nature of the
assignation.

'*Kaffee und Kuchen, bitte,*' Peter said, rather peremptorily to
the waitress. Then he leant across the table and took my hand.

'Today, Margaret,' he said softly, 'I think you will enjoy
your tour of our beautiful town. We have many places of note
for you to see.'

'We are going to the town hall and the castle and then to the place where the Werra and Fulda change into the Weser. And tomorrow there's a trip to see the border with the East.'

'Why will you go there? There is nothing fine to see. No-man's-land and border posts and a few watchtowers only. They are very ugly, I think.'

'We don't just go to beautiful places. We are here to see what Germany is like, now the war has been over for some time.'

He said nothing, but shrugged his shoulders, as if he couldn't believe the stupidity of the English.

He was still holding on to my hand and only let go when our coffee and cakes arrived. The coffee was strong and the cakes were more like tarts with whole plums on them, piled high, as usual, with lots of whipped cream. I remember I was so nervous that the sight of them made me feel slightly queasy. I started to drink my coffee.

'You do not like our cakes?' He made it seem like a personal slight.

'Yes, they are very good. But I am not very hungry, I'm afraid.'

The door of the café opened and, much to my embarrassment, Fritz came in, followed by another young man and an older woman. I looked down at my cake and tried to pretend I hadn't seen them. But Fritz came straight up to our table.

'Hello, Margaret. And Peter. This is my brother, Gunter, who works at the *Apotheke* next door – the apothecary, I think you say – and this is my mother.'

Peter and I stood up and we all shook hands.

'Now,' said Fritz, 'we will go to our table and leave you both together.'

I felt a mixture of relief and dread. Relief that we would be alone again, dread because I thought that it was inevitable now that he would say something about meeting us to the family and to Gudrun in particular, which I knew would not go down well, to put it mildly.

What did we talk about? Did he perhaps quote some more poetry at me? Talk about the concert? I can't remember. But I do remember him taking my hand again, and can picture the blue of his eyes as he gazed at me, the cake uneaten on the table between us. And then he suddenly got up, as if coming to a sudden decision.

'Now, Margaret, we will go for a short walk and I will show you my home, until it is time for you to meet your friends.'

Fritz smiled at me as we left the café and I thought I saw the suspicion of a wink. I wondered if he was tacitly telling me that he would keep the knowledge of my secret assignation to himself.

I have to get out my photos again to remind myself what the town looked like. I study one showing a narrow street with tall timber-framed houses crowded on either side. Although the photo is black and white, I do remember that the walls were painted in various colours, making it look almost like a stage set. But there are no pantomime or operatic characters walking down the street, only quite ordinary people, the men in suits and ties, the women quite smartly dressed and a couple of cars, including a Volkswagen Beetle, driving along the road.

Peter took me to a house in one of the streets close to the centre of the town.

'This is the house in which I was born,' he said. And although he didn't say so, it was also presumably where his mother died. Then he led me down towards the river and stopped outside a large, detached house, surrounded by trees.

'This is now my home,' he said, starting to walk towards the front door. 'My father is not in. He is at a meeting in the town, I believe. But I will show you. You will think it is beautiful.'

As indeed it was. The front door led into a spacious hall with several doors leading off it. He opened a door to the right, and I followed him into what was obviously the living room. A grand piano stood in the bay window and he immediately sat down and began to play. I recognised the Mozart sonata he had played the day before at the school concert. I remained standing awkwardly by the piano, not quite knowing what to do.

In spite of its size, the room was actually quite claustrophobic. There seemed to be far too much furniture in it and the curtains at the window were dark and heavy, cutting out too much light. On the floor, the carpet was deep red, intricately patterned and covered with faded, oriental rugs. The brown leather chairs looked uncomfortable and uninviting, placed in a rather arbitrary fashion around the room as if to discourage intimate communication of any sort. Every spare surface was filled with ornaments – porcelain figures, elaborately decorated vases and carved wooden figures. Against the walls were several glass-fronted cabinets containing more porcelain, silver coffee pots, jugs and spoons. Photographs in heavy frames stood on a highly polished table in the corner. And pervading everything was a faint, almost musty smell.

Peter came to the end of the first movement of the Mozart. He looked at me, obviously waiting for some sort of reaction.

'Wonderful,' I said.

He immediately launched into the opening bars of the Brahms rhapsody once again, but came to an abrupt halt after the end of the opening theme.

'It is time to go,' he said, standing up and coming towards me.

And that seemed to be it. But then he came closer, so that I could feel his breath. He put his hands to my face, looked into my eyes, then ran his fingers through my hair.

'On Thursday, I shall again visit to the Schmidt family. Until then, we will think of each other I think. "*Ich bin bei dir, du seist auch noch so ferne, du bist mir nah!*" Goethe says, "I am with you, however far away you may be, you are near me." Do you think that also, Margaret?'

'Oh, yes, I do, Peter,' I breathed, 'I do.'

And of course I did. That afternoon, I never stopped thinking about him. Looking back, I suppose the secrecy only added to the romantic image I had of him. Because, so far, meaningful conversation had not been exactly prolific. Not enough, anyway, on which to base hopes of a future life together and a "happy-ever-after" scenario. I have to refer to the diary again, as I can't remember where I met the others, or where we went.

We had to meet outside the House of the Youth. The man who took us round hadn't got a very good German accent – some sort of dialect – and we had difficulty in understanding him. First of all we went to a monument to the First and Second World Wars, but which was built ages ago – it was a sort of little round building with iron gates. We then went to a castle opposite the Mittelschule. From the tower of this, about two years ago a man had put a rope across to another building and, to get some money, had started to walk across, watched by most of the inhabitants of Hann. Münden. But half way across he fell off and was killed (a nice, cheerful story!). We then went to the town hall and saw a large room with the history of Hann. Münden painted round the walls in murals. We ended up outside the church, which has a clock and above this a ball, which shows the phases of the moon. We went and watched the river for a little by a sort of weir, where the water was very foamy. We then went further down the river, over a bridge, to see the Weserstein – the stone

*marking the spot where the Werra and Fulda change into the
Weser.*

My entry seems to imply that my German, by this time, had
improved enough to understand the gist of what the man with
"some sort of dialect" was saying. I remember that Barbara
noticed how quiet I was during the tour. Of course, she put it
down to "that hairdresser boy," as she had begun to call him,
much to my annoyance. By the time I arrived back at the
village I was so lost in my own thoughts that I was totally
unprepared for what happened next. We were in the middle of
the evening meal – the usual bread, cold sausage and tomatoes
– when we heard someone knocking loudly on the door
downstairs. Gudrun ran down the stairs and I could hear
Barbara's voice. I had never heard her sounding so agitated
and upset, almost hysterical. She burst into the room, tears
running down her cheeks.

'He's been shot. They think he's dead, but they don't
know.'

'Oh, Barbara, not Helga's brother? How absolutely
dreadful. Was he trying to escape?'

'Yes. He got through some woods, but then he started to
swim over the river – such a silly thing to do, wasn't it? The
border guards must have seen him and started shooting. A
man arrived just now with the news. I think he's from some
sort of organisation helping people to escape to the West.'

'This is very bad news,' said Herr Schmidt. 'I must go to
the family at once.'

He got up from the table, his food uneaten, and hurried
downstairs, while Gudrun explained to her mother what had
happened.

'My mother says you must come to stay here with us,
Barbara. You will sleep in the room with Margaret.'

I felt I had known Johannes through the framed photograph on the mantelpiece in the Altmeyers' house. I thought of how Helga was close to tears when she spoke about her beloved brother; of Herr Altmeyer's obvious pride in his son; the guitar by the desk, waiting for its owner to claim it; Frau Altmeyer's sudden fierce embrace. I could feel the tears start to roll uncontrollably down my cheeks. How would the family ever recover from such a tragedy?

And now, sitting in my bedroom in Blackheath, thirty-five years later, the memory of that evening still shakes me. Now that the wall has come down, it looks as if East Germans will be free to cross the border whenever they want to. What happened then seems even more futile. I look through the box beside my bed to find the letter to my parents. Did I tell them about it, or was it briefer even than my diary, just the usual sanitised version of events? I find reference to it at the end of my first letter.

> *Tuesday 17*[th] *11pm*
> *Today we received some awful news. The brother of one of the girls at the school has been shot trying to escape to the West and we believe he has died. I'll post this letter now and tell you more about it when I write next.*
> *Love from Margaret*

My diary says little more. I glance back at the rest of the letter. I wrote so little that I had not even filled two sides of the writing paper and had told them nothing at all about the visit yesterday to the Edersee.

Barbara went back later in the evening to collect some of her belongings. I remember the feeling of disappointment that my lovely bedroom, with its window seat looking out over the valley and my desk in the corner, was no longer my own. She took over the room entirely. She didn't seem to put anything away. She left her clothes hanging on the backs of the chairs and strewn on the floor. I realised I must find a safe place to keep my diary from her inevitably prying eyes. Even when we went to bed, I couldn't be alone with my thoughts, couldn't re-live my conversations, such as they were, with Peter, or let my imagination range freely. She had, as my mother so accurately said, "verbal diarrhoea", and kept up a whispered conversation with me till the early hours, until, in exasperation, I eventually had to tell her to shut up. I remember thinking that now I had no chance at all of preventing a meeting between her and Peter. From the time I began sharing my bedroom with her, everything seemed to go wrong.

By now, I can hardly keep my eyes open. I put away the diary, the letter and the photos, and fall into a deep, undisturbed sleep...

CHAPTER EIGHT

Part One

Thursday 28th December 1989

...so that when I wake up, I take a moment to get my bearings. And then remember. And feel happy. And wonder what he's doing now. Wonder if he's thinking about me. And hope so. I can't remember when, if ever, I have felt like this before. Because thirty-five years ago I was never wholly, unreservedly happy. With Peter, I was always nervous and awkward; my feelings were always tinged with anxiety. With Jonathan, I am secure and comfortable. I feel a little stir of excitement when I remember our walk this afternoon. I find I'm smiling to myself.

I'm still smiling when I get downstairs.

'You look happy, darling,' says Ruth. 'Don't forget we're meeting Val for coffee this morning. And I want to collect the photos before we go.'

'I'll go now if you like. I need some fresh air and it looks as if it's going to be a nice day. I can take Bella. I shan't be long.'

Ruth gives me the slip for the photos, looks at me and gives me a quick hug. It's only when I'm walking down the steps that I realise I haven't had any breakfast. I walk briskly across the heath. The early morning mist is clearing already. As I pass the church, Geoffrey is coming out. He raises his hand in greeting, but doesn't stop. I notice that Shirley is hovering in the porch, but that she doesn't make any move to follow him.

I'm back at the vicarage in about half an hour. Ruth and I sit at the kitchen table and spread out the photos on the table in front of us. Most of the pictures are of the choir, taken at a concert about a month ago. The ones I'm interested in, though, are the two Ruth took on Boxing Day.

In the first one, we are all looking expectantly at the camera, not quite knowing when the flash will go off. We are a very odd assortment of characters. I'm sitting on the sofa, in a red waistcoat and matching headscarf pulled down rather too far over my eyes, a middle-aged, middle-class gypsy. Jonathan is standing behind me, wearing a black eye-patch and oversized top hat; a twentieth century highwayman. Helen, sitting beside me, has a tinsel crown perched crookedly on her head and Ian stands behind, rather sheepishly holding a matching wand; escapees from a down-market pantomime. Ruth wears a jaunty black moustache and Geoffrey has a garland of tatty crepe paper flowers round his neck; refugees from a bad South Sea Island film. Val is in the nurse's outfit I remember the girls wearing when they were little, and Martin is clutching a toy stethoscope, with a bright red scarf as a makeshift surgeon's mask; leftovers from *Carry on Doctor*. The boys are sitting on the floor in front of us, Jack as a knight in plastic armour, complete with helmet, breastplate and sword; Max in a huge cowboy hat, which comes down over his eyes. Even William and Marcus, who were too embarrassed at first to join in, had eventually put on false beards. They had tied a scarlet ribbon to Bella's collar and she is sitting beside them, head on one side, one ear up. Jane is on a separate chair, slightly aloof, her head swathed in a tasteful silk scarf, the only one of us not to look silly.

In the second picture – the one taken as the camera slid off the books and tilted forward – we are all bending down, trying to keep level with the lens, mouths open, frozen in the middle of hysterical laughter. I wonder whether, ten years from now, I shall have forgotten the man standing behind me? Or shall we look at this photograph together, remembering that it was taken just after we met?

'Have a look at these, boys,' says Ruth, as Jack and Max come crashing through the door from the garden into the kitchen. 'Take your shoes off first though, please.'

Jack, predictably, lets out a whoop of laughter, but Max studies the picture carefully. He climbs up on to Ruth's lap and puts his thumb in his mouth.

'Where's me, Granny?'

'There, darling. With the big hat.'

He looks at Ruth then back at the photo.

'Hm,' he says, as if the whole thing is of no further interest.

'I think we've got a tired boy here, Auntie Meg. Let's see if we can find a drink.'

'Me too! Me too! I want coke.'

'What else do you say, Jack?'

'Please, please, Granny!' he cries, running round the table. 'I want coke, I want coke!'

Suddenly, the kitchen seems full of people and noise. Ian and Helen decide to go into Greenwich with the boys and take them to the *Cutty Sark*. By the time they've gathered them all together in one place, got them into suitable clothing and made sure they've all been to the loo, it's almost half past ten. As the front door closes, Ruth and I heave a united sigh. I put the photos in my handbag to show Val. We decide to take the car down into Greenwich, as we need to do some more shopping on the way. As we drive, I'm preoccupied thinking of this afternoon – what I imagine will happen and what I hope will happen. I try to suppress thoughts of a romantic "Heathcliffe and Cathy" type meeting in the park and grin to myself, but say nothing. Ruth is equally silent.

'You know, the more I think about it, the more convinced I am there's something Geoffrey's not telling me,' she says eventually. 'When he came back from the church this morning, he disappeared into his study even more quickly than he usually does and I could hear him on the phone to someone for ages. It was obvious the other person was doing most of the talking. When Geoffrey did speak it was as if he was, well, defending himself, I suppose.'

'Who do you think it was?'

'I've no idea. The bishop, possibly. Geoffrey doesn't usually take any notice of anyone else. Anyway, I suppose it will all come out eventually, whatever it is. The awful thing is, Meg, I don't really care anymore.'

Ruth is by now concentrating on parking the car and we don't mention Geoffrey again, until we've done the shopping and are walking towards the café.

'It's odd, but I suspect Shirley is involved in some way. Nothing I can put my finger on, but I'm pretty sure Geoffrey is worried she's going to say something she shouldn't. The more I think about it, the more I'm convinced that the scene in the church was not just Shirley getting worked up because she'd heard he was leaving.'

'You're surely not having second thoughts about any hanky-panky between them?'

'Not really, although nothing would surprise me anymore,' she says, laughing, opening the door of the café.

Val is here already, sitting at a table in the corner, surrounded by carrier bags. I tend to forget what good company she is, especially when she starts on her hospital anecdotes. We sip our coffee, eat our Danish pastries and get out the photos. We all laugh immoderately. Just what Ruth needs at the moment. But then Val puts down her cup, leans back in her chair and looks at Ruth.

'Now then,' she says, 'what's all this about Geoffrey retiring?'

I suppose it's inevitable Ruth will try to make light of the whole thing. She shrugs.

'Don't quite know what to make of it. Bit unexpected, actually. But then, that's Geoffrey, isn't it?'

'Come on, Ruth. I know you and I know things haven't exactly been rosy lately. But there's something else, isn't there? I can tell you're furious with him, isn't that right Meg?'

'I haven't seen her so upset for years. No,' I go on, as Ruth tries to interrupt me, 'I think Val deserves to know everything. Geoffrey is behaving very badly. Look, we can't really talk properly here. Why don't we pay the bill and go for a bit of a walk.'

I always have the feeling that Val is closer to Ruth than anyone, including her family. She was the first proper friend Ruth made when she and Geoffrey came to Blackheath. She had only recently married Martin, and Marcus hadn't yet been born. At that time she was on the committee of a local concert society and it was through her that Ruth got involved in all the musical activities, which have now become such an essential part of her life.

Once outside, we make our way towards the river.

'Now, tell me.' Val takes Ruth's arm.

'Well, we know he wants us to go and live in Wales when he retires. What we don't know is why he's retiring so suddenly. He says it's because he's lost his faith, but I think there's more to it. The question is, what?'

'Well, the obvious ones are either sex or money,' says Val. 'But then neither of those really seems likely, knowing Geoffrey.'

'I hadn't really considered money. There's a thought. I just hope he hasn't done something really silly though. I heard him on the phone for ages this morning. I told Meg I thought it was probably the bishop. Geoffrey sounded like a naughty schoolboy being told off for flicking catapults in the classroom. Anyway, Val, you might have a lodger on your hands in the summer, because there's no way I'll go and live in Wales, or wherever he decides to go to escape his pursuers.'

'You would be very welcome, you know that, but I can't imagine it getting to that stage.'

'You think I don't I mean it, don't you. Actually, I've never been more serious in my life.'

By now we're beginning to get cold. Val shivers.

'Look, I've got to get back; I'm on duty later. Promise me you'll let me know as soon as there are any further developments. I'm absolutely dying to know what he's been up to.'

Ruth has noticed I've been surreptitiously looking at my watch.

'And we must go home too,' she says. 'Meg's going for a walk with Jonathan after lunch.'

'Oh, I'm so glad. Martin said he's been asking about you. He's such a nice man.'

'I'm sure it doesn't mean anything,' I mutter.

'Anyway, I must dash. Enjoy your walk, Meg. And don't you dare let Geoffrey lure Ruth away to darkest Wales. We'd all miss her far too much.'

It's half past two before he phones, by which time, of course, I'm convinced he's either forgotten, or is having second thoughts.

'I'll be with you in about ten minutes. I'm leaving now.' And he puts the phone down.

No time to change. My skirt and sweater will have to do. Perhaps some heavier shoes. Warm coat. Scarf. Gloves. Hat?

'Uncle Jonathan!' shouts Jack, looking through the sitting room window. He runs to open the door and I follow him. 'Can we fly my kite, Uncle Jonathan? Please!'

'Another day, Jack. I want to have Auntie Meg all to myself today.' He smiles at me. 'I thought we might walk down through the park and go to The Queen's House, if you haven't been there already?'

'That would be nice. Ruth and I meant to go last summer, but we never got round to it. Do I need a hat?'

'Probably.' He takes it gently from my hands, puts it on my head and pulls it down over my ears.

'You're teasing me,' I say, laughing.

'Yes, I am. You're very teasable. Isn't she, Ruth?'

'She takes herself far too seriously. You're doing her a lot of good, Jonathan. Now, off you both go.'

She opens the front door and shoos us out. We look at each other and smile, suddenly awkward, not quite knowing what to say. We start walking across the heath towards the park, in silence. It's as if we are both suddenly aware that other people have expectations of our relationship, but that we ourselves need time to catch up before we can fulfil them. When we do speak, it's about Geoffrey.

'Val thinks the real problem may be to do with money, rather than any grand passion. What do you think?'

'Has he got access to any money – I mean apart from his own?'

'Presumably there are church funds. I know they've had an organ fund on the go for some time. He could have borrowed from that, I suppose, although I don't know why he would need to. They always seem to have managed all right up till now. I can't see him having a gambling problem and there aren't any signs of fast cars or loose women.'

The picture this conjures up makes us both laugh. We wait to cross the main road and he takes my hand and keeps hold of it until we're in the park. We do not comment on this slight development.

'Do you feel ready to tell me more about Germany yet?'

I pause, not quite knowing how to begin.

'Last night, after I got in, I read some more of my diary. I came across something really dreadful. It had nothing to do with Peter – you know, the German boy. I'll tell you more about him later. I hadn't really forgotten about that evening, but it came as a real shock when I read about it again. And with all the recent developments in Eastern Europe, what happened seems so unnecessary and stupid.'

'Tell me.'

'The brother of one of the girls at the school in Germany was shot trying to cross from the East. It was only later we learnt what happened. I don't know if you remember, but until 1961 there wasn't actually much of a physical barrier between East and West Germany, just a wide area of neutral territory. I've got a photograph of my friend Barbara and me with the Russian zone in the background behind us, with no barrier or barbed wire in sight. In fact, Helga – that was the girl's name – and her family had actually walked across the border in Berlin the previous year, with her little brother in a pushchair, with just the clothes they stood up in, a photo album and a guitar. Apparently, quite a lot of people worked in the West and lived in the East. And people were allowed to visit relatives until the infamous wall went up, so it was actually quite safe. They just had to report to the officials in the West and ask for political asylum. The wall wasn't built for another seven years or so after we were there in 1954'

'I'd forgotten that. You tend to think they put barbed wire and watchtowers in place immediately after the war was over. Why didn't the brother come the same way?'

'He was living just the other side of the border, quite a long way from Berlin. By that time, his family had been re-housed in the village we were staying in, only a comparatively short way from the border on the other side. So he thought he would make his way at night through the woods and then swim across the river. He had the confidence of youth, I suppose. But, of course, the border guards saw him. It turned out he was actually in no-man's-land when they shot him. No one from the West could reach him – or even knew what had happened for some time. He just lay there. He bled to death.'

We stop walking. Jonathan says nothing. People pass us. I feel tears running down my face. He turns me to face him. Passes me a handkerchief. And embraces me. And kisses my forehead. After a few minutes, he takes my hand and we walk on. We say nothing until we arrive at The Queen's House.

'Do you still want to do this? We can leave it till another day if you like.'

'No. I'd like to, I'm all right now. Silly really.'

'No, not silly at all.'

Walking round the magnificent rooms, we make comfortable remarks to each other. We stop in front of a portrait of James II when he was still the Duke of York. We look at each other and back at the painting. He is standing bare-chested, one hand on his hip, the other holding a staff. He is wearing a tunic, a pink cloak and a blue ribbon at his waist. But it's the sight of the open toed sandals – laced up his leg, encrusted with jewels, finished at the top with a cross between a lion and a man's head, with big floppy ears – that makes us start to giggle uncontrollably. We get some strange looks from the museum attendant, so move through to another room. A painting of someone called John Everett by Sir William Orpen catches my eye.

'He reminds me of someone,' I say, puzzled.

'Not someone I'd immediately warm to, I must say.'

He is sitting casually in an armchair, cane in one grey-gloved hand, wearing a black suit. I note the long nose, the eyes, slightly shielded by his black top hat, looking directly at me, the superior and supercilious expression. I suddenly realise who he looks like.

'You haven't met Phillip, have you. Well, take away the top hat, the beard and whiskers, and it's him to a tee.'

The visit has done me a lot of good. I have scarcely given the events in Germany another thought.

Afterwards, we walk along to The Bosun's Whistle café next to the Maritime Museum. It's getting dark outside and we are the last customers of the day. We order tea and sit at a table by the window.

Jonathan puts down his cup and looks at me. I'm already becoming familiar with the way he leans back in his chair, one hand behind his head.

'Do you need to get back for supper?'

'Not really, no. Although they will be expecting me.'

'Because I could rustle up something at home, if you like? Nothing spectacular. Just some pasta or something.'

'I'd like that very much.'

I feel myself start to flush and hope he doesn't notice.

'I'm afraid it means a bit of a walk again, but no more than going back to the vicarage. We can go up Maze Hill.'

'I'm fine. I'm quite resilient really.'

Half an hour later, we are walking up the drive to a largish, detached house in a quiet road on the eastern edge of Greenwich Park.

Jonathan opens the door.

'Come in and let me take your coat. The house is too big, really, so I rattle around rather, but it suits me. I can walk to the hospital from here, so it seems a bit silly to move.'

He picks up some leaflets from the doormat, then turns to hang my coat up in a cupboard in the hall.

'When Anna died, the children were still at home. But now my son is married and my daughter's in Birmingham during term time, so I don't need such a large place. I suppose it will be nice if and when I have grandchildren. No sign at present though.'

He leads me straight into the kitchen.

'You could go into the sitting room if you like, while I see what I've got in the fridge.'

'I'll stay in here and talk, if that's all right. Can I do anything?'

'No need. I'm a dab hand. I always used to do most of the cooking anyway, even when Anna was alive. It relaxes me.'

I laugh. 'It has the opposite effect on me. I'm hopeless.'

'Well then, we're an ideal partnership, aren't we?'

He pours two glasses of wine from a bottle on the table, which is already opened, hands me one and clinks his glass against mine.

While he gets out pasta, fills a saucepan with water and tips some bolognaise sauce from a bowl in the fridge into another pan, I sit at the kitchen table, sipping my wine. Once again, I watch his hands. He works quickly and precisely, moving easily round the kitchen.

'I suppose I ought to let Ruth know where I am.'

'The phone's out in the hall.'

Ruth answers. I can hear the boys in the background and music coming from the radio.

'Of course I don't mind, darling,' she says. 'I'm delighted. Have a nice time. Be good. See you later.'

I put down the phone. I stand in the middle of the hall for some minutes and take stock. The only sound is the ticking of a long-case clock, which somehow emphasises the sense of calm I feel. Here I am, in an unfamiliar, ready-made environment. It could be said that I'm a usurper, a trespasser. Someone else has created all this. Jonathan and Anna arranged the furniture precisely where it belongs, hung the pictures on the walls in just the right place, placed the lamps where they would cast just the right light.

When I go back into the kitchen, Jonathan is straining the pasta and the table is already laid.

'You don't mind eating in here, do you?'

'Of course not. It smells absolutely wonderful.'

I want to say that, at this moment, there is nowhere else I would rather be and that I have an overwhelming feeling that I have arrived home. Jonathan tops up our glasses, puts the food on the table and sits down opposite me. We eat in silence for a few minutes. I can feel my cheeks beginning to glow with effects of the wine.

'Oh, I forgot, I've brought the photos of all of us Ruth took on Boxing Day. I'll show you when we've finished eating. We all got a bit carried away and silly, didn't we?'

'No harm in that sometimes.'

When we've finished eating, Jonathan makes coffee and we take it into the sitting room. There is a grand piano at one end, an impressive looking audio system along one wall and bookshelves lining another. I sit down on the sofa and he sits beside me. I get out the photos.

'I see what you mean about us all looking rather silly.'

'Except Jane, of course.'

'She's always very elegant, isn't she? I don't know her very well, but I can't imagine her ever being remotely dishevelled.'

He peers at the photo again.

'You look very fetching, I must say. And I look as if I'm about to whisk you off and have my wicked way with you.'

His head is close to mine, so I can't see his face. I remember his fleeting kiss last night. We drink our coffee.

'I've been on my own now for over seven years,' he says at last. His tone is matter-of-fact, but I have the feeling that what he is about to say will break new ground.

'When Anna died, she'd been ill for less than a year. She had a particularly virulent form of cancer. She was a doctor, too, you know, so we both knew that she had months, rather than years, to live. It was particularly distressing for the children of course. Robert was seventeen, working for his A levels. Sarah was only thirteen. Two weeks before Anna died – she was still able to get about then – she visited their schools, as if she knew this would be the last chance to, well, tidy things up, I suppose. And she wrote letters to each of us, to be read only after she died.'

He pauses. I wait. A car goes by outside. A dog barks in the distance.

'She died peacefully and very suddenly. I woke up one morning, and she had died in her sleep. I've never said this to anyone before, Meg, but I'm almost certain she helped herself. By then she was on morphine and I think she just took more than was prescribed. We had often discussed it in principle, of course. But there seemed no point at all in saying anything to anyone at the time. Afterwards, I was too busy coping with Robert and Sarah to feel very much myself for a long time. Then it hit me quite suddenly. I suppose I had some sort of breakdown. Rob was at university by then, so Sarah and I were by ourselves. She was wonderful. She was only fifteen, but I don't know how I would have coped without her. It took another two years for me to recover properly – to feel I could live a normal life again.'

He reaches out and takes my hand.

'I suppose I shall always miss her, Meg. She was such a strong person; someone you couldn't ignore. But I've got so used to being without her, that I realise sometimes I haven't even thought about her for whole days at a time.'

I dare not move, let alone look at him. If I do, he might not go on to say what I think he's going to say. What I hope he's going to say.

'I never imagined I would ever meet anyone else. Thought I was quite content to be by myself. But then I turned round after playing the Brahms that evening, and there you were, standing in the doorway. And it was as if I'd always known you. I knew who you were, of course, because Ruth said you were coming for Christmas. But it was more than that. Does that sound silly?'

'No,' I say. 'To quote you, not silly at all.'

I don't know what else to say and I don't think Jonathan does either. I'm just as much at a loss as I was thirty-five years ago. The clock in the hall starts to strike and I begin counting: eight. We look at each other. And smile.

'I'm really out of practice at this,' Jonathan says, beginning to laugh. 'I've not had to use a chat-up line since, well, since before they were called chat-up lines, for all I know.'

'Is that what you're doing – chatting me up?'

'I have a distinct feeling it is.'

'And I've never encouraged anyone to chat me up, so I've no idea what I should be doing either.'

We lean back, still holding hands, and start to giggle. Jonathan's foot knocks the edge of the table, making the coffee cups rattle alarmingly. I let out a little shriek, lean forward to steady them, and knock into the table again. The photographs slide off on to the floor. We are behaving, it occurs to me, as we would have done if we'd met thirty-five years ago; as I should have behaved with Peter. But giggling with Peter was never an option. Life for him was far too serious a matter.

'I rather think I want to kiss you properly. Is that all right?'

'Very all right,' I say, as he leans towards me. And realise that, for the first time in my life, it is.

Before our German holiday, Barbara had spoken a lot about "French kissing", as she called it, but refused to tell me what it involved. She took great pleasure in taunting me.

'You'll find out soon enough,' was all she would say.

But when I did eventually find out, I was appalled. It had absolutely nothing to do with what I thought of as "romance". At university I positively discouraged the attempts of fellow students to seduce me after college dances. My lack of enthusiasm meant that I got a reputation for being frigid and the offers soon dried up. In my final year I did actually have an "official" boyfriend, but he was as inexperienced as I was. We never got beyond embarrassed fumblings, still fully dressed, in his room, or during otherwise chaste expeditions on our bicycles into the countryside at weekends. After we graduated, he got a job in Yorkshire and I returned to Dorset. The relationship soon petered out. Since then, I have always ignored any incipient sexual feelings I may have felt, terrified, I suppose, of being let down, knowing the devastating effects of betrayal. The spectre of Peter has never really left me.

Until now. Because now my body is involuntarily behaving in a distinctly odd and unfamiliar way. I am very far from feeling revolted. And I don't want the kiss to stop. Jonathan begins gently to explore the curve of my back. I move one of my hands up to his head. His hair is slightly springy. The smell of him is already familiar. What I feel, I suppose, is quite simply, joy. Why did nobody tell me it would be like this? Life will never be the same again.

It turns out that he has been thinking as much about me over the last few days as I have about him, which we both find rather amazing. We agree that the chemistry between people is extraordinary; that age has nothing whatsoever to do with it; that inside these two middle-aged bodies, there are two adolescents struggling to get out.

'If you carry on looking at me like that,' Jonathan says, putting his hand to my cheek, 'I'm not going to be responsible for my actions.'

'I think,' I say carefully, 'that I need to tell you what happened in Germany – to get it out my system. But I don't think I can cope with doing that today.'

'And I wouldn't ask you to. I don't want to rush you, Meg. We have all the time in the world. I just want you to be happy.'

He gets up and goes over to the shelf of CDs.

'What would you like to listen to? More Brahms? Or Schubert, maybe.'

I lean back and consider.

'Something gentle would be nice.'

'How about this? I've just discovered it. See if you can guess who it's by.'

The piece is for string quartet and begins with a soft, rising phrase, which is oddly familiar.

'I'm sure I've heard it before and wondered what it was, but a long time ago. It reminds me for some reason of a warm evening, watching the sun go down.'

'We must listen to it again, then, in the summer.'

'I've no idea who wrote it though.'

'It's by Puccini. "Crisantemi." Rather different from *Madame Butterfly* and *Tosca* isn't it!'

I let the music wash over me, soothing, mesmerising even, as if someone is stroking my hair. I lean back and close my eyes. When I open them again, Jonathan is standing in front of me, watching, smiling.

'I'm glad you like it. There's such a lot to learn about each other. For example, what is your opinion of, say, Bruckner?'

'Would it offend you if I said I've never really got on with him?'

'Good,' says Jonathan, grinning. 'Just testing. I don't much care for him either. Too long-winded for my taste. Apart from some rather nice motets the choir sing sometimes.'

At about ten o'clock, we decide that, as Jonathan has a busy day tomorrow, he should take me home. Outside it's cold, but we decide the walk will do us good. I take his arm and match my stride to his.

'I'm going to fetch my mother on Saturday. She's been staying with my sister in Colchester. I suppose you wouldn't like to come with me, would you? I'd like you to meet her.'

So, we agree that he will come to the vicarage tomorrow when he finishes at the hospital and that perhaps we'll go out to eat. Then he will call for me on Saturday morning and we'll drive to his sister's. We pause below the vicarage steps. He takes both my hands in his.

'This reminds me of taking my first girlfriend home; she always insisted on going straight in. I was allowed one very short kiss, more a peck really – said her father would be watching to make sure I didn't take advantage of her.'

'Well, I'm sure Geoffrey won't be glued to the window this evening, so you're quite safe.'

Our embrace is hampered by thick layers of clothing and his lips are cold.

'In you go. I'll see you tomorrow. Sleep well.'

'And you.'

Once again, I stand, feeling rather dazed, in the hall. Already the evening seems as if it's a half-remembered dream. The house is quiet and at first I think everyone must have gone to bed. But then I see a light coming from the sitting room. The door is half open, so I put my head round to say goodnight to whoever is there.

Ruth is sitting on the sofa, staring into the last glow of the fire.

'Hello. Are you all right?'

'Yes, darling, thank you. Just thinking about things, that's all. Did you have a nice time?'

'Yes, thank you,' I begin, then realise we sound ridiculously formal. 'Yes, yes, I did. And I don't quite understand what's happening to me, Ruth.'

'Darling, all I know is that you look very happy. I think probably that's enough to be going on with.'

'I suppose you're right. I just want to take things one step at a time, but I'm rather afraid I'm getting carried away.'

'I think you're the last person that's likely to happen to.' She looks at me carefully, smiling. 'Aren't you?'

I shrug.

'Maybe,' I say, grinning. 'We'll just have to wait and see. Anyway, I assume there aren't any more developments on the Geoffrey front, are there?'

'No. He had a meeting this evening and when he came back, he went straight into his study. I think I heard him go up a little while ago. No good night, not even any television. Not like him at all, in fact. No doubt it will all come out eventually. Anyway, I think we both need an early night.'

I know that tomorrow I need to tell Jonathan about Peter. I could, of course, actually tell him exactly what happened without reading another word. But when I get upstairs, I realise I'm reluctant to open the small, green notebook lying on the table beside my bed. It's almost as if I'm afraid of what I'm going to find. When I read what actually happened, I might wonder what all the fuss was about, just as, when I at last actually looked at the photograph of Peter, what I saw was just an ordinary young man. Or perhaps what I wrote has miraculously been altered in the intervening years. I decide there's only one way to find out. I undress and get into bed. I pick up the book and carefully turn the pages...

PART TWO

Wednesday 18th August 1954

...and, finding the page, remember that, with a dreadful irony, it was the day we went to the border with the Russian zone. Once again, my diary told only part of the story.

Barbara is now staying with us and sharing my room. We had to get up early to go into Münden.

It had not been a good night. After Barbara stopped talking, I lay awake for a long time, unable to get thoughts of Johannes Altmeyer out of my mind. I dozed off eventually, but slept only intermittently. I was not used to sharing a room with anyone. Barbara was a restless sleeper and frequently muttered incoherent remarks in her sleep. The moon was shining in at the window and I could see her flailing about as she turned over in the bed next to mine. When I woke the next morning, she was already up and dressed, banging the wardrobe door, opening and shutting drawers.

'I've got to bring the rest of my stuff up later, so you'll have to move some of your things, Mags.'

'Not now, for goodness sake, Barbara.'

'All right, all right. No need to snap.'

When we got downstairs, Fritz was just finishing his breakfast. No one else was about.

'*Guten Morgen,* James!' Barbara started to put on her "Fräulein von Hügel and the butler" act. I could hardly believe she was behaving so frivolously and was relieved that Fritz refused to play the game that morning. When he started to speak directly to me, she shrugged her shoulders and disappeared into the kitchen.

'Margaret, Herr and Frau Schmidt have already gone to visit the Altmeyer family. I think they will stay with them and only I will teach the children today. Gudrun is in the garden, as she must feed the dog, Max. She says she will return when it is time to catch the train.'

I sat down at the table and found I had nothing to say.

'I think,' said Fritz after a while, 'that you have not known anyone who has been killed before?'

'No. Not even in the war. It's so dreadful that people can do that to each other.'

'One day, Margaret, I will tell you of how Herr Schmidt helped people in great danger during the war. He is a good man.'

'I know he is, Fritz.'

We went to school in the morning. After lessons we walked in the town and bought some postcards. We then had coffee and cakes – with cream and fruit – in the Café Hargemann, (not the Café Obst, because Gudrun says it isn't so good). We saw Fritz's brother, Gunter, in the Apotheke *as we went passed and he waved to me.*

There doesn't seem to be any reference to either Johannes Altmeyer or Peter in my diary. I write as if it were a completely normal day. But I know I was thinking constantly about both of them.

We went to the Russian border this afternoon. The coach we had was dedicated to Doktor Eisenbaht, whose Fest *they celebrate here each year. He was an eighteenth century doctor who made blind people walk and lame people see again.*

Reading that again now, I wonder whether I really meant to write that. Perhaps it was intended as an example of German humour.

The coach was decorated with flags of various towns and districts (including the Lorelei Rock) and little emblems and pictures (including those that were obviously of the driver's family). A model of Doktor Eisenbaht himself smiled venerably down at Miss Harris and Miss Smithson, who, being quite oblivious of this, offered a great contrast to him by munching apples and smoking cigarettes. We were taken first to a youth hostel called Ludwigstein. It is surrounded by beautiful woodland overlooking the River Werra and was once a castle. It has a little chapel that you get to by going through a small door from the courtyard.

I remember now. I had sent my parents a postcard from there and I'd taken a photograph from one of the balconies overlooking the cobbled courtyard. I get it out of the folder. Barbara is standing on the balcony opposite, waving. Down below, I can see Gudrun about to go inside the building. I'd forgotten that the German girls had come with us on that occasion.

The next photograph is of Barbara and me standing by the border itself. We are wearing coats, so the day must have been chilly, in spite of the time of year. Barbara, gesticulating in the way I remember so well, is in the middle of talking to whoever took the photo. I am standing beside her, head down, not looking at the camera. The black and white image immediately brings back the feeling of desolation I experienced that day. In the distance there is a range of forest-covered hills. Behind us I can see a glimpse of what must have been a river. Is this the river Johannes swam across in his bid for freedom? And is the patch of scrubby ground in front of it where he lay bleeding to death? As if to emphasize the bleakness of the scene, to our right is a small, spindly, emaciated tree, leaning slightly to one side. In front of us, a small, muddy puddle.

I can't remember if we went anywhere else that day. My diary doesn't say. I wonder if Barbara and I talked about Johannes at all. She had seemed so upset the previous evening, yet that day she was her usual exuberant self. By the time we got back to Volkmarshausen I was exhausted, but Barbara was as lively as ever.

Herr Schmidt was out visiting the Altmeyers again and Barbara went back there to collect her things when we returned. Fritz's mother, brother and aunt came to visit and had the evening meal with us.

Fritz and I were left alone in the sitting room while Gudrun and her mother prepared the evening meal. For some time neither of us said anything. Then Fritz seemed to come to a decision. He stood up and went to look out of the window behind me. He spoke softly and with apparent urgency.

'You know, in the war, Margaret, that many Jews were taken to the camps. At first we did not know that many of them were killed.'

He paused. Gudrun came in to set the table and he waited until she had gone out again.

'A Jewish family lived in the village. The children – a girl and a boy – went to the school here. The girl was the same age as Gudrun and the boy was a little older – the same age as Peter, who was staying here while his father was away. At that time I lived in Münden, but my mother and my brother and I often came to the village, as my mother's sister lived here and taught at the school. My father was in the army, so he was not at home very often. Herr Schmidt and my aunt were worried about the family. One day, when the children were at school, soldiers came to the house and took away their parents. But when they came here to the school to look for the children,

Herr Schmidt told them that they had left already and had gone to live with their uncle in Münden. It was not true, of course.'

'What happened to them?'

'We never saw the parents again. We learnt later that they were taken to a camp and killed. The children remained here, hidden upstairs in this house, until arrangements could be made to take them to a safer place. They were the first of many children to be helped in this way. Where better to hide children than in a school?'

It occurs to me now to wonder if Gudrun knew about what her father was doing. I suppose she was too young at the time. But what about later, after the war? And did Peter know? Or, more importantly, his father? Fritz asked me not to say anything about what he had just told me, so I never did and I still haven't.

'Now,' said Fritz, 'I can see Barbara coming up the path. I will go down to help her carry her bag.'

Barbara's luggage seemed to have expanded greatly in the short time since our arrival. When I went up to the room later, every available surface seemed to be covered with her belongings and she spent a considerable amount of time for things she thought she had lost.

Soon afterwards, Fritz's mother and brother arrived and I spent an anxious few minutes hoping they wouldn't say anything about seeing me with Peter. Although when they shook hands they said they had met me briefly the previous day, they made no reference at all to Peter. Shortly afterwards, Fritz's Aunt Freda arrived. She still lived in the village, although she had retired from teaching at the school.

The conversation around the supper table, inevitably, was largely of the Altmeyers and was mostly in German, so I had difficulty following what was being said at times. But I knew enough to understand how worried they were about the family – in particular Herr Altmeyer, who seemed to have lost the will to go on and just sat in his chair all day, staring ahead of him. Frau Altmeyer said little and continued with her household tasks. Helga was tearful while helping to care for her little brother, who was alone in not understanding what had happened. In my mind's eye the image of the guitar leaning against the wall beside the desk refused to go away. It had become the symbol of a seemingly insoluble problem. And the image is just as clear today. The problems remain. Boundaries and borders are created and demolished. Only the locations shift.

There was one last drama that day. Until I read further in my diary, it was another incident I had forgotten all about and which, with hindsight, could be seen as another example of how, after Barbara's arrival at the school, everything seemed to go wrong.

Gudrun went outside to feed Max, the dog, again. I went into the kitchen to help Frau Schmidt clear away and wash up, but Barbara went with Gudrun, as she had not yet seen Max. The next thing we heard was Barbara running up the stairs, shouting for Herr Schmidt to come quickly. Gudrun had been stroking the dog and said that Barbara could try to stroke him too. He would not normally allow strangers near him, but Gudrun thought it would be safe if she were there. But as soon as Barbara put her hand on him, he knew it was different and turned round, but instead of biting Barbara, he bit Gudrun. Herr Schmidt immediately took Gudrun to the doctor in the village. When they came back, she had her arm in a sling and had had an injection. She has to have another tomorrow, but she felt much better and was no longer in pain.

After her initial panic in the garden, while they were gone Barbara seemed remarkably composed. She even seemed to be enjoying herself. Later, though, she must have been having second thoughts, or perhaps it was a case of delayed shock.

'Just think, Mags,' she said, when we were finally in bed with the light out. 'It might have been me. I might have been bitten by that dreadful dog.'

'But it was just as bad for Gudrun. Worse, in fact, because it's her dog – the dog she's been perfectly safe with up till now.'

'That's a matter of opinion, isn't it. Any way, it's their fault for keeping it chained up. It's bound to make it vicious. I don't know why I ever went near the thing. I've never really liked dogs. And do you know why they call it Max? It's after some cartoon character, which makes it sound all cosy and sweet. Gudrun was telling me before the dog turned on her that Max and Moritz are a pair of cheeky little boys who get up to all sorts of pranks and are supposed to be loved by all German children. They used to have another dog, too, called, of course, Moritz, but it died last year.'

She was quiet for a moment and I thought she must have fallen asleep. I just wished she would go away. At home I was accustomed to being on my own a lot of the time, so Barbara's incessant chatter was already becoming unbearable.

'Oh, yes, Mags, I didn't tell you, did I?'

'How should I know, Barbara, if you don't say what it is?' I didn't attempt to hide the weariness I felt.

'Your hairdresser friend, Peter, is coming here tomorrow evening. Gudrun told me.' She paused, as if for dramatic effect.

'He usually visits on a Thursday,' I said, trying to sound casual. 'I do wish you wouldn't talk about him like that, though. His name means a charcoal burner, not something to do with hair. It just sounds stupid.'

'I won't call him that in front of everyone else. It would be far too difficult to explain and they probably wouldn't understand the joke anyway. I don't think the Germans do puns. And before you get yourself in a tizzy, I didn't tell Gudrun about you and him and what you've got up to, stealing her chap. Like the good girl I am, I did what you asked. Still, it might be difficult when he's actually here for me to remember, don't you think?'

I'm surprised, looking back, that I still counted Barbara as my best friend. When I was younger, it wasn't uncommon for her to reduce me to the verge of tears. That year in particular she had begun to take an apparent delight in making unkind, barbed comments and remarks, which could almost be seen as a threat of blackmail, if I'd known what she wanted as a consequence. Perhaps it was just a need to be superior. Although she was bright and quick and good at games, academically I left her standing. Mocking my love of reading and my lack of interest in boys was the only way she knew of making me feel inferior. It was only recently that I had begun to see through this ploy.

Lying there in the darkness, I could feel my anger rising. I told myself not to rise to the bait, to remain calm.

'Oh, for goodness sake, shut up, you stupid girl,' I eventually blurted out through clenched teeth, just about managing not to raise my voice above a hoarse whisper. 'You're just jealous because someone has taken an interest in me for a change. Just be quiet and go to sleep.'

And with that, I suppose, I metaphorically threw down the gauntlet. The challenge was one which Barbara was unable to resist, one which was to be my undoing.

CHAPTER NINE

PART ONE

Friday 29ᵗʰ December 1989

It's after midnight when I eventually switch off the light, but I find it difficult to get to sleep. I know it's ridiculous, but I can't help imagining alternative endings for my German story. "If only I hadn't", or "I should have", or "perhaps if'" all lead to endless possibilities. And there are just as many "what ifs" in the English story that I'm in the middle of now.

One overwhelming doubt lies lurking at the back of my mind. My automatic reaction has always been to recoil from any form of physical contact. Even Ruth and her family's enthusiastic embraces have always, if I'm honest, slightly embarrassed me. And yet a few hours ago, I actually enjoyed being kissed by Jonathan. As I lie here now I try to imagine what it would be like if he were lying beside me. It's a situation completely beyond my experience. I've convinced myself over the years that the last thing I want is actually to become intimate with a man. I smile to myself. The euphemism exactly sums me up. I have never said out loud any of the words for the more embarrassing parts of the human body, male or female – I can't even think of the words without cringing – let alone the intimate act itself. But there is the undeniable fact that just a few hours ago, I felt the first stirrings of what can only be called sexual desire.

Ruth's words of yesterday echo in my mind. *She takes herself far too seriously. You're doing her a lot of good, Jonathan.* Then I hear Jonathan's voice. *If you carry on looking at me like that, I'm not going to be responsible for my actions.* And imagine him putting his hand to my cheek and starting gently to explore the curve of my back. And feel enormous pleasure.

I look at the clock. Nearly half past one. I start to panic. What on earth shall I look like tomorrow without any proper sleep?

But the next thing I know is I'm waking up to the sound of the boys in the middle of the sort of argument only children seem to have. Their door opens and I can hear Jack crashing down the stairs, followed by William's more measured steps, both calling out to Helen, who presumably will be expected to sort out the quarrel without having the remotest idea what it's all about. I lie here, luxuriating in the knowledge I don't have to do anything about it and feel a slight stir of excitement as I think about this evening. It's nearly half past seven. Six hours sleep. It seems enough. I feel energised, eager to start the day, although not quite ready yet to face the family hurly-burly. I have a long shower and dress slowly.

The post is being put through the letterbox as I come downstairs. I'm just going to pick it up when Geoffrey comes out of his study and almost races me to the front door.

'Expecting a letter,' he mutters, as he bends down. He selects a buff coloured envelope, then goes back into his study and shuts the door. I take the rest of the post through to the kitchen. Ruth is sitting by herself at the table.

'Where is everyone? It seems uncannily quiet.'

'Ian and Will have gone to Greenwich and Helen's taken Max to Sainsbury's. Jack's watching television.'

I hand the post to Ruth.

'Geoffrey seems very anxious about one of his letters,' I say. 'Do you know what it can be?'

'No, except that it has to be to do with what he's not telling me, hasn't it? What was it like?'

'Just an ordinary brown envelope. I couldn't see it properly, though. He scuttled away too quickly.'

Ruth gets up to make some coffee.

'That presents me with what I can only call a moral dilemma, doesn't it? I'm sure I could find out the full story quite easily if I had a look through his papers while he's out of the house. On the other hand, I really want him to tell me himself. Not just brush everything under the carpet, which is what he's always done throughout his life, and which is what he's doing now.' She turns round to face me. 'What do you think, Meg?'

'It's very tempting, isn't it? I'd help you, if that's what you want to do. Act as lookout, anyway.'

Ruth comes and sits down opposite me. We look at each other.

'I think,' she says carefully, 'I'll give him one more chance to say something himself. I've never even thought of doing anything like this before, not even when he decided to give up the law. If I had delved into his papers then, I think I would have found there was more to it than he admitted. I never really believed in his sudden conversion, as you know. But I won't hesitate this time if he obfuscates again.'

She butters a piece of toast and spreads it thickly with marmalade.

'Anyway, espionage on moral grounds always seems justifiable to me.' She bites into her toast with precision.

The doorbell rings.

'I'll go,' I say, but once again Geoffrey beats me to the door.

'Come in, Shirley,' we hear him say, but we can't hear her reply and he immediately hustles her into his study.

'Well, well!' says Ruth. 'I think I was right. Shirley has definitely got something to do with it. I think I'll go in and take them some coffee.'

'You're hardly likely to catch them in a compromising clinch, are you?'

'No, but he might be showing her the letter.'

She pours out two mugs of coffee, slops in some milk, stirs some sugar into one of them and puts them on a tray. She carries it out into the hall and opens the study door. Geoffrey stops in mid-sentence. From the sitting room comes the sound of the television. *Sesame Street* is in full swing. Ruth comes back into the kitchen.

'Well?'

She makes a wry face and shrugs.

'They were just sitting there. No letter that I could see. But I was obviously not welcome.'

She starts loading the dishwasher. Breaks a glass. Curses.

'Oh, Meg, I'm just about at the end of my tether. I'm far too old for all this.'

'Here, let me do that. He's got to tell you what it's all about. You can't go on like this. If you don't ask him, I will.'

'No, no, I must do it. You don't want to get involved.'

'But I am involved Ruth. I hate to see you so upset.'

'I'll leave it till after lunch. Helen and Ian and the boys are going to see Ian's mother this afternoon, so we'll have the house to ourselves.'

'Where's Jane, by the way? I didn't see her at all yesterday, now I come to think of it.'

'She's taken Bella out again. I think she needs time by herself to come to terms with everything. We had a talk when you were out yesterday afternoon. I told her I thought there was more to Geoffrey's retirement than he's told me. I was surprised she felt so angry about it. I know she and

Geoffrey haven't seen eye to eye on quite a few things in the past. But now, I think, it's all muddled up with what's happened with Philip, so she's just against men in general. She also told me she's got an offer of a job in New York, which she's going to accept. I'll miss her, but it's probably the best thing for her to do. I shall go out and see her once she's settled. I've never been to New York – well, I haven't been anywhere other than the odd trip to France when the girls were small. Before Geoffrey got religion. When we were comparatively rich.'

'Geoffrey's not exactly the intrepid world traveller is he? Would he want to go?'

'I shouldn't think so for a moment. But then I wasn't planning to take him along anyway.'

It seems the matter is closed for the time being. Ruth seizes a bag of rubbish and goes into the garden to put it into the dustbin. I sit down at the table to finish my coffee and start to read the headlines in the paper. The main news is still about Romania. Ceausescu's supporters and relations are being rounded up and there is sporadic fighting on the streets of Bucharest. The world seems to have accepted that the Romanians were right to execute Ceausescu and his wife straight away. I still can't help feeling uneasy about it, though; even the Nazi war criminals had a proper trial.

Suddenly, I seem to be besieged as, almost simultaneously, Ruth comes in from the garden, Jack bursts out of the sitting room, demanding a drink of coke, and Jane returns from her walk, carrying a couple of shopping bags. Bella trots in, goes to her water bowl and takes a long and noisy drink. She comes and lovingly puts her head on my lap, soaking my skirt. Then Helen staggers into the kitchen under the weight of several more plastic bags, followed by a tired and grizzly Max.

'Thanks for doing that, Helen.' Ruth picks Max up, sets him down on a chair at the table and opens the fridge. 'Right,' she says, briskly, 'who wants coke, who wants milk and who wants coffee?'

Her moment of doubt has passed, at least for the time being, and she is back to her capable, cheerful self.

'Where my doggy, Mummy?' says Max, putting his thumb in his mouth, looking close to tears.

'You must have left it in the car, darling. Jack, can you go and see if you can find it please. And while you're there, can you bring in the other bag?'

'Oh, Mum, must I?'

'Yes,' says Helen, firmly and finally. 'And make sure you shut the car door properly, please.'

"Doggy" is a scrap of fur – Max's equivalent to a comfort blanket – which is now unrecognisable as the original Snoopy dog it once was and which can be the cause of a major panic at bedtime if it can't be found.

Jack stomps out of the kitchen and returns after a minute, making a great play of dragging the bag of shopping and holding "doggy" between his thumb and finger, as if it's contaminated. He drops it on to the table beside Max and resumes drinking his coke.

Ruth and I look at each other, as we hear Geoffrey and Shirley coming out of the study. Helen, in turn, looks at Ruth and raises her eyebrows. Ruth imperceptibly shakes her head and Helen carries on putting the shopping away. I know she will ask what it's all about once the children aren't about. Geoffrey now comes into the kitchen with the coffee tray. Jane pointedly turns her back on him and looks out of the window.

'What did Shirley want? She's beginning to get a bit of a nuisance, isn't she?'

Good old Ruth – that's blunt, anyway.

'No,' says Geoffrey, rather irritably, 'on the contrary, she's being a great help at the moment. She's helping me sort quite a few things out.'

'Such as? Are they not things I could be doing instead?'

'I don't think so.'

And with that, he goes out of the room. Moments later we hear the front door shut. No one says anything and even Jack is silent, sensing perhaps that this is more than just idle talk.

'Please can you take Max into the sitting room, Jack?' Ruth says. 'Wasn't that *Sesame Street* I heard just now?'

'It's finished. Can't Dad look after Max? I want to play football outside.'

'Daddy and Will have gone into Greenwich, you know that. They won't be long. We need to start the lunch. Go on, off you go.'

This is obviously going to be a family conclave. Ruth seizes the boys by their hands and leads them out of the room.

I've noticed that, whenever Geoffrey gets irritable with Ruth, it's rarely actually as a result of anything she herself has done. A disgruntled parishioner might have upset him, he might have scraped the wing on the car; whatever it is, it's Ruth's fault. She obviously hasn't been patient enough on the phone, she's left the car too near the wall. This time, he'll probably imply it's something to do with Ruth's lack of faith. Always a case of transferring the blame if he possibly can.

Jane, Helen and I sit at the kitchen table, a committee waiting for its chairman, not sure what the agenda will be. Jane is the first to break the silence.

'Well, I don't know about you two, but I think that was just plain rude. How dare he talk to Mum like that! If she doesn't have it out with him soon – before I go back tomorrow, in fact – I'm going to say something myself.'

'Meg and I have already decided that a bit of spying might be the thing to do, if he won't tell me himself.' Ruth has returned in time to hear the end of Jane's outburst. 'I quick rifle through his papers shouldn't be too difficult. I always knew sitting through all those James Bond films would come in handy one day.' Ruth has already broken the tension. By treating the idea as if it's just a clever wheeze to defeat the enemy, she has turned the whole idea into an adolescent game in which no one will get hurt, because none of it is real.

'Anyway, I just wanted to say that I intend to confront him this afternoon; give him a last chance to confess. So, if you find blood in the hall, you'll know what's happened. If that fails, I'll call in the reinforcements. Now, we really ought to start preparing lunch, because I know you want to get off early this afternoon, Helen, don't you?'

She tips out a bag of potatoes into the sink and starts to scrub them, rather more violently than is strictly necessary. By the time Ian and William get back, it's as if nothing untoward has happened. At lunch Ruth and Geoffrey are acidly polite to each other, but the boys are no less exuberant than normal.

'I hope Granny Knight hasn't forgotten to get our presents,' says Jack, waving his knife in the air. 'Did you give my list, Mummy?'

'Yes, darling, I did, and please put your knife down.'

'What's my present, Mummy?' Max seems to have perked up considerably now he's had something to eat.

'I don't know, sweetheart, you'll have to wait.'

'I want to ask Granny Knight about my family tree, Dad,' says Will. 'I've put in a lot of Mum's relatives, but not many on your side.'

They all pile into the car straight after lunch. Jane and I decide it might be diplomatic if we went out too, since Ruth has rejected our offer of moral support.

'It's best if I do this by myself. Just give me an hour; that should be enough. I want to catch him off-guard. If he sees a whole deputation advancing on him, he might try to dodge and weave again.'

Bella looks rather surprised as we call her to come for another walk. She heaves herself out of her basket and stands in the hall, wagging her tail in a rather desultory fashion, waiting for her lead to be put on. It's overcast and chilly once we get outside. Not a day to be trooping about on the heath for an hour or more. We decide to go and see if Val is in, as it's only a five minute walk from the vicarage.

'Hello, this is a nice surprise. I'm afraid the place is in a bit of a mess.' Val bends down to give Bella a pat and a scratch behind the ears. 'Come through into the sitting room.'

I have to move a pile of music from one of the armchairs before I can sit down.

'We're refugees at the moment. Ruth has decided at last to have a proper talk to Geoffrey and we thought it best to leave them to it.'

'About time too.'

Jane flushes and raises her voice. 'I'm so angry with Dad. Mum's been so loyal and he just walks all over her.'

'This isn't like you, Jane,' says Val. 'I always think of you as taking everything so calmly.'

'Well, I'm not calm at the moment. And I expect you've heard all about Philip, haven't you? But did you know that he came round the day before yesterday wanting to come back!'

'I hope you said no.'

While Jane and Val are talking, my mind wanders. I wonder what's going on in the vicarage? We can't really go back for another half an hour. And what about this evening? Perhaps Ruth and I will both look back on today as the turning point in our lives.

'Now, Meg, what about you? How did your date go yesterday?'

'Don't call it that Val! It makes me sound about sixteen. If you mean my walk with Jonathan, I enjoyed it – we went to The Queen's House.'

'Then?'

'Then supper at his house.'

I grin, in spite of myself. And feel embarrassed.

'Excellent,' is all she says.

'Anyway, Meg,' says Val, as we eventually get up to go, 'I can't wait to know all about Geoffrey's shenanigans.'

'I promise I'll get Ruth to phone you when we know what it's all about.'

Walking back to the vicarage, Jane and I are both lost in our own thoughts for a while.

'You know, Meg, I feel quite nervous.'

'Me too. It's silly isn't it? Let's just hope your father hasn't done one of his famous vanishing tricks. That really would be something of an anticlimax!'

The vicarage is unlit and utterly silent when we get in. No raised voices. And, thankfully, no blood on the carpet.

Bella heads for the sitting room, so Jane and I follow. Ruth is sitting on the sofa, staring straight in front of her.

'I really don't know where to begin,' she says at last.

I go over and switch on the lamp. 'How about a cup of tea first?'

'That would be lovely, darling. It's all so complicated. I've got to get my head round it first.'

She bends down to fondle Bella's ears. I go into the kitchen and put the kettle on for the tea. There is no sign of Geoffrey. Is he contrite at last? Or has he stormed out in a huff? But then, just as I'm putting the tea on to the tray, he comes down the stairs.

'Sorry, Meg,' he calls out cheerfully. 'Can't stay. I'm late over at the church as it is.'

And he hurries through the hall and out of the front door. As usual after any sort of crisis, he appears to be behaving as if nothing untoward has happened. In the sitting room, Ruth grins at me.

'You heard that, presumably,' I say, handing her a mug of tea.

'Yes. He never ceases to amaze me, you know. Once he'd told me everything – and I hope it really is everything – he actually seemed relieved.'

'Right, Mum,' says Jane, firmly. 'Tell us the whole sordid story.'

'Well, it's not exactly sordid, darling. More tacky. He's been really, really stupid. And, yes, Meg, it does involve Shirley, but not in the way we thought.'

'For goodness sake, Mum, tell us.'

'Well. I need to go back to the time Shirley's husband died – two or three years ago, I think.'

'Nearly three,' I say. 'When we were manning the urn together at the carol concert, she told me her husband had left us three years ago this coming March. I assume she meant he'd died.'

Ruth smiles. 'Yes, that sounds like our dear Shirley. Apparently she discovered that, far from being comfortably off, Norman had left her with some very hefty debts. Rather out of character, I should think, because I remember him as a rather boring, holier-than-thou sort of man. Not at all the sort to go in for speculating on the stock exchange. But he seems to have been rather too easily influenced. Apparently he got friendly with a stockbroker when they moved here, who advised him to use his retirement lump sum and also take out a substantial mortgage on their house, to buy shares, or stocks, or something. Norman thought he'd make a nice profit, because it looked as if the stock market would carry on going up forever. You'll understand all about this, Jane. This was shortly before he upped and died – very suddenly, I seem to remember. Shirley's solicitors advised her to sell the shares and pay off the mortgage once they had sorted out his estate, which would have been fine. But of course, before she could do anything, about six months later, Black Monday happened – something I've never really understood, or cared about before now.'

'That's all very well, Mum, it must have been a shock for Shirley, and I'm sure we all feel very sorry for her. But what's it got to do with Dad?'

'Well, put it this way. I think he thought of the church organ fund as the equivalent to a solicitor's client account for his parishioners. Except, of course, even client accounts are not supposed to be dipped into for the benefit of all and sundry.'

She suddenly stops talking and puts her hand up to her mouth.

'You don't think, do you, that he did just that when he was in practice – you know, before he "found God"?'

'Left under a cloud, you mean?' It wasn't something I'd thought about before.

'Yes. It would explain a lot. Suppose his partners found out he'd been, shall we say, generous in handing out money? Then, rather than create a scandal for the practice, they just hushed it all up. I'm not saying he would have pocketed it for himself; just lent it rather rashly, which is precisely what he's just done now. Shirley came to him for advice when she realised what it meant when the bank said her account was overdrawn. Would you believe it? Even I know that means a bit of a problem! They decided she'd have to sell her house, but of course it was about the time house prices were falling, so they thought she ought to wait. But in the meantime she still had to pay the mortgage her husband had taken out and the interest rates were rising. So Geoffrey thought there was no harm in helping her out with what I think they call a "cash-flow" problem. He says he was quite sure it could all be put right, once Shirley sold the shares. Neither of them thought to find out what they were actually worth and Shirley hadn't realised the implications of Black Monday. I cannot believe he was so stupid. He's been trying to cover it up ever since.'

'What's he going to do, Mum? Does anyone else know?'

'Oh yes. There's more to come. The auditors found out in the autumn and the bishop's involved. So your father's voluntary retirement on the grounds of loss of faith is really a case of jumping before he's pushed. You can't help feeling sorry for him. He must have gone through hell these last months – if that's the right expression in the circumstances!'

She pauses. Jane and I say nothing. As so often happens in moments of shock, our reactions are unexpected. In spite of myself, I feel an overwhelming urge to giggle. I catch first Ruth's, then Jane's eye. It's as if, at this moment, we have a choice of how to behave. We are teetering on the edge and in the end plump for frivolity. In no time at all, all three of us are laughing uncontrollably, practically rolling around on the sofa. It's the sort of hysterical behaviour I last remember indulging in as a schoolgirl – always at the most inappropriate moments. We are abruptly brought to our senses by the sound of the front door opening. We look guiltily at each other as we hear Geoffrey go into his study once more and shut the door.

'Oh dear,' says Ruth, wiping tears from her eyes. 'That was better than doing the weeping and wailing bit, I suppose. I must say I feel a lot better.'

She gets up and goes to the window and stares out into the darkness. I'm not quite sure why, but I feel a sense of anticlimax. For the last few days, we've been speculating wildly about what Geoffrey has done. Surely I don't feel disappointed that it turns out to have been about money after all? Did I secretly hope to see a headline in the *News of the World* along the lines of "Blackheath Vicar in Sex Romp"?

Jane starts to pile the tea things back on to the tray.

'And has Dad told you what he proposes to do now?'

'Having at last told me about what's happened, I think your father believes he's now handed the problem over to me.'

'That's nonsense. It's nothing to do with you.'

'It's not my fault, no. But since I can't escape the fact that I've been married to him now for forty years, I suppose my future is inextricably bound up with his whether I like it or not. I did say that the least Shirley can do is sell the shares, regardless of what they're worth now, and repay Geoffrey – or rather the organ fund – at least part of the money. And put her house on the market, of course, even though it might not be worth what it was when they bought it. It won't give your father back his reputation, but it'll be a start. What she does then is no concern whatsoever of either of us.'

'What did he say to that?'

'Oh, just muttered something about Shirley still needing his support.' She picks up the tray of tea things and starts to walk towards the door. 'If he hadn't said that, I might have decided to stay with him.' She disappears out into the hall. 'Looks like a fresh start all round, doesn't it?' she calls back.

I stare at Jane, not quite believing what I have just heard. She jumps up and follows Ruth into the kitchen.

'Have you told him?' I can hear her say.

'No, darling, because I've only just this moment decided to leave him.'

'Come on Ruth, is that really what you want to do?' I say, as I go in to join them.

I'm rather taken aback, when both Ruth and Jane start talking loudly at me simultaneously, so it's very difficult to hear what they are saying. As far as I can make out they seem to be in agreement that Ruth has put up with coming second for far too long and it's about time Geoffrey learns he can't always have his own way.

'All right, all right. I just think you oughtn't to be too hasty.'

'I'm not like you, Meg. You never do anything without making a list of the pros and cons and sleeping on it. And that's just whether to buy a new washing machine. I may put up with things just to have a quiet life, but once I've made up my mind, that's it. No turning back.'

'And I just think Mum deserves a life of her own, before she's too old to enjoy it.'

'Thank you darling. Not quite sure about the old bit, but I quite fancy going off the rails a bit and changing my image.'

The doorbell goes. I glance at my watch. Nearly five o'clock. Jonathan didn't say what time he would be here.

'I'll go,' I say, suddenly nervous.

When I open the door, he's standing there and I feel a little lurch inside me.

'Hello,' I say. 'Come in out of the cold.'

We stand in the hall and look at each other, as if once again uncertain about how to be behave. But then Jonathan comes towards me and holds me at arm's length, as he appears to examine my face in minute detail, before giving me a quick hug and a kiss.

'Yes,' he says, 'I think you'll do.'

Before I can respond, there is a shriek of laughter from the sitting room.

'Ruth's at last found out what Geoffrey's been up to. I think she and Jane are both a bit over-wrought. Better than crying, though, I suppose.'

'I can come back later if I'm intruding?'

'No, don't do that.' I stop myself from saying that he's practically part of the family now, which I feel might be a bit presumptuous. Instead, I lead the way into the sitting room.

'Perhaps I should dye my hair and invest in a glittery top with a plunging neckline for starters,' Ruth is saying as we go in. 'And swap my cello for an acoustic guitar. You could become a Goth, couldn't you, Jane? We could both get our noses pierced. Hello, Jonathan. Nice to see you. Sorry, you must wonder what the hell this is all about. You'll stay to supper, won't you?'

'Well, I was going to take Meg out.'

'You can do that another day. I don't think Jane and I could bear a threesome alone with Geoffrey just at the moment.'

Jonathan looks at me. I know that if we go out somewhere, I shall have to tell him about Peter and I realise I'm not quite ready yet. There's been too much drama already today. 'I think we'd all appreciate a dispassionate view about it all,' I say.

'I'll take you out tomorrow then, after we've collected my mother.'

'Good,' says Ruth, smiling at us both in what I can only describe as a "bless you my children" kind of way. 'Meg, you can fill Jonathan in with all the gory details before Geoffrey comes in. Come on Jane, let's make a start on the vegetables.'

Jane gives me an apologetic look as she follows Ruth, who turns back and shuts the door firmly behind her. We sit down side-by-side on the sofa. Jonathan reaches out and takes my hand in a nice, companionable sort of way. I try to explain what has happened as briefly as possible. When I've finished, he is silent for a moment.

'Do you think Ruth really means to leave him?' he says at last. 'Because if she does, I think he'll completely go to pieces. He likes to give the impression to the world at large that he's in control, that he's the one making all the decisions, but even I can see that Ruth is really the strong one.'

'You could be right. I suppose I'm bound to be rather biased. I've never felt especially close to Geoffrey – although I'm fond of him, of course. He's one of those people you can't help liking, isn't he? I suppose that's why he has such a devoted band of ladies in the church. Ruth and I call them his Angels of Mercy.'

'Including the dreaded Shirley, of course.'

'He's always just taken Ruth's loyalty for granted and assumes that she's going to take responsibility for the results of his own stupidity. And then expects her to change the whole course of her life without question.'

'Of course,' says Jonathan, carefully, 'sometimes there's nothing wrong with changing the whole course of your life.' He turns towards me. 'Is there, Meg?'

I don't know what to say. Is this a general observation, a serious question, a proposal even?

'There would have to be a very good reason,' I say, not looking at him. Have I gone pale, or flushed? I can tell I've definitely changed colour in some way. But before I can say any more, the door opens and Geoffrey peers in, mutters something and disappears again, unaware of his role as a "*deus ex machina*". We both laugh, the tension relieved. Jonathan pats my hand, gives me a brief kiss and gets up.

'P'raps not the best time to settle our future, Meg. Let's go and see if we're needed in the kitchen.'

The evening turns out far better than I expect – even jolly at times – helped, no doubt, by the two bottles of wine, opened with a flourish by Geoffrey. He doesn't seem to notice that he and Ruth drink most of it. He becomes more and more garrulous as the evening progresses, Ruth more and more silent. Jonathan seems quite happy to be on the receiving end of a stream of anecdotes from Geoffrey, most of which I don't follow and I don't think Jonathan does either. However, he laughs in the right places, makes suitable comments that seem to satisfy Geoffrey and manages to keep the conversation going nicely.

After supper Jane goes to pack as she is going back to her flat tomorrow, Geoffrey disappears as usual into his study and Ruth, Jonathan and I find ourselves in the kitchen clearing up.

'I can't tell you how nice it's been to have you here this evening, Jonathan,' Ruth says as she starts loading up the dishwasher. 'I'm only sorry I stopped you taking Meg out, but I just couldn't face an evening alone with Geoffrey – either discussing or not discussing things. I need to sleep on it all and see how I feel in the morning.'

'You know, don't you,' I say, 'that whatever you decide to do, we'll be on your side?'

'I've been bottling it all up for so long now, it's just a relief to be able to talk to someone about it.' She turns back to the dishwasher and starts clattering cutlery. Sniffs. Fumbles for a handkerchief. 'Sorry, Jonathan. You must think you've got yourself involved with a bloody odd family.'

Jonathan puts his arm round Ruth's shoulders and gives her a quick hug. Dare I imagine it's a "future brother-in-law" type hug?

'On the contrary, I'm flattered to be included. But don't be too hasty, will you?'

'You sound just like Meg. I know it's early, but I think I'll go to bed when I've cleared up. I didn't sleep very well last night. Can you say goodnight to everyone for me?'

'You leave it to us, darling. Off you go.'

I give her a kiss and shoo her out of the room.

We don't say much as we finish loading the dishwasher. But then, as I'm standing by the sink, Jonathan comes up behind me, turns me round to face him and gently kisses me on the lips.

'I think we've all had enough for one day. I'll see you tomorrow. Would about ten be all right? I've said we'll be at my sister's in time for an earlyish lunch.'

I stand at the top of the steps and wave goodbye as he drives off. I'm just about to go inside, when I see the headlights of another car coming round the corner and stopping outside. The door opens and Jack practically falls out and dashes up the steps.

'Hello, Auntie Meg. Look what Granny Knight's given me.' He holds out his wrist. 'It's a proper watch; it tells the date and everything. It's better than Will's. You gave him his last Christmas, didn't you? You said I wasn't old enough then, but I am now, aren't I? He just got money from Granny Knight this time, which I think is really boring.'

Ian leans into the car and lifts out Max, who is sound asleep, clutching his doggy.

'Hello, Meg. Come on, Jack, it's long past your bedtime too.'

Jack automatically lets out a yell of protest, but it's only half-hearted, and he trails upstairs after Ian. Even William says a mumbled goodnight and follows them up.

I go out and help Helen unload the car.

'Well?' she says. 'Did Mum have her heart-to-heart with Dad?'

'Indeed she did. She's absolutely exhausted, though, so she's gone to bed. She asked me to say goodnight. I'm sure she'd like to see you though and tell you about it herself. Ian's putting the boys to bed, so why don't you go up now? Geoffrey's still in his study.'

'I think I will. I don't think I would sleep without knowing.'

'Don't worry, he's not eloping with Shirley or anything as dramatic as that.'

I go into the sitting room and put another log on the fire. When Ian comes down I tell him briefly what's happened. We sit there, not saying much, until Helen joins us.

'Well,' she says. 'I suppose in a way it's both better and worse than we imagined. No wild women – if you discount Shirley – quite a disappointment!'

'Anyway, there's nothing we can do tonight, is there? Let's hope Ruth gets a good night's sleep.'

We hear the study door open.

'Hello, you're back then.' We all start almost guiltily at the sound of Geoffrey's voice. 'I think we all need a drink. Whisky, Ian?'

'Thanks, that would be nice.' Ian sounds rather taken aback.

'What about you girls? And where's Ruth?'

'Not for me, Dad. Mum's gone to bed.'

'Bit early, isn't it? Never mind, she's had a busy day, I suppose. How's your mother, Ian?'

'She's fine. I think she found her Christmas a bit tiring though. As you know, she went to my brother's. Apparently the new baby hardly seems to sleep at all and has a very efficient set of lungs, as she puts it. And Lucy, who's only just two, does a good line in tantrums. Believe it or not, she said having our lot for the day was a delight, by comparison!'

Am I alone in thinking the whole situation is rather unreal? Here is Geoffrey, dispensing drinks and bonhomie as if nothing has happened, having just been revealed as a fool, at best, or a thief, at worst. I feel if I sit here any longer, I shall say something I shall regret.

'I think I'll go up too, if you don't mind. I'll make myself a hot drink.'

Helen must feel the same, because she gets up too and follows me into the kitchen.

'Am I intolerant, or is my father really rather a shit?'

'You're certainly not intolerant, darling.'

I pour some milk into a saucepan.

'You don't think Mum will really leave him, though, do you? In spite of everything, I think she'd be absolutely lost without him.'

'Jonathan actually said he thought it would be the other way round. That your father would go to pieces.'

'Maybe. Anyway, sorry, Meg, I didn't ask about your evening. Did you go somewhere nice?'

'We stayed here, actually. We thought Ruth and Jane needed moral support. I'm going to meet his mother tomorrow, though, and his sister.'

'That's great, Meg. About time you got yourself a man!'

I grin, in spite of myself, as I pour the hot milk into our mugs. 'I wouldn't put it quite like that, but, yes, I certainly enjoy being with him. I think I'll take this up, if that's all right. Sleep well.'

Upstairs, I undress slowly, sipping my hot drink, then get into bed and pick up my diary…

Part Two

Thursday 19th August 1954

…and start to read the next entry.

> *We went by coach to the Harz Mountains all day today and travelled through the most gorgeous scenery – high hillsides densely wooded with fir trees.*

Nothing about my argument with Barbara the previous evening.

After my outburst she had said nothing more, but it was obvious, by the way she pointedly turned her back on me and then kept tossing about in her annoyingly creaky bed, that she was in a big huff. I eventually got to sleep, but spent another restless night. And once again she was up before me in the morning, slamming drawers and muttering to herself.

Early that morning Gudrun went to the doctor for her second injection and had her bandage changed. When she came back, it was left to me to ask her how she was. Barbara was too busy upstairs looking for yet more mislaid belongings.

'There is not so much pain now, thank you, Margaret. The doctor says now it should heal well.'

The German girls were coming on the excursion with us, so we all caught the train into Münden together. When we got to the school, the coach was waiting for us. Barbara pointedly sat down beside Anne Simmonds, completely ignoring me and I found myself sitting next to Ursula Hegel – the girl whose parents knew Fräulein Schaefer. I was in no mood to keep up a continuous conversation – let alone in German, which still required a good deal of concentration on my part – so after a few initial remarks, we were mostly silent. Gudrun, I noticed, was wedged into a window seat beside Fräulein Braun, the headmistress of the school, and was looking distinctly uncomfortable and embarrassed. Fräulein Braun was obviously asking about her bandaged hand, and once or twice they looked over in Barbara's direction.

The Harz are not too far from Hann. Münden. On the way to the highest parts of the area we stopped at a wonderful lake called Odertalsperre, in the middle of the mountains. We bought some postcards, then walked along the dam wall. The lake is a reservoir and also provides electricity (I think) for Denmark. It was very beautiful. The light was shining on the water, making magical silvery patches and the mountains, disappearing into the distance, were a misty greyish-blue.

I imagine that my description of the lake owed something to my newly found romantic view of solitude and nature, prompted by my constant thoughts of Peter. Among my postcards there is one of the Odertalsperre, written to my parents. It seems from the lack of any more proper letters in my collection that my intention of writing home at length, adding something every day, had gone by the wayside, to be replaced by the occasional postcard.

Dear Mummy and Daddy,

I expect when this gets to you, you'll be home. Did you have a nice time in London? This is a lake in the Harz Mountains where we went today. The scenery is wonderful, especially the wooded mountains. I shall post this card in Goslar. Give my love to Ruth and the girls. I hope Jane has recovered from chickenpox and that Helen hasn't caught it.
Love Margaret

The postcard neatly sums up my preoccupations at that time. Even after thirty-five years, I feel a sudden sharp pang of nostalgia; an almost painful longing for the security of the close and loving family of my childhood. For an adolescence which was as yet untainted by betrayal, but which was about to be shaken in a way that would affect the rest of my life.

We then went on further and drove up very steep, windy mountain roads, which was alarming. The views down through the trees, however, were beautiful. We then got to Goslar, which is a very old town and stopped at the market square. It is surrounded by very old timbered houses – the newest was built in about 1400. In the middle is a fountain with a golden eagle on it. We went into the town hall, which is hung with many pictures and then went along a tiny passageway into another, smaller room, also covered with paintings – the ceiling as well – and also very old books. Two ghastly looking German boys sort of tagged along with our party and Miss Smithson called them our "pilot fish".

I remember taking some photographs in Goslar, and manage to find them in my box. One is of Gudrun, complete with bandage, leaning on some railings and looking down at what must be a river or stream. Behind her is a whitewashed, timber-framed house with small dormer windows in a steeply sloping tiled roof. Another shows three or four storey buildings on either side of a cobbled street, empty apart from a motorcycle parked by the kerb and a young woman walking along the narrow pavement. By the fact that the buildings are more or less vertical and the focus more or less sharp, I was obviously getting the hang of using the camera, which I think I had borrowed from my father.

We were then free to look round by ourselves, so we went to a hotel in the market square and sat outside at a table to have coffee.

I think it was then that Barbara made a tentative effort at a reconciliation, or at least had temporarily forgotten our quarrel. I remember her chattering on about the German boys in the town hall and how one of them had, as she put it, lured her away from the group to show her a painting of two nearly naked men, and had, as we would say now, "chatted her up", which she seemed to find immensely flattering and exciting.

> *We then looked round the town a bit more and it was quite late by the time we got back to the coach. Typically, the members of staff were the last people back. We stopped once more and saw some cattle with bells round their necks. The German girls started to sing in the coach and it was lovely jogging along to the accompaniment of the cheerful German music. The tune was the same as the record we have in England of a children's choir singing "The Happy Wanderer", so we all joined in too. They taught us the German words and we taught them the English ones, and we even managed some of the harmonies.*

I remember there were several verses, but I can only remember one – in English, not German – together with the unbelievably jolly chorus:

> *"I love to go a-wandering*
> *Along the mountain track,*
> *And as I go I love to sing,*
> *My knapsack on my back.*
> *Val-deri, Val-dera,*
> *Val-deri*
> *Val-dera-ha-ha-ha-ha-ha*
> *Val-deri, Val-dera,*
> *My knapsack on my back."*

Thinking about that song, even after all these years, fills me with a mixture of anticipation, excitement and dread. I was beginning to get anxious that we wouldn't be back in time to see Peter that evening. I had been thinking constantly about seeing him again, with growing excitement. At the same time I remember the feeling of dread at the prospect of Barbara meeting him at last, knowing she would take every opportunity she could of making snide remarks about our relationship.

As we got lower down the steep mountain roads our ears went deaf and it was a most peculiar feeling – it was very difficult to get our hearing back again. The light was beginning to fade when the coach dropped Gudrun, Barbara and me off in Volkmarshausen and Herr Schmidt was cross at first because he thought we must have gone somewhere else after coming back from the Harz.

It was obvious Peter had already arrived at the school house, as we could hear the piano being played upstairs. Barbara raced up in front of us and burst into the room, just as he had finished the final chords of the Brahms rhapsody.

'You must be Peter,' she said, somewhat breathlessly. 'I'm Margaret's friend, Barbara. I've heard such a lot about you!'

He looked somewhat taken aback, but got up from the piano, holding out his hand to shake hers.

By the look on Gudrun's face, she was far from pleased. After she had explained to her father that we had come straight back from the trip to the Harz Mountains, her mother called to her from the kitchen. She gave Barbara another black look and went to help prepare the evening meal. Herr Schmidt followed her. Fritz was sitting at the table engrossed in a book and seemed to be taking no interest in what was happening.

'*Komm mit, Peter,*' said Barbara. 'I want you and Mags to come out into the garden so I can take a photograph of you both together.'

She rummaged in my bag until she found my camera and proceeded to hurry down the stairs.

'Hurry, before it gets too dark.'

Peter looked at me and shrugged his shoulders.

'I'm afraid she's always like this,' I said apologetically. We followed her into the garden.

'Come on, stand here,' said Barbara. 'No, no, closer than that, Peter. Put your arm round her shoulder. Now, smile.'

She clicked the shutter.

'Now,' she said, handing me the camera, 'you must take one of me and Peter.' She took my place beside him, putting her arm through his. And yes, I remember now. I looked through the viewfinder, saw her leaning her head on his shoulder and smiling into the lens. And didn't take the photograph, which explains its absence from the folder of negatives. Barbara was too wrapped up in the moment to notice my act of defiance.

Upstairs, Gudrun and Herr Schmidt were still in the kitchen, so that only Fritz knew we'd left the room. He didn't say anything, but he gave me a slightly rueful smile, as if he understood precisely what I was feeling.

Gudrun, enveloped in her usual pinafore, came out of the kitchen and started to lay the table, one-handedly placing knives and spoons noisily but precisely at each place.

'Can we help?'

'That would be good, Margaret,' she said, rather abruptly. 'It is difficult for me with the bandage on my hand.'

I followed her out of the room, expecting Barbara to come too. But when I returned carrying bread and salad, she and Peter were sitting side-by-side on the piano stool. She looked up at me with what I can only describe as a look of triumph on her face.

'Peter says he will teach me a duet after supper, Mags,' she said smugly.

'But you can't play,' was all I managed to say.

'I only have to play two notes. Peter says it's very easy.'

Peter looked embarrassed and said nothing. He got up from the piano and sat at the table. Barbara followed him, humming rather tunelessly, executing a rather odd, sideways dance step and sat down next to him, placing her arm across the back of his chair. When Gudrun came in from the kitchen again she paused in the doorway, looking at Barbara disbelievingly.

'You must sit over here, Barbara,' she finally said, peremptorily. 'That is my father's place.'

In fact, she had taken Gudrun's own place, next to Peter; Herr Schmidt, I knew by now, always sat at the head of the table. Barbara pushed back her chair noisily and flounced round to the other side of the table.

'Anyway,' she said, leaning forward, putting her elbows on the table and giving Peter one of her dazzling smiles, 'I can see you just as well from here, can't I, Peter?'

I don't think I had ever hated anyone as much as I hated Barbara at that moment. The situation had a kind of dreadful inevitability about it. I had thought that she would limit herself to making pointed remarks to Gudrun about my relationship with Peter. I didn't think she would be interested in Peter for herself, especially bearing in mind her derogatory comments about him.

But it was becoming obvious that her intention was to usurp both Gudrun and me in Peter's affections. I had seen her too many times practising the art of flirtation, to know that I couldn't compete. She had too many well-practised ploys – her ability to capture her quarry's attention by raising her eyebrows, fluttering her eyelashes and widening her intensely blue eyes; her wide smile, her fly-away auburn hair, even her freckles; all were irresistible. Previously, her targets had always been the "spivvy" boys I so despised, boys who would give her "a good time" and who apparently shared her obsession with "Pretty Little Black-eyed Susie", sung by her current heartthrob, Guy Mitchell. Not boys who quoted Romantic poetry and played "boring" music on the piano.

During the meal Peter said very little, even then only in reply to something Herr Schmidt asked him. My only hope was that he would refuse to succumb; that afterwards he would draw me to one side and say how devoted to me he still was. He would touch my cheek, run his hands through my hair and recite some appropriate poetry, at the same time pouring scorn on Barbara's pathetic attempts at seduction. However, I gradually realised that, in spite of his apparent indifference, he was far from being oblivious to her. In fact, he could scarcely keep his eyes from her. And it soon became obvious that she was only too aware of his attention.

Her response was to show off. She started by trying to play the "James, the butler and gnädiges Fräulein von Hügel" game with Fritz. But Fritz refused to join in for long, once again catching my eye. Changing tactics, she proceeded to say what wonderful scenery we had seen that day, when I knew she had scarcely glanced out of the coach window; and what magnificent paintings there were in the art gallery in Goslar, when I knew that all she was interested in were the depictions of the scantily clad mythological characters. All I could do was watch helplessly, a slow, cold feeling of dread seeping through my body.

Gudrun's response was to start telling him in minute detail, in German, how Barbara had been instrumental in making her beloved dog attack her and how painful her hand had been and how she had scarcely slept. Barbara responded by saying, also in German, how very upset she had been at the time, how she too had lain awake, full of guilt at what had happened.

All three of us were playing a complicated, manipulative game, in which I was hoping to come out on top by remaining passive, looking soulful and, I hoped, incurably romantic. And was he worth all the trouble we were taking? With hindsight, the answer is, of course, no. But he was my first and, I thought at the time, my only love, the love of my life. I certainly wasn't going to give up without a fight.

It looked as if Barbara had the upper hand by the end of supper. No one seemed to have noticed that I had hardly eaten anything, and had just been picking at the food in front of me. I knew it wouldn't be long before Peter would have to catch the last bus back to Münden. Time was running out. I hoped Barbara had forgotten the promised duet. But once everyone had finished eating and got up from the table, she seized Peter by the hand, led him to the piano and sat on the stool beside him. To my delight, it soon became obvious that she had no idea even what the notes on the piano were called, for, when Peter told her to play an F sharp, she looked at him blankly. Peter addressed me directly for the first time that day.

'Margaret, you will come and show Barbara what she must do. Sit here, please.'

The duet turned out to be a simple version of "Chopsticks" and I had indeed to play only two notes. I understood immediately what I had to do, much to Barbara's dismay. Even following our demonstration, she was still at a loss. It was one of the few moments of hope and triumph I had that evening.

Barbara soon lost interest. When she got up from the piano stool and stood beside him, Peter began playing a few soft chords up and down the piano; his eyes never left Barbara's face. I stood by the window, mesmerised, unable to speak or move. I could hear the clatter of cutlery from the kitchen as Gudrun and her mother cleared away the supper things; the door to the schoolroom below opening and shutting, as Herr

Schmidt and Fritz busied themselves preparing for the next day's lessons; the dog barking outside in the garden.

Suddenly, Peter got up. 'Now, I must go. The bus will leave shortly.' He came over to where I stood and took my hand tightly in both of his and gave me the briefest of kisses on the cheek. 'Goodbye, Margaret. We will meet again soon, I hope.'

'Oh yes, Peter, I do hope so.' My mouth was dry; I could scarcely get the words out. I wanted to say how much I loved him; that I thought about little else but him; that I wanted him to play just for me; that I wanted him to look into my eyes again, to talk about the peace of the mountains, to say that I was like a flower, his flower. He smiled down at me, but said nothing more. And I knew Barbara was watching my every move.

I suppose, actually, he was hedging his bets. Keeping me in tow. Stringing me along. Just in case.

He went into the kitchen to say goodbye to Gudrun and Frau Schmidt. Barbara and I stared at each other in silence. Then he was back, opening the door, going down the stairs. I still didn't move, but Barbara did. She hurtled down the stairs after him. I could hear them talking to Herr Schmidt outside the window. I turned and looked out, just in time to see Peter and Barbara going out of the gate, down the lane, disappearing from sight. I could only guess what she was saying, what they were doing. But almost immediately she came back and walked quickly towards the house. Had he told her to go away? I doubted it. Had he given her a passionate embrace and kiss? There had hardly been time. I could hear her clumping up the stairs towards me, humming tunelessly to herself.

And I fled up to our bedroom, knowing only that I had to get away. Not even stopping to turn on the light, I threw off my clothes and climbed into bed, pulling the duvet over my head, so that I could scarcely breathe. Too numb to cry, I lay there, not moving, curled round, arms crossed, hugging my shoulders, giving myself some sort of false comfort. Eventually, I heard Barbara come upstairs, put the light on, crash around for a bit, mutter to herself, put the light out, get into bed and start snoring almost immediately. Outside, I could hear an owl hoot and some time later the last frantic shrieks of a small animal, a mouse perhaps.

Now, thirty-five years later, I look back on my young, naive self with a mixture of exasperation and pity. To have had such high expectations of a practically non-existent relationship and then to have been plunged into such a state of hopeless despair seems, with the benefit of experience, the height of folly. And to have let the events of a few days cloud the whole of the rest of my life seems, with hindsight, plainly ridiculous.

I look at the diary again, but all I said was that Peter came for supper again. When did I write it? Certainly not that evening. I also see that there is only one more entry, for the following day. After that, just blank pages. I decide to wait until tomorrow before reading to the end, though. It's getting late and I want to get a good night's sleep…

CHAPTER TEN

PART ONE

Saturday 30th December 1989

...and, unlike the night thirty-five years ago, I sleep soundly and peacefully, until about eight o'clock. My first thought is that Jonathan will be here in two hours. My second is to wonder whether Ruth has changed her mind about leaving Geoffrey. It's only when I see my old diary still open on the bedside table that I remember my German story is approaching its conclusion. And that I've promised to tell Jonathan things I've never told anyone before. Am I ready yet? As ready as I'll ever be, I suppose.

Through my window I can see the boys outside in the garden playing football. Jack, already covered in mud, hurls himself to the ground, picks himself up and hurtles towards William, who calmly kicks the ball past him between the makeshift goalposts. Max is playing his own quiet, independent game, kicking his football backwards and forwards, well away from the hurly-burly.

When I get downstairs, Jane's case is already in the hall and I can hear her talking to Ruth in the kitchen. I gather from Jane's exasperated tone that Ruth has either not made up her mind or has decided to stick it out with Geoffrey after all. I pause in the hall, not quite knowing whether I should interrupt them or not.

'Anyway, Mum, I must be off. I want you to promise you'll phone me this evening. I'm out all day, but I shall be back by six.'

'Yes, darling, I will. I may not have much to say, though.'

I decide it will seem as if I'm eavesdropping if Jane finds me listening at the door when she comes out. Anyway, I want my breakfast. Bella greets me enthusiastically and looks pointedly at her bowl.

'Have they forgotten all about you, you poor old dog? Shall I give her some breakfast, Ruth?'

'Oh, darling, would you? I'm in a bit of a muddle this morning.'

'She's still vacillating, Meg. Not like her at all.' Jane sounds exasperated.

'It's a big step to take,' I say. 'We don't want her to regret what's she's doing.'

'But he's behaved outrageously. She shouldn't put up with it any longer.'

'I am still here, you know, you two,' protests Ruth. 'Anyway, Jane, you must go, or you'll be late.'

'I'm meeting my boss to give him my answer about the move to New York, Meg, then I'm going to see Philip. He's been staying at the flat since the lovely Debbie kicked him out on Wednesday. I'm going to tell him he must find somewhere else to stay until I go away.'

She gives Ruth and then me a hug. We go to the front door with her and watch her drive away round the corner. Back in the kitchen, I give Bella her breakfast then put some bread in the toaster.

'I know Jane thinks I should make a clean break,' Ruth says. 'But our situations are entirely different, aren't they? For a start, I've not really had any life apart from my marriage, so I'm not financially independent like Jane is. Also Geoffrey's not in the remotest bit like Philip. Thank goodness!'

She pauses, pours out coffee for us both.

'We've been through a lot together,' she says, not looking at me. 'And in spite of everything, I'm actually still quite fond of him.'

'You're trying to talk yourself out of leaving, aren't you?'

'I suppose I am – for the time being, at least.'

Having told Ruth last night not to make any hasty decisions, I now find myself feeling inexplicably disappointed that she hasn't; rather like finding out Geoffrey wasn't going to feature on the front page of the *News of the World* after all. Up until now, I had no idea that I have such a penchant for drama and gossip.

I glance at my watch. Nine o'clock.

'What time is he coming?' I might have known Ruth would see me.

'He said about ten.'

'The others are all going to Ian's sister for lunch. I shall have a good think while you're all out. And then, perhaps, a talk with Geoffrey – if I can find him and pin him down, that is. He got up very early and went out. I haven't seen him since.'

The phone rings, making us both jump. Ruth hurries out into the hall.

'Hello, Nick, you're back early.' She sounds puzzled. 'We weren't expecting you till next week.'

Nick is Geoffrey's curate, who has been away since Christmas, visiting his family in Wales.

'Really? He didn't say anything to me. When did he ask you?'

There is a pause.

'I see. Yes, of course. He's not here at the moment. Look, why don't you come round. There's something you ought to know and it's difficult to explain over the phone.'

She hangs up and comes back into the kitchen.

'Apparently,' she says, 'Geoffrey phoned Nick yesterday and asked him to come back early, so he could take the services over the weekend.'

'How odd. Did he say why?'

'He just said that something had cropped up. He wasn't specific. It's pretty obvious, though, that Nick has no idea Geoffrey is leaving.'

'So where do you think Geoffrey is now?'

'If he's gone over to the church, he's been a long time. There aren't any dirty dishes in the sink, so it doesn't look as if he even had any breakfast. Do you think I should start worrying, Meg?'

'Of course not, darling. He'll just wander back in as if nothing has happened.'

The alternative headline "Blackheath Vicar Vanishes" flashes through my mind, but I don't say anything to Ruth.

'Before Nick arrives I think I'll just go and make sure he has actually gone out and isn't still in his study,' she says.

'No sign,' she says when she comes back, 'and his coat and scarf aren't hanging up in the hall. So where the hell has he gone?'

'Well, since we know our Shirley's mixed up in this, perhaps he's gone round there.'

'After what she said to me in the church the other day, I don't feel inclined to phone her to find out.'

'Would you like me to speak to her?'

'I don't think we ought to make too much of a fuss – not yet anyway. Tell Shirley, and before we can turn round, we'll have search parties combing the heath.'

The doorbell rings.

'That'll be Nick. Best not to tell him we don't actually know where Geoffrey is at the moment. But I think he deserves at least to know what is now public knowledge. Before the Angels of Mercy descend on him *en masse*, poor chap.'

'I'll leave you to talk to him and I'll make sure the boys don't barge in.'

I can hear Ruth greeting Nick affectionately. He has been in the parish less than a year and Ruth has taken him under her wing to a certain extent. He is a diffident, rather earnest young man and already has his own group of devoted Angels of Mercy, all somewhat younger than Geoffrey's. Apparently they almost came to blows about where he was to eat his Christmas lunch. Ruth leads him straight into the sitting room and shuts the door. I tidy up the kitchen and watch the boys through the window. Still over half an hour before Jonathan is due to arrive.

There's a sound at the front door and for a moment I think Geoffrey has come back, but it's the paper being delivered, so I go into the hall to pick it up. "Victory at last for Havel" it proclaims, over a picture of a triumphant new Czech president. Underneath another the headline says "Romanian Army is now in full control". I'm reminded of the Hungarian Revolution in 1956 and the Prague Spring twelve years later and can't help wondering whether we are getting our hopes up too soon about the apparent disintegration of the Soviet Union. Perhaps the euphoria and optimism will be shattered yet again in a few months' time. It could be just like China earlier this year. But because the struggle for independence is happening in so many places at once, this time it may actually succeed.

After I came back from Germany, I completely lost touch with everyone in Volkmarshausen. So I have no idea what became of any of them, or even whether they are still alive. How did the Altmeyer family cope with the death of their son? Herr and Frau Altmeyer may well have died by now, but presumably Helga eventually got on with her life. What must she be thinking now? The opening up of the Berlin Wall will surely have brought back the most painful of memories for her.

I'm brought back to the present as, almost simultaneously, the boys crash into the kitchen from the garden, Ruth and Nick come out of the sitting room and the doorbell goes.

'Hello, Jonathan,' I hear Ruth say. 'Meg's in the kitchen, I think.'

'I'm a bit early, I'm afraid.'

At the sound of his voice, I feel a little lurch inside me of – what? Excitement, anticipation? When he comes in, I'm smiling to myself with happiness.

'Hello, Uncle Jonathan! Have you come to take Auntie Meg out again?'

'Yes, Jack, I have. Do you mind?'

Jack looks uncharacteristically nonplussed and shrugs his shoulders.

'Where are you taking her?'

'To see my mother.'

'She must be very old.'

'She's getting on for a hundred.'

'Wow! Can I come too?'

'Sorry, old chap, not today. Another time perhaps.'

'You said that last time.'

During this exchange, Max comes quietly up to Jonathan, takes his hand, leans his head against Jonathan's leg and puts his thumb in his mouth. I remember noticing, during the kite flying expedition on Boxing Day, how totally at ease Jonathan was when the children crowded round him. I think he is one of those rare people who are able to attract young people without any apparent effort. My father was the same; when Jane and Helen were tiny, they would clamber all over him whenever they saw him. They were far closer to him than they ever were to Geoffrey, who would often ignore his daughters for days on end, then suddenly try far too hard to join in their games, tickle them until they felt sick or throw them up in the air just before bedtime.

'Shall we be off?' Jonathan smiles down at me.

As I go to get my coat, Ruth is standing in the hall, looking worried.

'It's obvious Geoffrey hasn't said anything to Nick about going. He seems genuinely sorry – and shocked, I think.'

'Did you tell him why he's leaving?'

'No, I didn't. That's up to Geoffrey, isn't it? He's got to take his head out from the sand soon and sweep the dust back out from under the carpet.'

'To mix your idioms,' I reply.

I'm pleased to see Ruth manages a rueful smile.

'If you don't mind,' I say, putting on my coat, 'I'll fill Jonathan in with the latest developments as we go. Are you sure you'll be all right, Ruth?' She looks pale and drawn.

'Of course I will, darling. Now, off you go – and have a lovely day.'

'Promise me you'll let me know when he gets back.' Jonathan comes out to join us in the hall. 'Could you give Ruth your sister's phone number, do you think? I'll explain why on the way.'

'I'll write down my mother's number too. We'll probably be there about teatime, I should think.'

'This is about Geoffrey, I suppose?' says Jonathan, as we get into the car.

'Yes. He seems to have disappeared. He went out early this morning, having asked Nick – you know, his curate – to take the weekend services. Poor chap had gone to spend New Year with his parents. I think Ruth is more worried than she's admitting.'

Jonathan leans over and gives me a quick kiss. For a moment, we look at each other, smiling.

'I think,' says Jonathan, as he starts the car, 'we ought to forget all about Geoffrey for a bit and concentrate on ourselves. Don't you?'

'That would be really nice,' I say, settling back into my seat. 'You must tell me some more about your family before we get there.'

'Well, my sister's called Rachel and she's been married to David for over thirty years. He's a solicitor in Colchester – a really nice chap, you'll like him. They've got four grown-up daughters and three grandchildren already. I'm not sure how many of them will be there today.'

'Goodness, it sounds a rather overwhelming. I must say, I feel a bit worried about meeting so many of them in one go.'

'I can guarantee they'll love you.'

'What have you told them about me?' I say, cautiously.

'I spoke to my mother on the phone yesterday. I just said that I wanted her to meet someone who I hope will play an important part in my life from now on. Is that all right?'

'That is very all right.'

Because Jonathan is concentrating on driving and not able to look at me, I feel we are both able to say more than we could face to face.

'What I should have said,' he went on, 'but didn't, is that I feel more attracted to this someone than I have to anyone for a very long time. And that I've been thinking about her ever since I met her.'

'And I could tell your mother that her son has made me feel things I never thought I would.'

'Nice feelings, I hope?'

I glance at Jonathan and see he is smiling to himself.

'Extraordinary feelings. Feelings I never thought existed.'

'I think my mother might be a bit startled if we launch into a conversation like that straightaway!'

We stop at some traffic lights. He turns towards me and kisses me on the lips. I can see the two young men in the car beside us grinning.

'Concentrate on your driving, Mr Jacobs. The lights are green.'

As he drives on, I look at him and have an overwhelming feeling of affection.

'I think,' I say after a while, 'that I ought to tell you a bit more about my time in Germany. At least get you up to date with what I've been reading in my diary.'

'Only if you don't think it'll be too traumatic.'

'Actually, I think it will be cathartic. Let's hope it'll get it out of my system once and for all.'

For a moment, I wonder where to start.

'During the few days I'd known Peter, I'd become absolutely obsessed with him; I could scarcely think of anything else. It had nothing to do with any sexual feelings, really. It just reinforced my belief in the existence of Romantic love. I'd got this notion that once you had met your soul mate, that was it. Neither of you would want anyone else ever again. And I really did think Peter was my soul mate. It was all mixed up with Romantic poetry of course, with nature and solitude. So when Peter started to quote Heine and Goethe to me, I immediately jumped to the conclusion that he felt the same way.'

The traffic is building up as we approach the Dartford Tunnel and we slow to a crawl for a while.

'I suppose in the normal course of events, my feelings would just have fizzled out, like all schoolgirl crushes do.'

'So what happened?'

'My friend Barbara happened. You remember I told you about the young man who was shot trying to cross into the West? Well, Barbara was staying with his family, so after we got the news of his death, she moved into the schoolhouse with me and shared my room. I was already beginning to realise that she was actually not a very nice person. She couldn't bear anyone else to have the upper hand. When she got to know about Peter, I suppose she just decided she wanted him for herself. And she was very attractive; not beautiful, or even pretty really, but she just had to look at a boy and he didn't stand a chance. So when she met Peter, that was the beginning of the end as far as I was concerned.'

'Poor old you.'

'From the perspective of now, it just seems so silly, but I thought it was the end of the world. There was more to come, though.'

I pause. I haven't read that bit of my diary yet and wonder how much I actually wrote about what happened that Sunday. Not much, if the previous entries are anything to go by, but I'm sure I shall be able to relive that day in minute detail without much help.

'Would you rather wait?'

'I think I would, if you don't mind. I'd like to concentrate on now – which I must say I'm rather enjoying!'

'Good.'

He glances at me, smiling, and takes my hand. We continue in silence for a while. By this time we're approaching the A12 and Colchester is already on the signs. I suddenly feel a slight pang of nervousness and realise that I'm worried that I won't make a good impression. And I really do want to make a good impression.

As we turn off the M25, the traffic thins out and we begin to speed up. Jonathan is a fast driver, but I feel completely safe. None of the involuntary stepping on imaginary brakes I find myself doing when Geoffrey is driving. Like most of the things my brother-in-law does, he drives extremely erratically, to say the least. I glance at my watch. It's only half past ten; at this rate we shall arrive much too soon. Jonathan notices.

'I know, we're early, but I wanted to get you to myself again. I thought we might stop somewhere near Chelmsford for coffee and a bit of a stroll.'

'That would be nice.'

'In fact, we've probably got time to go to Maldon. I think you'll like it. Lots of old boats and nice views.'

'I don't know Essex at all.'

'It's a very underrated county, I think. There are some very pretty villages and unusual churches.'

As we reach the outskirts of Chelmsford, Jonathan signals and turns off the main road. We drive through a couple of villages until we reach Maldon. He stops the car down by the river.

'This is the River Blackwater. Let's stretch our legs first before we find somewhere for coffee.'

He takes my hand and we walk along the towpath. There are several Thames barges moored three deep along the quay. Apart from an elderly man painting a large, gaff-rigged wooden boat, there is hardly anyone about. The sky seems vast and the air has an almost translucent quality. Only the plaintive sounds of seabirds break the silence.

'This is perfect,' is all I can manage to say.

'The sort of place to retire to, perhaps? As long as it's with the right person.'

'You're surely not old enough to retire yet, are you?'

'Well, not really, no, but it's a nice idea. I'll be fifty-seven next year, though.'

We walk back along the river and decide to go into The Queen's Head for coffee.

'I came one year with my sister's family to watch the Maldon Mud Race,' Jonathan says.

I giggle. 'What on earth is that?'

'Well, it started in the seventies, I think. Apparently the landlord here was challenged to serve a meal on the mud flats and it soon developed into a free for all. Everyone dashes over the river, through the mud and back and they all get absolutely filthy. We just watched. Anyway, I believe it was the last race this year for some reason. Probably all very unhygienic.'

We look at some photos of very muddy looking people on the walls of the bar. Our coffee arrives and we sit by the window and look out at the river. And talk and talk. I learn that his birthday is in March, he learns that mine is in September. We discover he went to school only a few miles from where I lived as a child and decide we might have passed each other on our regular bicycle rides round the Dorset lanes. We find out that we both spent childhood holidays in Cornwall and that he might have been playing cricket on the beach while I was still at the sandcastle stage.

By the time we get back in the car and set off again for Colchester, I can't believe we've known each other for just a few days. My life back in Dorset – school, friends, my house and garden – already seems remote. Perhaps once I get back home and into the familiar routine, today will just seem a distant memory too. I realise I don't want this to end. But the nagging doubt remains at the back of my mind. I'm not really sure at the moment whether I want to change the whole course of my life. Not that Jonathan has asked me to, of course, but I decide I ought to be prepared. To know what my answer will be if he does.

We don't go back on to the A12, but for the remainder of the journey drive through the Essex countryside, passing through some attractive villages and small towns. Jonathan's sister and her husband live on the outskirts of Colchester, so we arrive sooner than I expect and pull into the drive of a large detached house. Before we can reach the door, it's thrown open and a small girl rushes out.

'Come on, Uncle Jonathan!' she says. She seizes him by the hand and tries to drag him into the house. 'Come and see our new puppy.'

'This,' says Jonathan, turning to me, laughing, 'is Ellie. Ellie, say hello to Meg.'

'Hello Meg. Do you like puppies?'

'I certainly do, Ellie.'

'Come on then.'

We follow her through the hall and out to a conservatory where an enthusiastic chocolate brown spaniel puppy hurls itself at us.

'Down, Poppy!' The voice behind me is authoritative. 'Hello, Meg. Lovely to see you. Go through. I'm sorry about the chaos.'

I can see immediately that this is Jonathan's sister. She has his dark hair, his brown eyes, his smile.

'Lunch is nearly ready. I'm just going to rescue the potatoes, but David will get you a drink. He's around somewhere. Mother's in the sitting room.'

Jonathan gives my hand a quick squeeze as we go in. And there, sitting quietly in the corner, is a frail, bright-eyed, elderly lady.

'Mother, this is Meg.'

She looks up at me and holds out her hands. They feel thin, cool and surprisingly strong, as I take them in mine.

'My dear, I'm so pleased to meet you. You'll have to forgive me for not getting up. Sit here beside me and let me look at you. I'm afraid I can't see too well now – such a bore – but Jonathan was certainly right about you.'

Her voice is firm, her accent totally English, apart from the slightly guttural pronunciation of the letter "r", which betrays her German origins. I find it difficult to believe she is in her late nineties.

'We'll have plenty of time to talk later,' she says to me, conspiratorially, patting my hand. 'I've lost count how many of my family are here at the moment. My granddaughter

Hannah and her family called in this morning, but they've had to go somewhere else for lunch. So I think it's just Judy, Patrick and Ellie now – and the dog of course.'

'Hello, you old quack!' I turn to see a tall, balding man standing in the doorway.

'Judge!' Jonathan goes over to shake his hand. 'Meg, this is David. I try to boost his ego and he tries to take me down a peg or two.'

'We're so pleased you could come, Meg. What will you have to drink? I've started on the red wine myself, but we have all the usual things, I think.'

'A glass of wine would be lovely, thank you.'

'What about you, Jonathan?'

'The same, thanks David. I shan't be driving for a bit.'

'Lunch is ready.' Rachel stands in the doorway, glass in hand.

We take our drinks through into the dining room.

'Meg, you sit here, next to me,' says David. 'Jonathan, you can have her back later. Now, let's get the introductions over with. This is my daughter, Judy, and the rather dissolute looking chap next to her is my son-in-law, Patrick. I think you've already met Ellie.'

The talk at first over lunch is about people I don't know.

I let the conversation drift on around me. I'm beginning to wonder why I ever thought I might feel intimidated.

'Sorry, Meg, you must think us very rude,' says Rachel. 'We haven't seen each other for a bit, so we need to catch up. How was Christmas, Jonathan? You went to Rob's, didn't you?'

'It was fine. I didn't go to his in-laws on Boxing Day, though. I found I couldn't quite face them. As you know, I find it very difficult to work out who they all are when they have one of their huge family get-togethers. They're the sort of family, Meg, who give each other the most ridiculous nicknames, like "Smudge" and "Boodles", so I always feel as if I've wandered into a meeting of a rather exclusive club. Anyway, I got a much more enticing invitation, and I'm sure they hardly noticed I wasn't there.'

'Do we gather, Meg, that his invitation was something to do with you?' Rachel smiles at me across the table.

'It was my sister Ruth's idea, but I must admit I think she had an ulterior motive!'

'And do we also gather, Jonathan, that it worked?'

Jonathan laughs, and looks over to me. 'I think it probably did – at least I hope so.'

I'm starting to feel embarrassed, so am quite relieved when Rachel changes the subject.

'How's Sarah?'

'She's still staying at Rob's at the moment, then she's going to a party tomorrow in Birmingham, but I think she'll be home for a few days next week.'

The phone rings and Rachel goes to answer it. It occurs to me it could be Ruth, and I'm right.

'It's for you, Meg. It's your sister.'

'Excuse me,' I say, getting up and going into the hall.

'He's back, darling,' says Ruth.

'And?'

'I just wanted to let you know, that's all. I don't want to interrupt your day.'

'But he's all right?'

'Sort of, yes. I'll tell you later. It's a bit complicated. Anyway, he's not run away, or jumped off the church roof, or anything. See you this evening.' And she rings off. I don't know whether to be relieved, disappointed or even more worried. I decide I'm not going to dwell on it. Time enough later today. I go back and sit down. Jonathan looks at me enquiringly.

'It's all right, he's back. Sorry, everyone, it's a long story. My brother-in-law's having a few problems, that's all.'

I look round the table at them all. I seem to have known them forever. Feel affection, love even, towards them. Want to be part of this warm, welcoming family. Jonathan smiles at me and I smile back. So this is what it's like to be truly happy.

After lunch, Jonathan, David, Patrick, Ellie and I take the dog for a quick walk over the fields at the back of the house. Jonathan takes my hand and it feels the most natural thing in the world.

'Your mother never ceases to amaze me, Jonathan,' David says as we negotiate a muddy patch in the grass. 'No sign of flagging at all over Christmas, apart from a slight tendency to nod off after about nine o'clock. But then I do that all the time.'

'She finds it very frustrating that she can't see to play bridge any more. She and my father used to play every week with a group of friends, Meg. Feelings used to run very high sometimes.'

We are distracted for a while, as the dog finds a particularly muddy puddle to sit in and then proceeds to shake herself all over Ellie, much to the little girl's delight. By the time we get back, the light is already fading.

'I think we'll make a move soon,' says Jonathan. 'Is that all right with you, Mother?'

'Whatever you say, darling. I'm ready when you are. I'm all packed.'

I realise I don't want to go. It's partly a feeling of dread because I know that as soon as I'm back at the vicarage, I shall be absorbed with Geoffrey and Ruth's problems. I've hardly given them thought since I spoke to Ruth at lunchtime and I feel a slight pang of guilt. Mostly it's because any doubts I had about whether I want to change the whole course of my life have evaporated. I know what my answer will be if Jonathan asks me to do just that. I watch him as he listens to something David is saying. I know already that, when he laughs, the creases down his cheeks will be rather lopsided. He has one on the right hand side, but the one on the left divides halfway down. I want to lean over and run my fingers down them.

It's dark by the time we go outside to get into the car. Jonathan's mother insists I sit in the front, as if it's already my official place.

'I can't really hear what people are saying whilst we're going along,' she says, when I protest. 'And anyway, I can nod off in the back without anyone noticing.'

'Take care, darling,' says Rachel, hugging her mother. 'We'll see you next week.'

We sit in comfortable silence for some time. There is very little traffic and we soon reach the M25, this time turning north.

'I realise I don't know where you live, Mrs Jacobs,' I say, turning round to see that the old lady is very far from dozing off.

'My dear, that's far too formal. Why don't you do what David does and call me Helga. I'm afraid I moved into what they call sheltered accommodation a few years ago. It's near where I used to live – in Woodford Green. I've got my own kitchen, so I can be completely independent still, but there's a dining room in the main building if I don't want to bother cooking. It suits me very well, although I must say, I feel guilty having to ask people to do things for me.'

'What she really means, Meg,' says Jonathan, 'is that she can't bear to be told what to do.'

'Quite right, too,' I say. 'I hope I look half as well as you do when I'm in my nineties.'

'I'm sure you will, my dear. You've got the cheekbones. You don't know how lucky you are. A lot of people would give their eye teeth for your cheekbones.'

I know I must be blushing. I don't think anyone has ever said that to me before. I'm relieved when we drive into a large courtyard and stop in front of a low block of flats.

'You'll have to heave me out, I'm afraid, Jonathan. It's just one of the frustrations about getting old, my dear. I used to leap out of cars with no trouble at all a few years ago.'

She takes my arm while Jonathan gets her case out of the boot and opens the door of the flat. Inside, she leads me into her sitting room. The furniture, which I assume is from the family home, is on rather too large a scale for the room, which makes it look overcrowded. There are family photographs on every available surface and a collection of expensive looking china in one of the cabinets.

'Now, Meg, tell me all about yourself, while Jonathan goes and puts the kettle on.'

Jonathan shrugs and goes into the kitchen. I can hear him rattling cups and opening cupboard doors, while I try to summarise my life so far in a few sentences. She looks at me closely and unblinkingly while I'm talking, which I find rather disconcerting, until I realise she is rather more hard of hearing than she cares to admit and that she is probably partially lip-reading, not trying to read my mind. As I tell her about school, my house, visits to the theatre, concerts, it all sounds very banal.

She leans across and puts her hand on mine.

'You seem to have made a successful, interesting life for yourself, my dear.'

'But a very dull one, I'm afraid.'

'There were certainly times when I could have done with a bit of dullness. I don't know how much Jonathan has told you?'

'I know he was born in Germany and that you all came here before the war.'

'It wasn't an easy decision to make. And the worry didn't

stop there. During the early part of the war, there was a real danger that if the Nazis invaded, the persecution would start all over again. The name Jacobssohn would have given us away immediately, so my husband insisted we changed it to Jay. Cowardly, you might think, but practical. It was only afterwards we changed it back again, but decided to call ourselves just plain Jacobs.'

She pauses. From the kitchen comes the sound of rattling crockery, followed by a muttered curse as Jonathan drops a spoon on to the floor. We smile at each other. Tea is obviously going to be a little while. She becomes conspiratorial and lowers her voice a little.

'I'm sure he's already told you about Anna, but he probably didn't tell you that actually things between them hadn't been very good for some time. I was very fond of her, but she could be – well, I suppose "bossy" would be the word to use. They never said anything, of course, but we all sensed it.'

'No,' I say. 'He didn't tell me, but he did say he had some sort of breakdown after she died.'

'I have my own theory about that. I think it was because, after the initial shock, he realised he actually felt much happier without her. He's never said anything, of course, but I think in the end he couldn't cope with bottling up the feeling of guilt.

'But he seems fine now,' I say.

'Yes, he is, but he doesn't seem to have a real purpose in his life. So, Rachel and I agreed while you were all out for your walk, that you are the sort of calm, orderly person he needs to help him move on to the next stage of his life.'

'Have you told Jonathan?' I can't hide my surprise at this unexpected twist.

'No, no, of course not and you mustn't tell him. I just wanted you to know, my dear, that when he says something to you, we will all approve.'

I can't suppress a smile. It's beginning to seem rather too much like an arranged marriage – and I can't help noticing the word "when", not "if".

Jonathan appears in the doorway with the tea tray. He gives us both a quizzical look.

'You two both look very conspiratorial,' he says, pouring the tea. 'What have you been hatching up?'

'Nothing that concerns you, dear. Meg's just been telling me about life in Dorset.'

Jonathan looks doubtful, but doesn't comment further. As we sip our tea, it is evident that Mrs Jacobs – I can't quite bring myself to think of her as Helga – takes a keen interest in what's happening in the world, in particular the dismantling of the Berlin Wall.

'I've lived through so many changes and been on so many sides, I've become rather cynical in my old age. I just hope this will be the end of all the squabbling, but I'm afraid it won't be.'

Jonathan gets up and takes the tray back to the kitchen.

'Now, is there anything you need me to do before we go, Mother?' he asks when he comes back.

'No thank you, dear. I shall have a spot of supper then put my feet up in front of the television. You two run along.'

She insists on seeing us to the door, hugs us both in turn and kisses us on both cheeks.

'Now, my dear, make sure Jonathan brings you to see me again very soon.'

'I would like that very much,' I say, taking her hand. She stands at the door and watches us drive away.

But I'm supposed to be going home next week. Term starts the week after next and then I'll be plunged into my previous existence. It seems as if I'll be going back to someone else's life. Then there's the Geoffrey problem. Where had he been? And what did Ruth mean when she said he was "sort of" all right?

'Would you rather go back to the vicarage?' Jonathan must have been reading my mind. 'I had been thinking we could go home and have a boiled egg or something, but I don't think you'll be able to relax until you know what's happened, will you?'

'Would you mind?'

'As long as you let me lure you away again tomorrow.'

He switches on the radio and the car is suddenly filled with the most ravishing unaccompanied choral music.

'Tallis,' says Jonathan immediately. 'Forty part motet. The choir sang it in October with a few extra singers.'

We listen in silence, waves of sound engulfing us.

The vicarage is silent when we get back. Helen and her family are obviously still at her in-laws. Ruth comes into the hall.

'I'll leave you two together,' says Jonathan.

'No, no, please Jonathan,' says Ruth. 'I'd like your opinion about what's happened.'

We go into the sitting room. Jonathan and I sit on the sofa. He takes my hand and gives it a squeeze.

'Geoffrey's in his study,' says Ruth, standing over by the window. 'Can't bring himself to face you. He wants me to tell you everything. Same old Geoffrey, isn't it? Head in sand as usual.'

She starts to pace up and down. 'Would you believe that he's actually been let out on bail? He was at the police station this morning. Didn't tell me of course. They've charged him with embezzlement.'

'Oh, Ruth, darling, no.'

I'm immediately ashamed of the thought that involuntarily flashes through my mind – that the *News of the World* will have a field day.

'I never thought it would come to this.' Ruth is close to tears. 'I suppose I thought we could find a way of paying the money back and hush it up somehow. The auditors insisted it went further, though. And the stupid thing is that dear Shirley, apparently, hasn't been charged with anything.'

She looks at us directly for the first time.

'Of course, there's no question of my not standing by him now. Do you know, he actually broke down in tears when he came back from the police station? Kept on saying how sorry he was. I had to resist the temptation to say it was a bit late for that now. His solicitor doesn't think for a moment that he'll actually have to go to prison. The worst that can happen is that he'll get a suspended sentence.'

I'm stunned. Stupid, stupid man, I want to say. How dare he put Ruth through all this. But Jonathan seems in his element. He takes charge, gets up, pours Ruth a whisky, sits her down, puts a log on the fire and goes out of the room. Ruth and I sit looking at one another. We can hear him go into Geoffrey's study and shut the door. As Ruth sips her drink, the colour gradually returns to her face. Within a minute, the door opens again and Jonathan comes back, followed by Geoffrey, who looks only slightly sheepish, more like a naughty schoolboy caught pocketing a few sweets than someone being charged with misappropriating the organ fund.

Ruth launches into him straightaway, as if continuing on from their previous conversation. Her tone is firm and matter-of-fact.

'And there's another thing, Geoffrey. If we're going to support you through this, you mustn't hide anything else. Are you absolutely sure that you've told us everything we need to know?'

'Of course I have, darling.' Geoffrey sounds decidedly hurt.

Why don't I quite believe him? Is it because he's not looking directly at Ruth as he speaks? Or is it something about the set of his mouth, the movement of his eyes? I know that look. It's the look I get from certain known troublemakers at school, when they deny even the most trivial of misdemeanours.

'One thing I need to know pretty urgently is how long we've got before we have to move out of the vicarage. Do I have to order the packing cases straight away?'

'Don't be like that, darling. I'm sure the bishop will be reasonable about it.'

'Yes, he's a very reasonable man, but presumably he also wouldn't be too happy for you to carry on taking the services as if nothing's happened?'

'I really don't know, darling. Let's see what happens, shall we?'

'No, Geoffrey. I've been waiting all my life to see what happens. I'm not prepared to wait any longer.'

I'm beginning to suspect that Ruth wants Jonathan and me here, not to join in the discussion, but just to act as witnesses. I wouldn't put it past Geoffrey to deny certain vital parts of his story later on.

'If the worst comes to the worst, we can go to the cottage, or there's your mother's flat.'

'I've already told you. I'm not prepared to go to Wales. And since Meg owns half of mother's flat, she may not be prepared to let us live there.'

I open my mouth to say something, but Ruth ploughs on.

'In fact, I've got an idea. You go to Wales and I'll go to the flat.'

The dialogue seems to have come to an abrupt halt. Ruth suddenly looks exhausted and Geoffrey looks so miserable, I almost, though not quite, feel sorry for him.

'What I think we all need,' says Jonathan eventually, 'is something to eat. Meg and I will go into the kitchen and see what we can rustle up.'

'Oh, would you? You're an angel, Jonathan.'

And so, when Helen and her family get back from Ian's sister's, the four of us are eating scrambled eggs in front of the fire, all conversation exhausted. Jack is as exuberant as ever as he rushes into the room.

'We got more presents at Auntie Beth's. I got a new train for my railway, Granddad!'

'Not now, Jack,' says Helen, looking quizzically at Ruth, who shrugs her shoulders. They both go out of the room and I can hear them talking in the kitchen.

'That's excellent, old chap. You must show me properly tomorrow.' Geoffrey has suddenly metamorphosed into his role of the genial grandfather. 'What did you get, Will?'

'Auntie Beth said she didn't quite know what to get me, so I've got a book token.'

'Splendid, old man. You'll have great fun choosing.'

Ian puts his head round the door, carrying a very sleepy Max.

'I'm just going to put this one to bed. He can hardly keep his eyes open.'

Bella ambles in wagging her tail, greets the boys, then follows them out of the room and into the kitchen. It's once again as if nothing untoward has happened at all. Just a domestic, family scene.

But once he is left alone with Jonathan and me, Geoffrey leans forward in his chair and puts on a concerned expression.

'I know I've been pretending not to take my predicament seriously, but believe you me, Meg, I've had some sleepless nights recently. Trying to work out a way of getting out of this, without upsetting Ruth.'

'I don't really think you've succeeded, Geoffrey.' I don't even attempt to keep the note of sarcasm out of my voice. 'I think you ought to know that Ruth came very close to walking out on you yesterday. And if she had, I would have supported her without any hesitation whatsoever.'

Geoffrey sighs and puts his head in his hands. Then leans towards us again.

'You have my word, Meg, that I'll do everything I can to make things easy for Ruth from now on, but I suppose there is just one more thing. Something which, as they say in court, may be taken into consideration. I just couldn't bring myself to worry Ruth with it just now.'

It emerges that Geoffrey does in fact have something more to get off his chest. It turns out that our supposition about why he resigned so suddenly from the legal practice all those years ago was right after all. He had indeed "borrowed" quite a considerable sum from the clients' fund – "just for a few days". And of course, it was for the most altruistic of motives. Not for himself at all. Just for one his clients, another distressed widow. When his partners found out what he'd done, Geoffrey was just about to pay the money back into the account, the distressed widow's house having been satisfactorily sold in the nick of time. However, by mutual agreement, they thought it best if Geoffrey quietly resigned, rather than making the whole thing public.

'Really rather decent of them, don't you think? Anyway, it wouldn't have done the firm any good to make a fuss.'

I don't think I can sit here anymore, without saying something I'll regret. I get up, walk to the window and look out into the darkness. I suddenly feel so tired that it all seems unreal. Jonathan joins me and puts his arm round my shoulder.

'I think we've all had enough for today. I'll come round for you tomorrow morning. Say about half past nine?'

'Yes, please. I'd like that.'

'Say goodnight to Ruth for me, will you, and let her know that if there's anything I can do, she only has to ask.'

'That's sweet of you. Thank you.'

'I do have an ulterior motive, you know!'

We're whispering. Jonathan puts a finger to his lips, and I manage a guilty smile.

'I'm off now, Geoffrey,' he says out loud.

'Right.' Geoffrey pauses. 'And thank you Jonathan. You were right.'

We go out into the hall and I shut the door.

'What did you say to him in his study?'

'Just told him he'd feel much better if he faced up to what he'd done and got everything off his chest.'

When he's gone, I stand in the hall for a while, the feeling of his brief kiss still on my lips. And think how extraordinarily lucky I am. Then go into the kitchen to deliver Jonathan's message to Ruth. Helen has gone upstairs to put the boys to bed and Ruth is sitting by herself at the kitchen table.

'I'm sorry, Meg, I haven't asked you how your day was.'

'Don't worry, darling. I'll tell you all about it tomorrow.'

'No, tell me now. It might take my mind off things.'

'Well, they're all lovely – and his mother is amazing.'

'Did they approve of you?'

I smile to myself, remembering what Jonathan's mother said to me. 'Yes, apparently they did.'

'Good,' says Ruth. 'That's at least one bit of good news today.'

I pause for a moment. 'I think you need to ask Geoffrey if he's got anything else to tell you, because he did come clean just now about his reason for going into the church.'

'I think we'd guessed what it was anyway. Were we right?'

I nod and give her a hug.

'Anyway, I'm going up now. It's been a long day. And you look absolutely all in, Ruth. Geoffrey's still in the sitting room.'

Upstairs, I realise it's time to confront my German diary again before I go to sleep, although I suspect the entry for the next day will say absolutely nothing about the really important things…

PART TWO

Friday 20th August 1954

…and I'm right. There is no mention of my sleepless night either. Eventually I must have dropped off, because when I woke up the bed beside me was empty and I could hear Barbara's voice drifting up from downstairs.

> *In the morning we went to school with Gudrun. The lesson was scripture but I couldn't understand much – I think they were doing something to do with the Huguenots.*

Then yet another incident I had forgotten.

> *Because I am one of the few girls to have my own passport, I had to go to the bank with Miss Smithson and change some money. I didn't realise I was supposed to bring my passport with me, but the girl in the bank must have thought I looked honest because she said it didn't matter. Miss Smithson said that when she went just after we arrived, the bank clerk took ages comparing her photograph on her passport before she would let her have the money. Afterwards she took me to the Café Obst for coffee.*

I think Miss Smithson must have realised something was wrong. Perhaps she thought I'd got a temperature again, because she seemed quite concerned. I tried to assure her I was perfectly all right, but she didn't seem convinced. She asked me if anything had happened to upset me. Of course I said nothing, but remember feeling acutely embarrassed. I stood up and said I had to go back to Volkmarshausen and have my midday meal, otherwise I couldn't get back in time for the afternoon. We were going for a walk in the woods above the town and had to meet at the *Jugendhaus* at half past two. Some of the teachers from the school were coming with us and I think the object was to practise our German conversation.

Barbara and I had not spoken a word to each other that morning. Travelling back to the village on the train for lunch, Barbara went to sit with Werner, one of the boys who had come to the dancing with us the previous Sunday. She was on great form and I could hear her shrieking with laughter at something he said. I sat staring out of the window. In my mind's eye I could see Peter playing soft chords on the piano yesterday evening, his eyes never leaving Barbara's face; I could feel the brief touch of his lips on my cheek as he said goodbye; and I could see them disappearing down the path together when he went for his bus.

After lunch Barbara ran upstairs, muttering she had to get ready. Fritz came and sat next to me at the table. In front of me, my plate of food was almost untouched. He obviously knew exactly what was wrong.

'It is not good to be upset, Margaret,' he said softly. 'When you return to England, you will soon forget him.'

I could feel tears starting but was determined not to let anyone see how upset I was.

'And Barbara will forget him even sooner, you know. It means nothing to her.'

Fritz briefly put his hand on my shoulder. We could hear Barbara clattering down the stairs. She had changed out of the clothes she had been wearing in the morning and was wearing a bright red, full skirt, nipped in at the waist by a wide elastic belt with a metal clasp, and topped with a tight fitting white satin blouse. It was hardly what you would wear for a walk in the woods, so perhaps she wasn't coming with us. Had she made an assignation with Peter, or Werner perhaps? She left the house with me, flounced up the path to the station in front of me, got on to the train and then joined the other girls waiting outside the *Jugendhaus* in Münden.

We were going to walk to the Autobahn, through some woods. We climbed up quite high and looked down on Hann. Münden – it was a lovely view, but too misty to take a photograph. Miss Smithson and Harry strode out in front and Fräulein Schaefer and Belladonna were walking arm-in-arm at the back of the group. It was very slippery as we went downhill the other side and some of us fell over in the mud. Through a gap in the trees we could see the Autobahn, which is a very wide road, like a dual carriageway, only much wider and goes on for miles and miles and is usually straight. Apparently the main danger is that drivers often go to sleep while they are driving because it is so monotonous.

I had forgotten that, until the late fifties, there were no motorways in Britain, so the Autobahn was obviously a novelty and worth a special trip.

I took a photograph of it and then we went down further to a café called The Werrahaus. By now we were below the Autobahn and could see the bridge, called the Werrabrücke, under which the River Werra flows. On one of the brick supports are two figures – one representing a man who made the bridge and the other the man who designed it.

I get out the photographs and find a rather lopsided view of a fairly wide dual carriageway disappearing into the distance towards the hills. A solitary car is driving along it and a temporary sign on the side of the road announces *"Bauarbeiten"* – "Road Works". Why does this photograph give me a feeling of dread? Partly, I suppose, because of the association with my despair over the Peter and Barbara situation.

I suddenly remember the recurring dream I had for several years after returning home. I was always on the river below the bridge, sitting in some sort of boat – a junk perhaps. I knew there were people behind me, but I could never turn round to see who they were, though I knew they were the enemy. Suddenly there was a great roar and the figures on the bridge came crashing down into the water below. Huge cracks began to appear in the bridge itself until it too came crashing down. There was never any more to the dream than that, but the feeling of utter panic and confusion would always remain with me long after I'd woken up.

It was while everyone was sitting outside the café drinking coffee and eating cake, that I realised I hadn't seen Barbara since we arrived. At first I thought she must have gone inside the café. But no, when we set off again she was nowhere to be seen. I suppose she must have told someone she wasn't coming back with us, because no one remarked on her absence or suggested we should wait for her. We walked back a different way and as we rounded each corner I tried to convince myself that she would be waiting for us, that my fears about an assignation with Peter were unfounded. My head began to spin, my mouth to go dry, my legs to tremble. Needless to say, my diary says nothing of this.

After about fifteen minutes we reached the outskirts of the town and went past a few factories. Over the other side of

the river, there were some lovely old houses, all huddled
together and nearly pushing each other over. Belladonna
started to get quite poetical about the mountains and the
valleys and fir trees and said that most Germans, especially
the children, didn't appreciate them.

It was actually quite a relief that I didn't really know many of
the other English girls. Barbara and I were two of the oldest
and most of the others were in a class below us at school. So I
was able to walk back alone and no one seemed to notice I
didn't join in any of the conversations, either in German or
English. Once we were back at the *Jugendhaus*, I was able to
slip away and catch the bus back to Volkmarshausen. Perhaps
Barbara was feeling unwell. Perhaps I'd find her back in
Volkmarshausen, feeling sorry for herself. But at home there
was absolutely no sign of her. I went upstairs. Her bed was
still unmade and the clothes she had worn in the morning
were strewn all over the floor and draped over the back of the
chairs.

Downstairs, Gudrun was laying the table for the evening
meal.

'Where is Barbara?' she asked accusingly, as if it was my
fault she had not returned. 'She is not with you?'

'I don't know where she is,' was all I could say.

'We will not wait the meal. She will eat when she returns.'

I think it was while I waited for supper to be served that I
wrote the diary entry for that day. The last sentence is brief and
to the point.

Barbara hasn't come back yet for the evening meal.

It was the final entry. After that, the pages are blank, but I don't
need my diary to remember what happened next.

I began to be more and more convinced that she was with Peter, that they had arranged this assignation yesterday and that she had dressed up at lunchtime for his benefit. I started to feel physically sick at the thought of them together.

She had not come back by the time we'd finished the meal and it was beginning to get dark. In spite of myself, I began to feel anxious about her. However annoying she might be, I didn't want her to come to any actual harm. Herr Schmidt pushed his plate away with apparent impatience.

'The last train arrives at nine hours. If she is not on it, she must walk back to Volkmarshausen. I have responsibility for her now. I am most displeased.'

Gudrun could scarcely conceal her smugness. She got up and started to clear away the dishes, clattering the cutlery on to the plates, making sure I could see how well she was coping in spite of her bandaged hand.

Nine o'clock came and went. Herr Schmidt stood up.

'Margaret, I must now go and search for your friend. Fritz will come with me.'

I stood up also, ready to go with them. But Fritz laid a restraining hand on my shoulder.

'I think it is better, Margaret, that you remain here.'

And that, of course, is what I should have done. Then I wouldn't have seen what I did. Perhaps my life would have been set on a different course.

Gudrun and her mother were busy in the kitchen. I waited until I could hear Herr Schmidt and Fritz talking outside the window, then quickly went downstairs. I shut the door as quietly as possible behind me. Outside, it was already getting cold. I had left too quickly to think of putting on a coat and I stood shivering, trying to get my bearings. Although there was a moon, it was behind the clouds, so it was only after my eyes got used to the darkness that I could see them. They stood outside the gate on the path. Then Herr Schmidt started to walk down towards the village, but Fritz went up towards the station. I decided to follow Fritz.

He was holding a torch and I could see him pointing it down on to the path, then sweeping the beam around on either side, searching between the thickly planted fir trees. He was walking quickly and I had difficulty keeping up with him. I stumbled once or twice, tripping over tree roots beneath the path. I began to have difficulty catching my breath and was afraid that he would hear me and send me back.

Once he reached the station, he stood looking down the track towards Münden, as if at a loss to know what to do next, perhaps hoping the nine o'clock train was late. After a while, he turned sharply and I instinctively dodged behind a tree. Fritz began striding back down the path, pausing every so often to shine his torch into the darkness. About halfway down, the moon came out from behind the clouds and picked out something we hadn't seen on the way up: something white lying beside a tree. Fritz stopped abruptly. Before I could stop myself, I gasped out loud. He turned round.

'Margaret, why are you here? It is no place for you.'

'She was wearing her white blouse today.'

'I know. Stay here. Don't follow me.'

But I didn't have to follow him to know that what we'd seen was indeed Barbara's white satin blouse. A few yards further into the wood, I could see a bright red skirt draped over a low bush.

She's dead, I thought.

But of course, she wasn't.

As Fritz walked into the wood, I once again disobeyed him and stumbled along a few feet behind, until we came to a small clearing in the trees. At first all I could see was a strangely shaped figure, writhing about on the ground. It seemed to have too many limbs, limbs that gleamed in the light of the torch. And it was making a noise I had never heard before. A sort of moaning sound, which I instinctively knew was not one of pain, but of pleasure.

Fritz stopped dead in front of me and we both stared in disbelief. The two figures separated as they realised they were not alone. Two faces stared blankly at us, blinded by the light, then sprang apart. I had never seen naked bodies before. We were prudish in those days and even at school we didn't undress in front of one another. And I certainly had never seen a naked male before. I got the merest glimpse of Peter's body before he bent down to snatch his shirt from the ground, and made a desperate attempt to cover himself up. Barbara stood still for a moment, as if uncertain whether to brazen it out, before running past us, gathering up her discarded clothes and disappearing down the path.

I can't remember what Fritz said to Peter, except that I had never seen anyone so angry before. I do remember that I was shaking uncontrollably, with both cold and shock. That Fritz came over to me and put his jacket gently round my shoulders. Peter eventually dressed himself, fumbling with trousers and shirt, and started to follow Barbara out from the trees and down the path. If Fritz hadn't supported me, I don't think I could have moved.

Until that moment, I hadn't actually thought through the practicalities of the sexual act. We had been told the briefest theoretical facts by our biology teacher, who was probably more embarrassed than we were. When I had my first period, my mother had said in a vague, rather off-hand way, that sometimes an egg turned into a baby, as if that explained everything. I hadn't even in my wildest imagination thought that love – something I thought of merely as an idealised romantic concept involving the meeting of true souls and minds – would end up as this basic carnal struggle.

There were so many possible endings to this story.

Barbara could have arrived back before Herr Schmidt and Fritz set off. She most likely would have said that she had missed the last bus and walked back from Münden. I would never have known for certain that she had even seen Peter that day.

I could have stayed at the school and not followed Herr Schmidt and Fritz. Barbara would have come back, dishevelled, but safe. Again, nothing would have been said about what really happened.

I could have followed Herr Schmidt instead of Fritz and still seen nothing.

None of these endings would have changed the course of my life.

But what I saw caused so many emotions. At first the overriding one was anger. I hated Barbara with an intensity I had never experienced before.

I repeated over and over again as we walked down the path, 'I wish she was dead, I wish she was dead.'

And jealousy.

'I thought he loved me. Why did he do it? I don't understand.'

And horror.

Fritz didn't try to stop me. He must have instinctively known that the best thing for me was to somehow vent my anger.

Back at the school, there was no sign of Barbara or Peter. I must have looked completely exhausted, because Frau Schmidt insisted on taking me upstairs and into bed. As I lay there, I could hear Fritz talking to Herr and Frau Schmidt. Later, I could hear Barbara's voice. She didn't come upstairs. I have no idea where she spent the night or what happened to Peter.

I tried to convince myself it was all Barbara's fault and I suppose to a certain extent it was. She had obviously set out to seduce Peter the moment she saw him and there was no doubt that he had immediately become completely besotted with her. But that alone wouldn't have made him do what he did in the woods that evening. I wonder now whether in fact if it had not been Barbara, it might have been me. That his intentions were not entirely as platonic as I had imagined. I shall never know and now the question seems entirely irrelevant.

We were not due to return to England for another week. The next day, the rumour went round that Barbara had been sent home in disgrace, but no one seemed to know what she had done. I was certainly not going to tell them. The official story was that a relative of Barbara's in England was dangerously ill, so Miss Harris was taking her back early. I went around in a daze for the rest of the time. With no diary to remind me, I can't remember what we did.

Almost immediately after I got back to England, I fell ill with what was diagnosed as glandular fever. The fever left me only when I resolved, in my delirium, never again to get emotionally involved with anyone. I was able to return to school before Christmas and by then Barbara had left and I never saw her again. Was it all common knowledge by then? I doubt it.

Now, I just feel an overwhelming sense of relief. By confronting feelings I have been repressing for thirty-five years, I realise how irrelevant they seem today. I can at last move on. And tomorrow, I shall tell Jonathan…

CHAPTER ELEVEN

Sunday 31ˢᵗ December 1989

…so in the morning I wake early, with the feeling of excitement and anticipation I used to get as a child on my birthday. I'm downstairs before anyone else. I let Bella out into the garden and stand at the window, watching the sky gradually become paler. Two hours to go before I see Jonathan again. Two hours before I can finally rid myself of the trauma that's been hanging over me for thirty-five years.

In spite of the drama of yesterday, this morning seems like any other Sunday. Ruth is the first to come downstairs, looking only slightly fragile, closely followed by Helen and the boys. It's only when Geoffrey appears, dressed to take the morning service, that the cracks begin to show.

Ruth makes no pretence of hiding her exasperation. 'You're surely not going to church, Geoffrey especially since you asked Nick to come back specially from his parents. You're doing it again, aren't you? Sweeping everything under the carpet. Just as if nothing at all has happened.'

'Why can't Grandpa go to church?'

'He's not feeling very well, Jack,' Ruth says immediately.

'Is he going back to bed?' Jack sounds puzzled.

'I think that would probably be best, don't you, Geoffrey?'

Geoffrey looks confused. Then he quickly turns round and goes out into the hall, followed by Ruth. We hear his study door shut.

Max is sitting on the floor, engrossed in carefully turning

the pages of a favourite book, telling the familiar story to himself, oblivious of what is going on around him.

'Who wants breakfast?' says Helen, rather too brightly.

When the boys have finished their cereal, Helen takes them upstairs to get dressed. Left by myself at the kitchen table, I pick up yesterday's paper, still lying apparently unopened on the kitchen table. Underneath the photograph of Havel smiling and raising his arm in a triumphant salute, it says, "Freedom fighter's triumph: President Havel greeting the crowds in Prague yesterday after his election as Czechoslovakia's first non-communist President in forty-one years." The Czechoslovakian people have been waiting for this moment for all those years, since long before my German trip. It seems absurd how arbitrarily all our lives can be changed, just by being in the wrong place at a particular moment. And how will we use our freedom? It would be foolish to waste a once-in-a-lifetime opportunity for change, but equally foolish to assume that there will be no problems or setbacks in the future.

Eventually I hear Ruth coming out of the study, shutting the door firmly behind her.

'I've managed to make him see it wouldn't be sensible to take the services, especially as the news will be all round the parish soon and particularly if the papers get hold of the story. This is only the beginning of everything.'

She sits down opposite me, looking weary but resigned. For a while we drink our coffee in silence.

'You know, Meg,' says Ruth at last, 'I realised just now that he hadn't told me how he actually managed to get hold of the money. After all, it's not as if he could've done it by putting his hand in the collection and secreting the odd £5 note away. He had to get a second signature on any cheque he wrote. Eventually he admitted he had asked George Holloway – you know, the new churchwarden – to sign a cheque for umpteen thousand pounds. Said it was normal procedure to invest it in several accounts and all he was doing was transferring the money from one building society to another. He didn't actually forge anyone's signature, but what he did is just as bad. I still can't believe he could have been so stupid. And I don't think he realises even now the implications of what he's done.'

'I think the sooner you leave here the better. Don't wait for the bishop to say you can't stay. You can go to Mother's flat for as long as you like. We don't have to sell it yet. And when we do, the money from that and the cottage will give you enough to find somewhere else round here to live.'

'We ought really to use that to reimburse the organ fund,' Ruth says.

'Surely the sale of Shirley's house will cover that?'

'I should jolly well hope so. Trouble is, apparently the house is still worth less than the mortgage her husband took out on it, which was based on the assumption that house prices would just go on getting higher and higher, not suddenly plummet downwards. Anyway, that's her problem. At the moment I'd be quite happy to see her camping out on the heath if it means we can get on with our lives.'

Ruth gets up, puts her coffee mug noisily into the sink and starts to unload the dishwasher. She obviously doesn't expect me to reply.

'Anyway, Meg, when are you seeing Jonathan again?'

I glance at my watch. 'In about ten minutes I should think.'

'That's excellent, darling. You have a lovely time. It would be nice, though, if you could both come back here to see the New Year in, especially as it'll be our last one here. Helen and Ian aren't going until tomorrow, but the more people around the better.'

'We can talk to Jonathan when he arrives. I don't think we've got anything special planned.'

I'm surprised how quickly I've become accustomed to thinking of "us" and not just "me". And realise how happy that thought makes me feel.

Both Ruth and I jump as the doorbell rings. I get up to answer it and see that Ruth has tears in her eyes. She takes my hand.

'Don't worry, Meg, I'm all right. It's just a reaction to the tension of the last few days.'

When I open the door, Jonathan is standing there, smiling. It really is most extraordinarily nice to see him. He's muffled up against the cold, wearing a striped scarf and a Russian style hat, which gives him a flamboyant look I haven't seen before. He gives me a hug and a kiss. I lead him into the kitchen.

'Ruth has invited us both to see in the New Year here. Is that all right?'

'Of course,' Jonathan says, going up to Ruth and putting his arm around her shoulders. 'A new decade is really rather special and I can't think of anything I'd rather do than see it in with some of my favourite people.'

'That's really sweet of you, Jonathan,' says Ruth, smiling up at him. 'I've asked Martin and Val, too.'

'Splendid,' he says. 'Can you spare Meg if I whisk her off for the day? What time would you like us back?'

'Say supper about eight o'clock? And don't worry about coming back before then. Helen and I will manage. I did the shopping yesterday. And Val says she and Martin will come early and give me a hand. Anyway, I need to tell them about the latest developments in the Geoffrey saga.' Ruth is beginning to look her old self again, cheerful even.

'Are you taking Auntie Meg out again?' Jack is coming downstairs as we go out into the hall. 'Can't you just stay here? We could fly my kite again.'

Jonathan laughs and pats him on the head. 'Sorry, Jack. We'll be back later though.'

Jack shrugs his shoulders and goes past us into the kitchen.

'We're off now, Ruth,' I call out, gathering up my coat, hat and scarf.

'I thought it might be nice to go for a walk, then have lunch out somewhere,' Jonathan says as we get into the car. 'Then, maybe back to my house in the afternoon for a cup of tea or something?' he adds, putting on his seat belt, not looking at me. I smile to myself as I reach round for my own belt.

'That sounds very much like a chat up line to me.'

'I suppose it must be.' He starts the car. 'Anyway, how about going to Rochester? It's not far. Just down the A2.'

'That sounds nice. I don't know it at all.'

'We used to live there for a while when the children were small. I worked at the hospital. It's got a castle and a lovely cathedral. And wonderful music. And a good café.'

'Perfect.'

And it is perfect. I feel no awkwardness as we drive along in silence, just contentment. There is no need to fill every moment with talk. I remember a young teacher at school, glowing with the excitement of a new relationship, saying how she and her chap hardly ever stopped talking. One of the other teachers asked her, with the wisdom of cynicism and experience, what their silences were like. And she looked puzzled as if silence were a bad thing.

We get to Rochester in about three quarters of an hour and manage to park the car just down from the cathedral. Jonathan takes my hand as we cross over the road. He gestures towards a huge tree in front of the west door.

'That's the famous Catalpa – it's very rare. Robert and Sarah used to get into trouble climbing up it.'

'It looks a very precarious.'

'Highly dangerous, looking back. They're talking about putting railings round it now. Shall we go in? I think there's probably a service on, but we might be able to slip into the back and listen to the choir if you'd like to.'

'I must tell you that I take the same view of the church as Ruth does,' I say as we walk towards the cathedral. 'I love the music, but I'm not so sure about what to believe. What about you?'

'Well, in theory, of course, I'm Jewish, but very lapsed I'm afraid. Neither of my parents were ever very devout either. It's ironic that we had to escape from Germany because of our religion and yet to us it seemed so unimportant.'

We go in and sit at the back of the cathedral. The service is drawing to a close and the choir starts to sing a final anthem, which we learn from the service sheet is a setting of "Oh Lord Support Us", by the cathedral organist. There is nothing quite like the sound of English choirboys in an English cathedral. And of course they always look so innocent, which of course I'm sure they're not.

After the service has finished, we wander round. The winter light is coming in through the stained glass windows. The cathedral must have been built in stages, as practically every architectural style seems to be represented. Jonathan tells me the most recent addition was the spire in the early 1900s. We pause in front of various tombs of bishops and deans, all with effigies on top, including one of Dean Hole, the founder of the National Rose Society in the 1870s, his very modern looking shoes rather charmingly resting on a wreath of roses.

It's not too cold outside so we walk round the garden, which is in middle of the ruins of the old monastery and dominated by a huge magnolia tree. Despite being near the main road, it's very peaceful and we are almost the only people here.

Jonathan suddenly turns and kisses me on my nose.

'Come on, let's go and have some lunch. Your nose is quite chilly.'

'And red, I'm sure.'

'Well, yes, but it's still a very nice nose.'

We have soup, making my nose glow even more, which has been a source of embarrassment to me for most of my life, but which Jonathan seems to find very endearing. He leans across the table and tucks a stray strand of hair back from my forehead.

'Shall we go home?'

'I think,' I say, 'I need to finish telling you my German story before we go back.'

So, we make our way out into the garden again. While we walk round the paths, past the herb garden, the magnolia tree, the box hedges surrounding the flowerbeds, I tell him everything. Things I've not even dared to think about in the intervening thirty-five years, which have been hidden deep in my memory, until I lived through them again last night. It leaves me trembling, but relieved, the weight finally lifted. Jonathan says nothing, just takes me in his arms. Eventually, he leads me out of the garden, back through the cathedral to the car and still we say nothing as we drive back to Greenwich. It's as if I'm going home.

Inside the house, we stand in the hall facing each other, unsure of what to do, suddenly awkward. Jonathan takes a step towards me. Holds me at arm's length, looking carefully into my face, as if trying to commit every detail to memory. Comes nearer. Then we are holding each other, clinging together, as though trying to prevent each other from falling. Not moving. Then kissing. Properly. For a long time.

There is no going back. We have gone beyond the point of no return.

I'm utterly bewildered by what is happening to me. How did I not know until now that such intense feelings existed? The answer, of course, is that I have never allowed myself to get to this point before.

'We don't have to do anything more yet, you know, my darling,' says Jonathan gently. 'We have all the time in the world. I can wait.'

'But I want to, more than I've ever wanted anything.'

Upstairs, Jonathan says he's a bit out of practice. So there's a bit of fumbling and a few giggles, as buttons and zips fail to undo. And then, suddenly, there's the unbelievably wonderful feeling of his bare skin against mine. It seems the most natural thing in the world. There is no vestige left of any sordid association with what I saw in the woods that evening in Germany.

And later, as we lie there, the light almost gone, a bird starts to sing outside the window. Just a few notes, but I know that whenever I hear birdsong at dusk on a winter afternoon in years to come, I shall feel undiluted joy.

'I never imagined,' I say at last, 'that there could be anything so wonderful.'

Later still, when we are downstairs, Jonathan sits at the piano and plays the Brahms rhapsody again. Thirty-five years ago, it stirred in me all my over-the-top romantic feelings. In the intervening years, if I heard it unexpectedly on the radio, I could hardly bear to listen, hearing only menace in the phrases I'd once thought so exciting, knowing it would bring back memories I thought I had suppressed. But now it seems like a different piece of music. There are moments of great tenderness as well as of passion. Above all, of affirmation and certainty. Jonathan plays from memory and I watch him as he concentrates on the keyboard, lost in the music. I want to put my arms round him, touch his face, his hair. He plays the final two chords, turns, looks at me and smiles.

'I have a very nice bottle I've been keeping for a special occasion like this.'

'You weren't planning all this by any chance, were you?' Because there, already sitting on the small table beside the settee, is a bottle of red wine, together with two glasses and a corkscrew.

'I could always have put it away again if you'd rejected my bold advances.' He opens the bottle, pours out two glasses and sits down beside me.

'There are so many things I want to say to you that I don't where to start.' He pauses, sips the wine. 'It's all been rather overwhelmingly sudden, but I think we both know that this isn't something that will go away when you have to go back to school next week. So, I have a proposition to make. No, that sounds wrong.' He continues straight away, before I can say anything. 'I knew the moment I saw you that you were the person I wanted to spend the rest of my life with. You don't have to say anything yet and I want you to think very carefully, because it will change both our lives, but would you be prepared to marry me? Please.'

He looks so anxious, almost pathetic, that I can't help smiling. I decide not to tell him what his mother said to me yesterday. Or that I have already made up my mind what to say.

'Do I really not have to say anything yet?'

'Well, I'm only too aware I've sprung this on you without warning. We've only known each other for a few days after all and you might at least want to find out if I've got any annoying or revolting habits.'

'I might have some too, for all you know. And you haven't seen me first thing in the morning.' I pause. He looks at me expectantly, his glass of wine in his hand. I pick up my own glass and touch his.

'I really don't need time. Yes. Yes, please.'

And I know, without any doubt, that it's the right thing to do.

Jonathan fumbles in his pocket and brings out a small box.

'My grandmother's engagement ring,' he says simply. 'Don't worry, Anna didn't wear it when we got married. My grandmother was still alive then.'

He opens the box, and there, on the deep blue satin lining, is the most beautiful ring. A single sapphire stone flanked by two small diamonds, set in platinum.

'If you don't like it, I'll buy a special one for you.'

'I love it,' is all I manage to say. He picks it up and takes my hand. Inevitably, though, my finger is much too big and it won't go over the knuckle. We both laugh as the little ceremony is abruptly halted.

'Never mind,' says Jonathan, 'I know a very good man in Greenwich who'll fix that for us. We'll go in on Tuesday when he opens again.'

So, by the time we leave to walk up the hill, back to the vicarage, having drunk a considerable quantity of wine, my future has been mapped out. I'm astonished at how simple it all seems. I shall leave school in the summer and move to Greenwich. I realise that I shall actually be relieved to give up teaching, at least for a while, as I've been stuck in a rut for some time now without any obvious goal in sight. We'll get married in the summer, Ruth's choir will sing, but we think it's highly unlikely in the circumstances that Geoffrey will be able to take the service. We have even got as far as agreeing it would be best to sell Jonathan's house, which after all holds so many memories for him, and buy a house we can plan together, but that it would be rather nice to keep mine as a holiday home in Dorset. I tell Jonathan how, in Volkmarshausen, I'd spent that restless night just after I'd met Peter, planning my future as the wife of a famous concert pianist, regardless of the fact that I'd devised the plot and the dialogue myself without even considering what he might feel and how I have been wary of making plans ever since.

When we get back to the vicarage, I'm rather taken aback to hear the sound of laughter and chatter coming from the sitting room. Ruth is by herself in the kitchen.

'You've got something to tell me, darling.' she says. 'I know that look. Is it what I think it is?'

I look at Jonathan, who is smiling rather sheepishly. 'I never could hide anything from you for long, could I, Ruth? Jonathan's asked me to marry him.'

'I hope you said yes.'

'Of course I did.'

'I can't tell you how pleased I am for you both. I need something to buck me up. But you must wonder what you're getting yourself into Jonathan. We're landing you with a whole lot of problems.'

She comes up to us and gives us both a hug.

There is a particularly loud burst of laughter from the sitting room. It sounds unexpectedly jolly. I had expected a rather more muted gathering.

'What on earth is happening in there?'

'Words fail me,' says Ruth. 'I always knew Geoffrey would move on to another role eventually, after he had stopped being a vicar, but I didn't think it would be so soon.'

'What's he decided to be now? A stand-up comedian by the sound of it. '

'Just go into the sitting room and have a listen,' says Ruth. 'You won't believe it. We've given Max his tea and put him to bed, but apart from him, everyone is in there. All I'll say is he's decided to come clean about everything and now has plans.'

As we open the door, Geoffrey is standing in front of the fire, holding forth to an attentive, if obviously bemused, audience. Only Jack, lying on the floor with Bella, doesn't appear to be listening. Helen sees us and gives us a despairing grin. Geoffrey appears not to have noticed us and ploughs on.

'... so while I'm waiting for the trial, I shall do some preparatory work.'

We seem to have missed the funny bits, as everyone is now listening intently. It gradually transpires that, far from dreading a possible spell behind bars, Geoffrey can't wait to start his sentence. He plans to keep a prison diary, to be published after he's released. His new mission will be to improve the lot of the average prisoner by giving literacy and numeracy lessons to his fellow inmates and organising entertainments for them, which is presumably where the comedy element will come in.

'And I thought you could bring the choir in too, couldn't you, darling?' he adds, as Ruth comes into the room.

'I'm not sure whether a Bach motet is what the average inmate will have been waiting for all this time,' is Ruth's only comment. 'Anyway, supper is ready, so I'd appreciate some help carrying things in, please Geoffrey.'

In the past few days, it's become obvious that the relationship between Ruth and Geoffrey is changing quite radically. Ruth has always been forthright in expressing her views on anything ranging from what to have for lunch to religion, but has always eventually gone along with Geoffrey's life-changing moves. Now, though, she has definitely become the one in charge and he obediently follows her out of the room. For a moment there is silence.

'Why is Grandpa going to prison?' Jack seems to find the prospect exciting. 'Is he a wicked person?'

'We don't know that he will have to go to prison, darling,' says Helen, 'and no, Grandpa isn't wicked. He was just trying to help someone by lending them some money.'

When we finally sit down round the supper table, we all carefully avoid the subject of Geoffrey's future. At first the conversation is muted, as if none of us can think of anything more interesting to talk about than the weather. Then, by an unspoken mutual agreement, everyone starts talking at once in small groups. I notice Geoffrey is not included in any of them. Helen, to his right, is turning away to ask Val something. William, to his left, bursts out laughing at something Marcus has said. I'm just happy to be sitting next to Jonathan. At the other end of the table, Ruth is already on her second glass of wine. She is beginning to look flushed and is engaged in an animated conversation with Ian and Martin. She looks up, catches my eye and mouths something to me. When she points to her ring finger at first I think she's trying to show me that she is no longer wearing her engagement ring, although her wedding ring is still in place. Then it dawns on me she's trying to ask if she can make an announcement.

'I think,' I say to Jonathan, 'that Ruth wants to tell everyone our news. Is that all right?'

Jonathan just leans over and gives me a kiss.

'I take it that's a yes,' I say, smiling at him.

'Yes,' I mouth back to Ruth.

I'm still in a euphoric state, hardly believing how my life has changed in what amounts to a few hours. Have I done the right thing? Will I regret it tomorrow? Perhaps if everyone knows, it'll seem more real.

Ruth taps her glass and everyone stops talking.

'I've just heard some very good news,' she says, standing up. 'I think we all need something to cheer us up after what my dear husband has got himself into. Although,' she adds, looking over towards Jonathan and me, 'I expect you can all guess what it is anyway.'

'If it's what I think it is,' says Martin, 'you certainly don't hang about, Jonathan, do you?'

Embarrassingly, once again I feel myself blushing.

'You can't get out of it now, Meg,' Jonathan says, smiling at me. 'And yes, Martin, she actually said yes with surprising speed.'

'There ought to be a tune for an occasion like this,' Ruth says, 'like "Happy Birthday."'

Jonathan takes my hand and gives it a squeeze. And then everyone is raising their glasses to us. And I feel I've never been happier in my life.

'What's Uncle Jonathan done now, Granny?'

'He's going to marry Auntie Meg, Jack.'

'Cool,' says Jack, and everyone laughs.

As we all get up from the table I feel in a complete daze, as if suddenly I'm public property. I'm definitely not used to being the centre of attention like this. I'm touched when even William joins in the general congratulations and gives me a quick, if rather embarrassed, hug and a kiss on the cheek. I notice that Geoffrey is still sitting at the table, looking somewhat bemused. I suspect he's rather put out that he is no longer the centre of attention. Eventually he gets up, shakes Jonathan by the hand and gives me a rather formal embrace.

There is still a considerable time before we see in the new decade, which, after all, is why we are all here together. When we go into the sitting room Ruth switches on the television for the news. The screen is filled with images of the New Year celebrations around the Berlin Wall. It's absolutely covered in graffiti of every conceivable colour. On top of it are scores of young people, arms waving, smiling, hugging each other, looking down at the people below them. Someone is hacking away at the top of the wall with a hammer. Someone else, carrying a coloured umbrella festooned with balloons, is dressed as a clown, white face, red nose, ginger wig. The camera cuts to the crowds in front of the Brandenburg Gate. It's just one huge, improvised, celebratory party and their mood is infectious. As we gather round the screen, we are all smiling too, but I can't help wondering whether the euphoria will be short-lived. So many times, all over the world, not just in Europe, hope of freedom has been dashed by violence. For now though, the atmosphere is one of undiluted joy.

The mood of the people of Berlin echoes my own. On the one hand, there is the excitement of a future filled with endless possibilities. But on the other, the nagging doubt that everything is moving on too quickly – that some things held dear might be lost in a new way of life.

Why do I even think like this when yesterday I was so certain that I knew what I wanted? Perhaps I've been settled in my ways for too long to make any radical change. With a sudden, involuntary pang of homesickness and nostalgia, I see myself opening my front door, going into the house and walking slowly from room to room. Everything I see is mine and has been lovingly collected over many years. Selfish perhaps, but part of what I am. And then there is the pleasure of knowing I can do exactly what I want, without having to worry about anyone else. And I actually enjoy being by myself. And supposing Jonathan eventually tires of me – or I tire of him – what then?

But suddenly my insides give a sort of lurch as I turn and see Jonathan, standing with his back to me, engrossed in watching the television screen. How can I possibly doubt my decision? He is already so dear to me. I know how he tilts his head when he's listening, how the hair at the back of his head curls slightly to one side, how he often stands with his weight on his left leg. I go up to him and take his arm. He turns and gives me a heart-stopping smile. Yes. Here is my future.

I'm acutely aware, though, that Ruth's future is far from secure and feel a slight pang of guilt. She is sitting by herself over by the window, staring at the television screen. When the news finishes, she gets up and goes out of the room. Geoffrey seems oblivious to what is going on around him and stays where he is, as Clive James starts to introduce a programme looking back on the decade, in his own particular ironic way, immediately changing the mood of introspection. Jack settles down beside him, thumb in mouth, something he only does now when he's tired and when he thinks no one is looking. I notice that almost immediately his eyelids begin to close. Soon he is sound asleep, leaning against Geoffrey's arm. Bella comes up and puts her head on his knee. On the face of it, a touching, domestic scene.

Still two hours to go before the new decade begins. Leaving Geoffrey and Jack in front of the television, the rest of us soon get up and leave the room. Will and Marcus take the guitar into the dining room; Will's technique is improving already by the sound of it. Jonathan is standing in the hall with Martin and Ian in what looks like a deep conversation, but which I suspect is the start of a joke-telling session. As I go towards the kitchen, Val and Helen are just coming out.

'I'm not quite sure, but I think I can see Ruth down the bottom of the garden.' Val looks anxious. 'I'm not sure if I should go out and see if she's all right.'

'Mum often goes out there when she's got something to mull over, doesn't she Meg? Mind you, not usually in the dark, but I think we ought to leave her for a bit.'

We go into the kitchen again and sit round the table. Val glances out of the window.

'I didn't realise how much things had deteriorated between Ruth and Geoffrey, Meg – even before the recent debacle,' she says. 'Anyway, she told me everything while we were getting the supper ready. Geoffrey doesn't ever seem to have taken her feelings into account. It's odd, isn't it, she always seems so positive and cheerful to me. He always seems to be so easy-going. It makes me feel I've never really known them at all.'

'That's just Geoffrey playing one of his parts. And Ruth's always just been my confident big sister, so I suppose I just took for granted that nothing was seriously wrong.'

'It was only when Dad had his sudden conversion all those years ago that we realised things weren't as rosy as we thought,' Helen says. 'But Jane and I were too young to do anything other than get on with our lives. And of course Mum never complained.'

We all start rather guiltily as the door opens and Ruth comes back into the kitchen, looking rather dishevelled, wisps of hair over her eyes, mud on her shoes.

'Right,' she says, sitting down heavily in the chair opposite us. 'I've decided.'

She pauses, looking down at her hands clasped together on the table. We look at her expectantly.

'Yesterday evening was the last straw, I'm afraid. I don't think he would have told me even now, if Jonathan hadn't persuaded him to come clean about absolutely everything. The trouble is I still don't really know whether there's something else. And look at him now. He's still behaving as if he's done nothing wrong and just assumes I'll always support him whatever he decides to do. Of course, up till now I always have. Well, he's got to realise it's all changed. The trouble is I don't think I shall ever be able to trust him again. And what's even worse, I suppose, is that I don't actually care anymore. Anyway, I decided out there in the garden. I'll stay with him while he gets through all this – but only as a practical presence – and then reconsider things then. I'll make my own life, do what I want to do, go where I want to go.' She looks up at last, giving us a wry smile. 'I suppose, if I'm honest, apart from anything else, I'm too proud to let people think I'm deserting him in his hour of need.'

Helen reaches out and takes Ruth's hand. 'I don't think you can do anything else, Mum. I know he seems at the moment to be making plans, but actually I can't imagine how he would cope without you.'

'You know Martin and I will always be here when you need us.' Val still looks anxious. 'And please don't let him persuade you to hide yourselves away in darkest Wales.'

'I've already made that quite clear – and that was before I knew everything. Anyway, he seems to be actually looking forward to a stretch in prison now, so he's probably forgotten about Wales.' She gets up. The conversation is evidently over as far as she is concerned. 'I suppose we ought to start thinking about getting the bubbly out. It hardly seems any time since we were seeing in this year and now here we are, doing it all over again.' She starts putting glasses noisily out on to a tray, picks it up and disappears into the sitting room.

After that, everything is a bit of a blur. We all seem to be marking time until midnight. Any effort to be jolly could have sounded a false note, so it's obviously a relief to everyone that Jonathan and I have provided a convenient excuse to be celebrating. And when midnight eventually arrives, we all gather in the sitting room. On the television, Big Ben strikes the hour, fireworks are let off, the crowds in Trafalgar Square cheer and sing "Auld Lang Syne". We all raise our glasses, hug each other and feel obliged to kiss everyone. It's always the same and yet this year everything is different, especially as I now have Jonathan, who leads me over to a corner of the room and gives me my first proper kiss of the New Year. When Ruth turns off the television, we can hear the crowds outside on the heath, fireworks being let off and the church bells ringing.

I suddenly feel very tired, so it's a relief when soon afterwards the party breaks up. Eventually Jonathan reluctantly goes home, too. I luxuriate in the knowledge that I'll be seeing him again tomorrow. I help Ruth and Helen clear up the glasses, but we decide that everything else can be left until tomorrow. Geoffrey has fallen asleep on the sofa, so we leave him there. Ruth will at least get the opportunity to have a good night's sleep. Upstairs, I climb into bed and...

EPILOGUE

Monday 1ˢᵗ January 1990

…reach over for my diary once more. If I'm to have a radical change of direction in my life, I need to write down my thoughts and feelings, if only to get everything clear in my mind. So I turn over the page from the last entry, pick up my pen and start to write.

> *It's an hour into a new decade. The fireworks and church bells have stopped now. In the distance, I can still hear people singing and shouting and cheering.*

I pause and consider what I'm going to write next. I haven't kept a journal for nearly thirty-six years. Am I just going to write down the bare facts of what I've been doing, as I did in Germany? There doesn't seem much point in writing that sort of diary. And who is it going to be for? If I want it to be a reflection of what I'm really thinking and feeling, it must be private. Just for me, then.

Will I have regrets about the decision I've made so hastily? Writing down any second thoughts I might have in the weeks to come will be cathartic, if nothing else. There's so much I don't know about Jonathan yet. I know the sort of music he likes, but not the kind of books he reads. I know about his lack of religious convictions, but not his political opinions. So much, and yet so little. Such a lot still to learn about each other. Will my reluctance to get up at the crack of dawn irritate him? And will my pedantic tendency to want everything to have its proper place annoy him intensely? Was he serious when he said he liked cooking? I'm only too aware that it's one thing to go on the occasional outing and enjoy the odd meal together, but quite another to live with someone day in and day out. All these questions and answers will have to be part of the journal I'm about to embark on. I continue.

I can't believe that ten days ago, we hadn't even met...

ACKNOWLEDGEMENTS

Particular thanks to David and Sally Beaton, for acting as my unofficial editors while I was writing the novel. Thanks also to Anne Lloyd, for checking the German dialogue; to Father Nicholas Cranfield, vicar of All Saints Church, Blackheath, for kindly showing me round the vicarage after I turned up unexpectedly on his doorstep; to Jim and Margaret Washington, for their hospitality in Blackheath; to Elke Smith (née Zimmerman) for telling me of her own escape as a child from East Germany; to Barry and Sandi Ferguson who told me about Rochester in 1989; Barry was organist at the Cathedral and composed the anthem *Oh Lord Support Us*. Thank you also to Maureen Griffin for a productiove weekend in Berlin. I should also like to thank my friends and family for reading the book, giving me encouragement and making so many helpful comments – Wendy Dimmick, Paula Street, Jeremy Isaac, Peter Darley, Sharon Street, Roger Street, Trish Street and De Ashton. Ans to Carolyn Date for nagging me to 'get on with it' in the first place.

SOURCES AND BIBLIOGRAPHY

German poetry from *The Penguin Book of German Verse*, introduced and edited by Leonard Forster. Pub 1957, reprint 1963. The translations are mine.

Information about the border between East and West Germany from *Along the Wall and Watchtowers*, by Oliver August. Flamingo 2000.

All headlines, straplines and descriptions of newspaper photographs from copies of *The Times*, 1989.

Descriptions of images and events at the end of 1989 from *Eyewitness to the 80s – A Moment in Time*, Rupert Matthews/Ted Smart, with photographs courtesy of Rex Features/Sipa Press. The Book People 1990.

The Heath by Neil Rhind, Blackheath Bookshop Ltd 1987.

Details of the Maldon Mud Race from:
www.essextouristguide.com

All facts about the villahe of Volkmarshausen and the town of Münden are from my own photographs and the diary I kept on a school exchange visit to Germany in 1954.

All the characters and the plot are entirely fictitious.